DEADLY REDEMPTION

A CAL CLAXTON MYSTERY

WARREN C. EASLEY

LUCASIAN PRESS

"When someone tries to drown Cal, he uses his fishing skills to good advantage. What a showdown finish! Easley's folksy style belies an intense drama revolving around corporate greed and espionage. The second outing in this action-packed Oregon-based series succeeds in quickly bringing readers up to speed."

–Library Journal

Never Look Down The third Cal Claxton Mystery

"Easley exquisitely captures Portland's flavor, and his portrayal of street life is spot on. Readers of John Hart and Kate Wilhelm will delight in trying this new author."

–Library Journal

"The Portland cityscape is as much a character as the colorful graffiti artist and the lawyer who walks Portland's streets with his dog, Archie."

–Ellery Queen Mystery Magazine

Not Dead Enough The fourth Cal Claxton Mystery

"Masterfully crafted, this tale of greed, deception, and revenge has an added benefit—the stunningly beautiful descriptions of the lush landscapes of Oregon's Columbia River country. Easley's characters bring enough complex complications to keep you reading long after regular bedtime."

–Anne Hillerman, New York Times bestselling author

"With a very likable sleuth, Not Dead Enough is sure to appeal not only to mystery lovers, but also to those interested in Native American history, Oregon culture, and environmental issues like salmon migration. Although *NDE* is the fourth in the series, it can be read as a standalone, allowing fans of Tony Hillerman or Dana Stabenow to dive right into Cal Claxton's life."

–*Shelf Awareness*

Blood for Wine The fifth Cal Claxton Mystery.

A Nero Wolfe finalist for 2018

"If you enjoy wine and a really good mystery, Blood for Wine is a must read."

–Phil Margolin, *New York Times*
bestselling author

"Warren C. Easley blends my favorite subjects—wine, food, a really cool dog, and of course a murder—into a tasty thriller sct in Oregon's wine country. With more twists and turns than a rain-swept coastal road, *Blood for Wine* is the fifth in this series with a tantalizing backlist just waiting for me to get my hands on. It promises to be a mystery maven's haven."

–*Bookreporter.com*

"Senseless acts of violence that hit too close to home upend Cal's personal life—but only serve to strengthen his resolve. Oenophiles and aspiring vintners will enjoy the wine lore in this well-wrought tale of love and betrayal."

–*Publisher's Weekly*

Moving Targets The Sixth Cal Claxton Mystery

"Intelligent dialogue, evocative descriptions of the landscape, and sly pokes at the current cultural climate make this a winner."

–Publisher's Weekly

"Easley continues in every installment in this series to get a better handle on his characters and the vital balance between principal and supporting plots."

–Kirkus Reviews

No Way to Die The Seventh Cal Claxton Mystery

"In Easley's satisfying seventh mystery featuring genial Oregon attorney Cal Claxton [he] creates authentic characters and relationships, and his eloquent descriptions of the Oregon wilderness are sublime. This well-plotted, character-driven series just keeps getting better."

–Publisher's Weekly

No Witness The eighth Cal Claxton Mystery

Winner of the 2022 Spotted Owl Award for best mystery written by an author in the greater Pacific Northwest.

"Easley should win new fans with this one."

–Publisher's Weekly

Also by Warren C. Easley:

The Cal Claxton Mysteries

Matters of Doubt

Dead Float

Never Look Down

Not Dead Enough

Blood For Wine

Moving Targets

No Way to Die

No Witness

Fatal Flaw

This is for Bettie and Dick
with a heart full of love.

"The past is never dead. It's not even past. All of us labor in webs spun long ago..."

–William Faulkner

"True Redemption is...when guilt leads to good."

–Khaled Hosseini

CHAPTER ONE

I'VE BEEN TOLD THE PAST IS THE PAST, THAT IT'S A STEP-pingstone not a millstone. Move on, the advice goes, stay in the moment. But what if the past is like a bad song stuck in your head? What if it plays in some dark corner of your psyche and refuses to shut the hell up? I found myself pondering those questions the day this story began.

I was thigh deep in the Middle Fork of the Willamette River in mid-April, a time when Covid had finally subsided in Oregon. I was drifting a Chubby Chernobyl, an artificial fly that looks more like a puff of cottonwood blossom than an insect that had crash-landed in the river. It was a splendid spring day, and I was hoping to tempt a rainbow trout or two into sampling my wares, knowing that rainbows in this river had a weakness for Chubbies.

I was in the Cascades at a spot where I'd caught a couple of nice eighteen-inchers just the year before. It had become my habit to go fishing on my deceased wife's birthday, alone except for the company of my Australian shepherd, Archie. I would spend the day thinking of Nancy and all that had happened. I guess you could call this a tribute, an act that said I hadn't forgotten, that I would never forget.

I saw a fish rise and slurp a bug in the eddy of a boulder forty feet ahead of me. I moved upriver a few steps as the current pushed strong and cold against my waders. I cast the chubby just beyond the lichen-crusted stone and tensed as the fly floated by. Nothing doing. Two more casts yielded the same result. Undaunted, I moved further upriver and repeated the process. Fly fishing is no sport for the impatient.

Thirteen years had passed, and I no longer grieved for my wife. In fact, I was in a serious relationship with a wonderful woman. Nancy had committed suicide—an overdose—and I hadn't seen it coming. Sure, she suffered from bouts of depression from time to time, but I never dreamed her illness would drive her to take her own life, an act that left not only me but our daughter, Claire, behind.

But the guilt lingered, unabated, a dull ache that hung like a persistent cloud over my life. It was me, I realized. It was my fault. I must have missed the warning signs. At the time I was a prosecutor for the city of Los Angeles, a demanding job that required a great deal of my time and attention. I loved the law, was damn good at my job, and my career seemed to stretch ahead of me like an ascending path. But how many dinners and soccer games were missed and vacations interrupted? And how many times had I fallen into bed, too exhausted by the stress of the day to even talk? Too many, by any count.

It became clear to me—I had put my so-called career ahead of Nancy's wellbeing. I had failed as a husband and as a father. There was no escaping it.

A breath of breeze danced across the river, and I saw another fish rise in a narrow, foamy seam between two current bands. I shrugged off my reverie and cast the chubby, which landed dead center where the fish had peeked its head up. I tensed again, and in a silvery flash a big trout snatched the lure and dove like a submarine for the safety of the river bottom.

"Whoa!" I cried out as my rod bent nearly double and the line began to scream off my reel. "Fish on!" I really didn't need to announce that fact since Archie spent his time on the bank watching my every move with intense interest. He came to his feet and began to spin in circles while his high-pitched barks shattered the mountain stillness. A fish on the line was always a treat for my dog.

The trout took a lot of line before it slowed down, and I was able to turn it around. I worked it back toward me in fits and starts and when it got close, it executed four writhing leaps to throw the hook. When I finally had the fish in front of me, Archie, curious as any cat, stopped barking and moved to the river's edge for a closer look. The trout was gulping watery breaths through crimson gills, and as it rolled on its side, sunlight ignited the iridescent band it was named for.

When I released the fish, Archie barked a couple of times as it vanished into the river. I looked at him as the adrenaline rush subsided. "Was that a nice fish or what, Big Boy?" He barked again in apparent agreement. I gazed up the river, which cleaved the fir-studded terrain rising steeply on either side. The sky was cobalt blue, the riverbanks were dusted with wildflowers, and boulders churned and roiled the oncoming water, which sang a tune I never tired of.

No question, fly fishing took the edge off a day spent in painful remembrance.

—/—

"How did it go?" Zoe Bennett asked not long after a couple of bars showed on my phone. I was heading home, having just turned off Hills Creek Road onto Route 58. Zoe was a Ph.D. psychologist who left an associate professorship at the University of Puget Sound up in Washington to open a private practice in the small town of Dundee, Oregon. Counseling was her day job, and she was damn good at it. But she was also writing a novel, her first, and that's where her passion lay.

"Caught a half dozen rainbows and kept two nice ones for dinner tonight," I said. "Care to join me?"

"Silly question. Of course. I'm chilling a 2018 Durant Sauvignon Blanc as we speak. I had faith in your fly-fishing prowess."

I laughed. "I take full credit for the ten percent that wasn't luck. See you in about two hours."

The traffic heading north on the 5 was light, and I made good time on the way home. I came to Dundee after taking an early retirement from the city of Los Angeles following Nancy's death. I bought an old, rundown farmhouse on five acres tucked in amongst the vineyards in the rolling hills above the town. I knew only one thing well—the law—so I passed the Oregon Bar and opened a one-man law practice, specializing in whatever came through my door. Keep it simple, I told myself at the outset. Find a balance between work and the rest of your life. But I was drawn to representing the most vulnerable among us, which was never simple. It was a rebirth of sorts, an effort to reinvent myself into someone I could live with.

I took the Aurora exit off the 5 and crossed the Willamette River before reaching Dundee. Sandwiched between the Red Hills and the river, the town stretched for two and a half miles along the Pacific Highway. The commercial section consisted of a collection of wine tasting rooms, small shops, and restaurants without a single chain store or national fast-food joint in the mix. I stopped at my law office on the north end of town to pick up my mail. A small, flat-roofed building, it housed the town's only barbershop back in the day. The old barber pole was still in place when I moved in, and I liked it so much I left it up even though it attracted the occasional walk-in looking for a haircut.

"Well, sounds like you and Arch had a fine time on the river," Zoe said after I arrived at The Aerie—the name my daughter had given my refuge—and finished describing the day's events. We were out on the side porch wearing fleece against the coolness of the late afternoon. She sipped her wine, swept a strand of ash blond hair from her forehead, and said, "Anything you want to talk about?"

I hesitated. She knew about the guilt I carried and always encouraged me to talk about it. But it was never easy for me to open up. No way I wanted to come across as someone who couldn't move on from the past. "It was pretty much like the year before except I caught more fish this time."

She smiled. "That was an evasive answer, counselor. Care to rephrase?"

I chuckled at that. "It got a little raw, you know, the memories and all, but I'm glad I went. Funny thing, a lot of the most painful memories—like my inability to socialize with our friends afterwards and my anger issues at work that cost me my job—those are slowly losing their sting. Kind of like photographs that fade over time."

Zoe nodded encouragement. "That's the normal course of things."

"Right," I said, my voice growing a little husky. "But the

day I found her up in our bedroom... *those* memories are still vivid and stark. That's the rawness I'm talking about."

Zoe flinched perceptibly. "That's the piece you're holding onto, the most painful, shocking part of the experience. Maybe this is how you punish yourself for your perceived complicity in her death."

I massaged my forehead for a few moments with my eyes closed. "Yeah. It's like if those memories begin to fade it'll mean I've let myself off the hook."

She smiled again and took my hand in both of hers. "We can't live this life without making mistakes and carrying some guilt around, unless we're sociopaths or raving narcissists. You've assumed responsibility for your actions, Cal. You've felt remorse, and you've made amends to your daughter. Maybe it's time to give yourself a break."

I paused for a long time before responding. "If the facts don't change, how in the world can I forgive myself?"

Zoe's mouth opened slightly as if to speak, but she held back. It was a tactical retreat. She respected the depth of my feelings on this subject. At the same time, I knew she felt she could help me. I wasn't so sure she could. I loved her for that, though, and for a lot of other things, too.

CHAPTER TWO

THE ORDINARY START OF THE NEXT DAY GAVE NO HINT of what lay ahead. I awoke as sunlight streamed into my second-floor bedroom. The old farmhouse I'd bought on an impulse was a classic, shiplap-clad four-over-four with a dormered roof and a porch that wrapped around the front and one side of the house. Perched on the edge of an abandoned quarry, it looked out on vineyards that fell away in the foreground and the Willamette Valley that stretched to the southern horizon.

I got dressed and took the back staircase down to the kitchen with Archie leading the way. I let him out to patrol his domain, much of it wooded with old-growth Douglas firs and made myself a double cappuccino at the kitchen sink. It was the day I set aside each week to offer legal services pro bono for anyone in the city of Portland lacking financial means. It was a commitment I'd taken on shortly after arriving in Oregon, and to say I was older and wiser for the experience would be an understatement.

With Beethoven's *Violin Concerto* playing during the twenty-five-mile commute, my thoughts turned to Portland, a city I'd grown to love. It was home to a warm, big-hearted populace but had recently fallen on hard times. A perfect storm of ramped-up gentrification, homelessness, civil unrest and, finally, a pandemic threatened to crush its vibrant, optimistic spirit. "Is Portland Over?" was the title of a series of special reports currently running on one of the local TV channels. The jury was out, I supposed, but my answer was "hell no," although I admit I wouldn't trade jobs with the mayor for all the bitcoin in the blockchain.

I worked out of a two-story building on Northwest Couch Street in Portland's Old Town district. Once the site of a neighborhood coffee shop called Caffeine Central, it had been put out of business by a Starbucks that moved in two blocks down the street. Like the barber pole on my Dundee office, I liked the old sign above the door, so I left it up. As a result, Claxton's Pro Bono Legal Services was known on the street as simply Caffeine Central.

I pulled into the small lot adjacent to the building at eight forty-five. A half dozen people were already queued up in front of the structure. I let Arch and me in through the back entrance, filled my dog's water dish, and set it down next to his pad in the corner. My appointment calendar showed no appointments that day so it would be just the walk-ins outside. Owing to a light breakfast, my stomach grumbled, but I'd vowed to jog along the river in lieu of lunch. I needed to shed some Covid-pounds.

My first client that morning teared up before she got her first word out. I pushed a box of tissues across the desk to her. "It's okay," I said, "this is a free-tear zone. What seems to be the problem?"

Worrisomely thin with short, spiky hair, she dabbed her mascara-stained eyes and sat up straighter. "Sorry. I have to move back to Phoenix to support my mom. She's sick, cancer, and can't work or take care of herself."

"I'm sorry to hear that. What are you doing here in Portland?"

"I'm going to Portland State, finance. It's early enough that I can withdraw without any problems."

"So, what's the hang up?"

"A lease. I signed a lease three months ago. I need to break it, but I don't want to wind up with bad credit or a collection agency hounding me. I think I see a way to break it, but a friend of mine told me I should talk to you first."

I read through the lease, which she'd extracted from her backpack. When I finished, I said, "Okay, tell me your idea."

Her face brightened. "Well, the dishwasher in the apartment never worked. They promised to fix it but haven't. And there's a leak under the bathroom sink. I have to keep a bucket there and empty it twice a day. I've documented all this." I nodded encouragement, knowing where she was going. "The lease says it's their responsibility to maintain the apartment, which they clearly haven't. I think those are grounds to break it."

"Bingo," I said, smiling. While she waited, I drafted a letter to the real estate firm, printed off a copy, signed it, and put it in an envelope. "Send this to them. I know this company. You won't have any trouble." As I saw her to the door, she knelt down to pet Archie, who'd gotten up from his spot in the corner. A tricolor Australian shepherd, he had a way with women. I wished her mom a speedy recovery, adding, "A finance major, huh? Maybe you should consider studying the law when you come back."

I'd like to say the rest of the morning went that smoothly, but of course it didn't. I had less sympathy for the next three clients. The first reeked of alcohol and had the dilated pupils of a user. I told him to come back when he was clean. The next two had been charged with first degree theft for stealing bicycles. I directed them to the public defender's office in the Kress Building on SW 5th.

"Aw, man," the more demonstrative of the two said, "We don't want some public pretender. They ain't worth shit and everybody knows it. A bro said Caffeine Central was the place to come, that you're the best lawyer in Portland."

"And you're free," the other man chimed in.

"I'm flattered," I said, "but I don't do criminal defense pro bono." I nodded towards the corner. "I have to feed my dog and pay the rent." I took a card out and wrote a name on the back. When you go to the Kress Building, ask for this woman. She's the best public defender they've got."

At noon, I hung a sign on the front door promising to reopen at one thirty and went up to the small apartment on the second floor and changed into my running gear. I let myself out the back door just as my landlord glided silently into the parking lot in his Tesla. Hernando Mendoza was also my private investigator and my best friend. A big man with an ample girth and a smile that could light up a dungeon, Nando was a Cuban exile who embraced our free market economy with the zeal of the newly converted. In addition to his PI business, he ran an office cleaning service and had extensive real estate holdings in southeast Portland.

"How's the Tesla running?" I asked.

He flashed a smile as he got out. "Purrs like the kitten." Always on the sartorial cutting edge, he wore a linen Havana shirt, designer jeans, and a pair of highly buffed Gucci loafers. He looked me up and down. "I was thinking lunch at Pambiche, but I see you have other plans."

I patted my gut. "I had trouble reaching my socks this morning."

He laughed, a clap of baritone thunder. "You are in better shape than most twenty-year-olds I know." He eyed Archie, who sat looking up at him. "But it looks like Señor Archie has his heart set on a run. I—"

"How 'bout we make it dinner?" I said. "Zoe's spending some time with Gertie tonight. Say, Pambiche at six thirty?" He nodded agreement, and I smiled. "I sent you a letter this afternoon requesting that you let a client of mine out of her lease."

He lowered his thick eyebrows and eyed me. "A lease is a lease, my friend. As a lawyer, you know this, *verdad?*"

"It's not binding if you don't fix the dishwasher and a leaky sink."

"Where is this?"

"Your triplex over on Southeast 16th, middle unit. A young student at PSU."

"*¡Qué fula!* It is Mateo," he said, referring to Mateo Rodriquez, one of his plumbers. "Ever since he got sick with the Covid, he has not been right. Repairs are slipping in the crack. I'll have it fixed tomorrow. No problem."

"Nando, the young student's mother has cancer. She has to drop out of school and go care for her in Arizona. Let the lease go."

He rolled his eyes and exhaled a long breath. "Okay, okay. It will be no problem, and I can bump the rent again."

"Thanks," I said. Sure, my friend was tight with a buck, but he was renting Caffeine Central to me at a fraction of what he could get for it. He'd grown up dirt poor in Cuba before he paddled a homemade craft to the Keys and was prone to ostentatious displays of his newfound wealth. But he was a generous man, and like me, he believed everyone deserved a fair shake.

After a hectic afternoon, I locked up and was hanging my *closed* sign in the window when someone knocked. I was tired and hungry, but I opened the door.

"You Calvin Claxton?" a man said. Black and fortyish, he was a couple of inches shorter than me, broad through the shoulders with ripped biceps, a shaved head, and a full, black beard. He gazed at me with careworn eyes the color of honey. They'd seen some bad shit. Not a thousand-yard stare, but something close to it. He seemed familiar in some vague way, too, but I couldn't place him.

"I am. What's your name?" I extended my hand.

"Can I come in?" he said, not offering a name or a handshake.

I stepped aside, and when I did, Archie got up from his mat in the corner and uttered a low growl. "Hey, cool it, Arch," I said, puzzled by his reaction. There was nothing threatening about this man, at least that I could sense.

"That's okay," he said, "I like dogs." Archie remained standing but stopped growling.

I offered him a seat as I took mine behind my desk and waited for him to speak.

He met my eyes. "My name's Dante Ellis." His voice was low and gravelly, and his gaze had turned expectant.

The name rang a distant bell, but I still couldn't place him. "Okay, Dante. What's on your mind?"

He sat there staring at me for an uncomfortable amount of time. Finally, he said, "You don't remember me, do you?"

I tried to smile. "No, not quite. I'm sorry."

"Ellis, Dante Luther Ellis," he repeated in a slow cadence. "Thirteen years ago, down in LA., you sent me to San Quentin for life." He reached into his jacket pocket and pulled out a big, shiny semi-automatic and leveled it at my chest. "Keep

your hands on the desk where I can see them. I got exonerated and now you're going to listen to how you wrecked my
life, and then I'm going to kill you, mother fucker."

CHAPTER THREE

THE MENACE IN DANTE ELLIS' VOICE, AND THE FACT THAT he was pointing a gun at me, set Archie growling again, this time with more feeling. "Hey, Big Boy," I said in as calm a voice as I could muster, "lie down on your mat. It's okay." He obeyed me but did not take his eyes off our visitor. I looked back at Dante and held his gaze, trying hard not to show the fear that clutched my throat. "Okay, Dante, let's talk about this."

He waved the gun angrily, and I flinched, thinking it might go off. "This isn't some negotiation, fucker. *I'll* do the talking. I've been waiting for this for a long time." He looked over at Archie, then back at me. "And keep your dog under control. I got no beef with him."

I nodded. By that time, my memory had kicked in. "I remember you now, although the last time I saw you, you had dreadlocks and no beard. This is about the Irena Krasnova case."

"That's right. You convicted me of her murder. The jury was out three days, so it was a squeaker. But you convinced all those folks that I did it, that I killed a beautiful young girl. I got life, no parole."

"I tried the case based on the evi—"

"Shut the fuck up and listen. I was happily married, my

girlfriend since high school. We had a beautiful son named Jamare." Dante grimaced and shook his head. "He was eleven then. The best of Shanice and me went into that boy."

I nodded, as more of the trial came back to me. We had him at the scene, he had a motive—he was having an affair with the victim, and it went south. At least that's the story I told the jury. Dante was right. The case was no slam-dunk, although his attorney—a public defender named Seth Conlon—was a notoriously weak adversary. I wondered if he planned to kill Conlon, too.

Dante's nostrils flared, and his eyes stayed cold and flat. I tensed again, thinking of his finger on the trigger of the gun, which looked like a cannon from my perspective. "You know what thirteen years at Quentin does to you?" He looked me over, his lip curling in disdain. "You wouldn't last a week there."

I didn't react. Although he didn't look all that proficient with the gun, if I made a move from behind the desk I'd never get to him in time. I pushed down my fear and waited for him to continue.

"Shanice was humiliated by my arrest and even more so by my conviction." His jaw trembled and he blinked away tears. "I swore to her I didn't do it, but she couldn't handle it—the newspapers, the trial, the pressure she got from everyone we knew. It was too heavy a load. She never came to visit me, and Jamare never did either. And I wrote letters to her and Jamare all the time, separate letters. Got nothin' back. Nothin'. Then after Shanice died I started getting the letters to Jamare returned to me."

"I'm sorry to hear that. What happened?"

"She divorced me and married some dude who abused her and finally killed her one night. He's doing time at LAC."

"Your son?" I ventured again.

His eyes filled, and a single tear traversed his cheek and disappeared into his beard. "Fostered-out with some family in Watts. Then Child Services told me five years into my time that he ran away from that family, and they couldn't locate him." He wiped a second tear with his fist. "He was only fourteen. Doesn't matter where he is. What's he want with a broken-down ex-con anyway?"

I sensed an opening. "He might surprise you, Dante. Kids never forget their dads."

He paused for a few moments, then smiled without warmth. "Nice try, fucker. You trying to make me forget why I came here? See, if you hadn't been such a hot-shot lawyer, talking all that shit about me in the trial, I might've gotten off. But you were too good, man. I could tell that jury was buying everything, every single lie you told. So I lay the blame on you, man. And you're gonna pay."

I looked him in the eye. "I was doing my job, Dante. The evidence pointed to you."

He scoffed. "Shit, I was set up, but you and the cops never bothered to consider that. You figured you could nail me for it. That's all that mattered."

I winced inwardly at the possible truth of his words. "Dante, you're free now. If you go through with this, you're going to get caught. You're the first person they'll look for."

His chin trembled again. "What do I care? I'll eat a bullet after I take you out, or maybe I'll take a few cops with me, you know, suicide by cop." He stood and leveled the gun at me. "Stand up, man."

I got up slowly, but Archie sprang to his feet and began growling again. Dante looked over at my dog, and I saw something in the man's eyes, the faintest glimmer of compassion. I said, "Dante, listen to me. If you shoot me, you'll have to shoot my dog, too. He'll go for your throat the moment the gun goes off. Don't hurt him, *please*."

He extended his arm with the gun aiming directly at my chest. Archie's growl went down an octave, and out of the corner of my eye I saw him crouch and look at me for guidance. The gun quivered in Dante's outstretched hand. "You're a free man," I said, stiffening for a fusillade. "Don't do—"

He lowered the gun and slumped back into his chair as tears began to pour from his eyes. He shook his head. "I can't do this. I can't kill a dog."

His arm dangled from the arm of his chair, the gun now pointing at the floor. I said, "Let's talk, Dante. I don't do prosecutions now. Maybe I can help you."

He looked up as if waking from a fugue. "Help me? How can *you* help me?"

"I can help you find Jamare, for one thing. He deserves to know his father is an innocent man. You could tell him how much you love and miss him."

Dante looked directly at me, laid the gun on the floor, and sat up straighter. "What else?"

Sensing the détente, Archie came over to me, and I scratched his head. "You have reparations coming from the state of California. I could help you with that, too. No charge."

He waved a hand. "The Innocence Project people are handling that. I wasn't worried about it, because I was planning on being dead after I killed you."

"Okay," I said, and before I had a chance to talk myself out of it, added, "You mentioned you were set up by someone. I do investigative work now. How would you like to find out who set you up? We could work together on that."

His eyes came alive, and he locked them on me. "You would do that? You would help me find out what happened?"

"Yeah," I said. "I'll help you. It's what I do."

He shot me a skeptical look. "You'll want all my reparations money, right?"

I shook my head. "No. I won't charge you. I *owe* you, Dante. I prosecuted an innocent man."

He picked the gun up off the floor, stood, and removed the clip. After laying the clip and the weapon on my desk, he said, "You can have these. Never liked guns." Then he added, "I've hated your guts for thirteen years, but I'm glad I didn't kill you. Maybe something good will come out of this."

"Yeah," I said as my knees stopped wobbling, "maybe it will, Dante, maybe it will."

CHAPTER FOUR

"SO, YOU ARE ALIVE BECAUSE THIS MAN COULD NOT shoot your dog?" Nando said in a tone of utter disbelief. We were seated at Pambiche an hour and a half later—at his usual corner table. I'd just finished describing what happened during my encounter with Dante Ellis.

"Something like that," I said after sipping my drink. Ordinarily, like Nando, I'd have a beer with Cuban food, but that night I started off with dark rum on the rocks to steady my nerves. I shook my head. "I'm still a little dazed, like did that really just happen?"

Nando drew his thick eyebrows together and frowned. "Indeed. It was a very close call, Calvin. What did you talk about after he put his weapon down?"

"We mostly talked about his son, Jamare. I told him I could find him. Dante seemed conflicted about it, like his son might reject him. But I think he'll come around."

Nando raised an eyebrow and smiled knowingly. "Let me guess—you want me to find this young man?"

"Yeah, I told him we could do that. Shouldn't be much of a problem for you." I slid a business card across the table with the boy's full name—Jamare Hakeem Ellis—and birth date. "He's twenty-six now."

Nando pocketed the card without looking at it. "Is there anything else?"

I took a swig of my rum to hide a sheepish look. "I, uh, I also told him I'd try to find out who set him up."

Nando rolled his eyes. "*¡Hostia puta!* A frozen case down in Los Angeles? This would be an enormous task, my friend."

"Could be."

"Why does this man care, anyway? He is free now."

"He wants payback, I guess."

Nando leaned in and rested his dark eyes on me. "And why do *you* care, my friend? And how do you know he's telling the truth about being innocent?"

I took another drink. "Let me finish telling you the story. All I'm sure of is that I owe him, Nando. What I remember of the case, it was strong, except we needed a motive. We decided Dante's victim must have spurned his romantic advances. But we didn't have a lot of evidence to back that up, so I had to sell it hard to the jury." I shook my head. "At that time in my life, it was all about winning, you know, padding my resume for the next promotion."

"It was your job to win."

I took another sip of rum while I mulled the comment over. "Yeah, of course. But it was my call to prosecute or not based on what our detectives uncovered. I made the wrong call, and it shattered Dante Ellis' life. Like I said, I owe the man."

Our food arrived—*ropa vieja* for Nando and *pescado con coco* for me—and after our waiter was out of earshot, we broke our cardinal rule of never talking shop over a good meal. Spearing a piece of shredded beef with his fork, Nando said, "Tell me about the case."

I chewed and swallowed a bite of red snapper before answering. "When Nancy died, my boss, the City Attorney, offered me as much time as I needed, so I took a couple of weeks off. When I returned, the case was on my docket. I was a mental and emotional mess, but I was still in ego mode, trying to prove how tough and dedicated I was." I puffed a breath. "By the time the trial rolled around, I wanted out, but I saw it through."

"You had a breakdown, *verdad?*"

"Sort of. After the trial, I roughed up an uncooperative witness in another case—damn near resulted in a lawsuit against the city—and told my boss to go screw himself on at least two separate occasions."

"Never a good idea," Nando said with a wry smile. "It must have been a painful time for you."

"It was, and that's when I realized how messed up I was, and my boss heartily agreed. I took an early retirement shortly after that and came to Oregon."

"And the rest is history," Nando quipped.

"Anyway, as I recall, Dante was having an affair with the victim, an undocumented woman named Irena Krasnova, Slovenian I think. She was found shot to death in her apartment. Dante was caught on a security cam entering and leaving the apartment around the time of the shooting. A subsequent search of his car turned up a gun consistent with the bullet that killed her."

"No ballistics?"

"The bullet was too fragmented."

"Brass?"

"No brass. Turns out she was killed by a pro, a man name Ferris Spielman, according to what Dante told me. He was doing life at Corcoran Prison for another murder, and after learning he had terminal pancreatic cancer, made a deathbed confession that he killed Krasnova. He knew details about the crime only the killer could have known. The Innocence Project got involved and secured Dante's release. It still took over two and a half years."

"I take it the deathbed confession did not include who hired the hit?" Nando said.

"That's right. Spielman took that information to his grave. Honor among thieves, I guess."

"There is no such thing," Nando shot back.

I laughed. "Of course. The contract was probably let on the dark web with complete anonymity. Anyway, that's where I come in."

Nando took a pull on his Cristal. "I am curious. What was Dante's defense at trial?"

"He claimed Krasnova called and asked him to come to her apartment. When he got there, she was dead. He panicked and took off. Said the gun was planted in his car. He testified they were just friends, that he wasn't having an affair with her."

"Was there a record of the call that summoned him?"

"Yeah, the call came in on his cell, as I remember it."

Nando pushed out his lower lip and nodded. "Not the most creative setup, but effective. The shooter forces the victim to make the call, then kills her and leaves while avoiding the security camera. Your man blunders in. Not surprising that he panicked and fled, unaware he was being recorded by a camera."

"Exactly. And Spielman subsequently planted the gun in Dante's car for the detectives to find. The only fly in the ointment was that the bullet was too damaged to be traced to the planted gun. Spielman should've left his brass behind. That would have done it."

"Why didn't he?"

"Force of habit, I guess. He was a pro. They never leave their brass behind."

"But you overcame that problem with the jury," Nando said.

"Yeah. It was a hard sell, because Dante took the stand in his own defense and made a strong showing. I really had to go after him on cross." I shook my head as memories of that encounter suddenly flooded back. "Not my finest hour."

Nando waved a hand dismissively. "Do not beat yourself. Your job was to win the case. And now you have a chance to help this man." He paused for a moment and stroked his chin absently. "A contract hit on a young, undocumented woman. That's very curious and very cowardly." He sighed and then smiled with resignation. "Okay, Calvin. You have managed to arouse my interest. It is against my business principles, but since you have apparently agreed to work on this case pro bono, I will donate my time to your noble effort."

I raised my glass, and he reached across the table and clinked it with his. "Thank you, Nando. I'll do most of the heavy lifting." I smiled back at him. "A thirteen-year-old cold case. How tough can that be?"

My friend's basso profundo laugh boomed across the restaurant. "Indeed. What could possibly go wrong?"

CHAPTER FIVE

THE NEXT MORNING BROKE COLD WITH A LOW, GRAY cloud cover, as if spring had never sprung. I fed Archie, had a double cappuccino followed by a bowl of granola and then headed out to my vegetable garden, hoe in hand. I was halfway across the field on the north side of my property when the sun broke through, putting a nice sparkle to the damp grass freckled with bright yellow buttercups and the odd gopher mound.

I was intent on weeding the plot where I grew vegetables every summer—tomatoes, beans, asparagus, artichokes, and the like. Archie was lying off to the side watching me work. A bright red frisbee lay in front of him. Every so often, he would pick up the disc, bring it over and drop it at my feet, and then look up at me with his big coppery eyes. Setting my hoe aside, I'd fling the disc as far as I could and watch as he raced after it, barking joyously.

"That dog of yours still has a lot of pup in him," a familiar voice said from behind me.

I turned and smiled to my neighbor, my bookkeeper and confidante, Gertrude Johnson. "Yep, gotta feed his inner puppy or he'll pester me all day. Top of the morning, Gertie."

She returned the smile, her robin egg blue eyes bright

in the spring light. She wore rubber boots, jeans, and an old flannel shirt—her gardening attire—and her pewter hair was up in a tight bun. "You think your artichokes wintered over okay?"

I glanced at the area where the three plants had thrived the summer before. It was covered with a thick mat of straw. "Hope so. The straw's supposed to provide some insulation, and we only had one cold snap."

We went on to discuss gardening and then cooking, particularly the art of preparing a good choke and the dipping sauce to go with it. Finally, Gertie changed the subject, saying, "What do you think of Zoe's plans?"

I stopped hoeing and leaned on the handle. "What's not to like? She's going to sell her place in Tacoma and find a place in Dundee. It'll take her a while to get her practice up and running, but there's such a shortage of psychological counselors that it shouldn't take her long."

Gertie nodded. "Yeah, I like that she's moving here, and you two will be together." Her forehead furrowed. "But damn it, I guess I'm old fashioned. Why the hell don't you marry her and have her move into the Aerie with you? I mean, two separate households?"

I laughed at that. "Maybe down the road, but no way that's happening right now. She wants to get established first. In case you haven't noticed, your niece is fiercely independent."

The creases in Gertie's forehead became more pronounced. "She's going to focus on the migrant community? She's doesn't even know the language."

"She's learning Spanish from Timoteo's mother, and Zoe's a fast study." Timoteo Fuentes was my part-time law clerk and assistant. "She feels like the migrant community needs more options for psychological care."

"And then there's the book she's writing," Gertie went on. "That seems to be all she talks about with me." She rolled her eyes. "She's taking on so much, Cal."

"Yeah, writing and counseling are competing passions for sure."

Gertie exhaled, shaking her head. "Well, you two make a good pair, that's all I can say. I suppose I'll have to keep the books for Zoe, too, so I can keep an eye on her the way I do you. Somebody has to have some financial sense around here."

I cringed a little inside. Wait until she hears about the case I just took on, I said to myself. Not exactly a move that made any financial sense.

—⊣⊢—

Later that morning, I packed Archie in the car and headed out to meet with Dante Ellis. I took my Glock 17—a gun Nando had given me years earlier—for this second meeting. I felt a little guilty that I lacked trust in the man, but as Nando put it the night before, "Dante could have a change of heart, you know. You can risk *your* neck, but do not endanger Archie again."

I offered to meet Dante in Portland, but he said he wanted to see a bit of Oregon, that he had a car, an old Ford F-150, and knew I lived out in the wine country. I arrived at my office in Dundee ten minutes ahead of him. I stashed my Glock in the top right-hand drawer of my desk and switched on my espresso maker. Archie took his customary spot in the corner as I tried to tamp down my nervousness.

Wearing a hooded sweatshirt and baggy cargo pants,

the first thing Dante said when he arrived was, "You a barber, too?" I explained the origin of the barber pole, which drew a faint smile from him, the first I'd seen.

Archie gave him a friendly greeting this time. Dante knelt and patted my dog's head. "I didn't expect to be here today," he said, blinking tears back. "Shit, didn't expect to be anywhere." He took Archie's head in both hands and stared into his eyes for a long time. "Thanks, boy. You saved me."

"He saved us both," I said, as my nerves began to calm.

A man who clearly disdained any show of emotion, Dante stood, recovering his composure. "Didn't see any grapevines around here."

"That side of the highway," I said, gesturing in a westerly direction, "up in the hills. There are around a hundred vineyards up there."

"Never drank much wine." He paused and eyed me as his smile became bitter. "The cafeteria at San Quentin didn't serve any. Maybe I'll try some to see what all the fuss is about."

"That can be arranged," I said, but he dismissed the suggestion with a look that made it clear drinking with me was not on his agenda. The room fell silent except for the drone of traffic out on the Pacific Highway. Finally, I said, "Do you mind my asking how you spent your time at San Quentin?"

"Worked out. Mostly weights. And when I wasn't working out, I was writing letters telling people I didn't kill Irena. And when I wasn't doing that, I was learning the game of chess."

"Chess," I said. "You still play?"

His eyes brightened, and he managed a thin smile. "Every chance I get."

"I suck at all board games. How's your game?"

Dante held the smile but diverted his eyes in modesty. "Took me three years, but after that nobody at Quentin could touch me, including the warden. Dude thought he was a hot shit player, too. I'm a little rusty now. Prison shut down all our board games for a year and a half because of Covid."

"Now you're free to play all you want," I said. Then, after making us each a cup of coffee—double shots in hot, foamy milk—we got down to the business at hand. First, I had him take me through some background information, which I jotted down on a legal pad. He told me he'd been married ten years at the time of the murder, was living in Compton, and worked as a bartender at an upscale bar and restaurant on West Pico called The Impromptu.

"Shanice and I had to get married," he explained. "I needed money, and the tips were good behind the bar. Dreamed about studying math at UCLA, but that never happened."

"It's not too late," I countered, but I saw no flicker of interest in his eyes. "As I remember it, you didn't have any priors, right?"

"Nothing, not even a parking ticket."

We fleshed out a few more personal details, but I didn't learn anything of note. It got more interesting when I began probing him about his relationship with Irena Krasnova.

"She hung out at the Impromptu. That's how I met her. She worked the place, you know."

I nodded. "A prostitute. She—"

"It wasn't like that," he cut in. "She didn't want anything to do with the life."

"Why did she stay in it then?" I knew the answer but wanted to hear his take on it.

"They had a lock on her. She owed them money for getting her out of eastern Europe. She was scared to talk about it."

"She was trafficked here," I said, remembering that part with clarity, "but I don't remember the investigation ever turning up who was behind it. Part of your defense was that her handlers might have killed her because she wanted out, but that didn't go anywhere. Did she ever mention any names?"

Dante leaned back and dragged a hand over his head as if smoothing hair that wasn't there. "Irena never breathed a word to me about who was running her. A dude hung out at the bar named Emile. Don't remember his last name or if I ever knew it. An enforcer, kept an eye on the girls."

"Okay, I need Emile's last name. It might be in the trial transcript or the investigative record, but it would be a lot faster if you can come up with it."

"Yeah, I can ask some people."

"What about Irena's friends or relatives—can you give me any names?"

"She didn't have family in this country. Two friends I remember, Anika and Lara. Both worked at the bar. They were tight, those three, good looking, classy. Men paid big bucks to have them hanging on their arms at fancy clubs and shit like that. Prostitution was always denied. Good Company—that was the name of the operation—was billed as an up and up escort business."

"Do you remember their last names?"

Dante pulled at his beard. "Uh, Novak, Lara Novak. Don't remember Anika's last name."

"Get it for me if you can." He nodded, and I added, "What else can you tell me about Irena?"

"She was different, you know? Smart. Read a lot. Had another gig, too—modeling."

"She was a model? Where?"

"I don't know. She never told me, but I knew it was something very special to her."

We both paused, and the room grew quiet, filled as it was with the ghost of Irena Krasnova. I said, "You've had plenty of time to think about this, Dante. Who do you think set you up?"

He shrugged with a puzzled look. "Still clueless, man. Somebody wanted her dead, and they needed somebody to take the fall for it. It was no secret the two of us were close."

"Her traffickers?"

"Maybe. But men couldn't resist her. Why have her killed?"

"What about a boyfriend or a john who was a regular?"

He paused for a moment, cocking his head. "She had a lot of regulars. One rich dude, a weird little fucker, kinda stalked her. She complained to Emile, but I don't think he ever did anything about it. First name was Tucker. Can't remember his last name."

"Get it for me."

He nodded, then brought his eyes up to mine. They were hard steel. "Look, man, it wasn't like you said in court about me and Irena. We weren't lovers. I cared a lot about her. Who the fuck wouldn't? She was a good woman. But I loved my wife and kid more."

A wave of shame hit me. I swallowed and managed to hold his withering gaze. "Yeah, I believe you, Dante. I don't expect you to forgive me for that, but I do ask that you give me a chance to help you now. It's the best I can do."

He finally broke eye contact and looked over at Archie.

"A man has a dog like that can't be all bad, I guess," he said, mainly to himself. "I don't forgive you, never will, but let's give this a shot, see where it goes."

"Fair enough."

CHAPTER SIX

"WHAT'S THE OCCASION?" ZOE ASKED EARLY THAT EVE-
ning. She was sitting in my kitchen sipping a Lange Estate
sauvignon blanc and watching me cook. It had clouded over
again, and the soft patter of rain rose above the kitchen
noise.

"The fish market in Newberg had Alaskan halibut, just
in this morning. I had to take out a second mortgage to
pay for it, but I figured what the hell." I held up one of
the filets, a thick slab with white belly skin. What I didn't
say was that it was a bit of a celebration, since I was still
breathing after my encounter with Dante Ellis, a topic I
needed to cover with Zoe.

"Yummy," Zoe said. She'd been out for a run and still
wore her Asics, sweatpants, and a maroon tee with *Puget
Sound Loggers* plastered across it. "How do you hear about
this stuff, anyway?"

"I have a mole at the market. He calls me whenever
something special arrives, like Clatsop mussels or Washington razor clams. The good stuff goes in a hurry." I eased
the halibut into a big frying pan simmering with olive oil
and butter and laid some thin Meyer lemon slices on top.
"How's the Spanish coming?"

She swept a lock of hair from her forehead and frowned.

"Slower than expected. I was pretty good after spending a semester in Madrid, but I've forgotten a lot more than I realized."

"It's in there somewhere," I said. "Your aunt's worried about your financial security. She thinks the immigrant community won't be all that interested in your services, and they won't have insurance or ready cash to pay you."

Zoe laughed and waved a dismissive hand. "Oh, Aunt Gertie's a worrier, you know that. My goal is to be able to counsel in Spanish for those who struggle in English or just prefer their native tongue. I won't attempt it unless I'm nearly fluent. And I'm not looking to get rich." She eyed me playfully. "Just like someone else I know who lives up here in the Red Hills."

I smiled as I gently turned the two filets over, then checked the baby red potatoes roasting in the oven before whisking up some salad dressing. We talked for a while about the challenges of providing psychological counseling to people from a different culture and language. "I'll be the first to admit I'm not a perfect fit as a counselor for migrants," Zoe said at one point. "But I know the need's there, and somebody has to fill it."

"Well, you've certainly done well in your counseling of Elena Fuentes," I said, referring to my office assistant's mother, who was severely traumatized by the murder of her daughter several months earlier. Timoteo says she's like her old self again, running the family with an iron fist."

Zoe laughed. "I happen to know that Elena's feistiness is her superpower."

I eased the fish onto a platter and whipped up my special wine, lemon, and caper sauce to go over it. The halibut was firm and flaky, and the sauce took it over the top. We clinked glasses and ate in silence for a while. I didn't broach the subject of Dante Ellis until we finished eating. After I described the initial encounter and the commitment I'd made, Zoe went over to Archie, knelt down, and threw her arms around him. "You're a miracle dog," she said and then looked up at me, her gaze fierce, her eyes wet with tears. "If you go down to LA, promise me one thing—"

I met her eyes and waited. Zoe accepted my penchant for becoming involved in violent crime investigations, but that didn't mean she liked it.

"You'll take Archie with you. He's your guardian angel."

I hadn't really thought that far ahead, but there were witnesses I wanted to interview at the very least. "Of course. We can drive down. He likes a good road trip."

She came over and hugged my neck, wetting my cheek with her tears. "It's good what you're doing for this man," she said, her voice husky. "Just finding his son will be a huge gift. The rest...finding who had that poor woman killed, well, that sounds...risky. And this will dredge up old memories for you, won't it? The painful kind?"

I took her head in my hands and gently wiped her tears away. Her eyes were deep blue like the sea. "Yeah, it might be a little scab-scraping, but I need to meet this head on. I screwed up, and I can never make it right. This is *something*, at least."

She kissed me, a soft meeting of our lips. "I understand. And I love you for it. But please be careful, okay?"

—/ /—

The next morning broke cool and cloudy. As was my habit,

I stood at the kitchen window, sipping a double cappuccino and taking in the view. Out near the horizon a wagon train of flat-bottomed, cumulus clouds scudded across the valley from the Coast Range to the Cascades. What sun there was breathed color onto the valley floor—greens, yellows, and ochres—and in the foreground, row upon orderly row of grapevines marched down the rolling hills, their branches speckled with the first lime green shoots of spring.

My heart swelled at the sight, like it always did.

Zoe was hunched over her laptop out on the deck, sipping a coffee and wearing a down jacket against the coolness of the morning. Archie was dozing at her feet. She was working on her book, a time when she didn't brook any disturbances. I carried a second cup of coffee into my study off the hallway, sat down at my desk, and began to jot down some preliminary thoughts on next steps in the Krasnova investigation. Beginnings were always daunting, but this case gave me a taste of what Hillary and Tenzing must have felt at basecamp below Everest. The thirteen-year time lapse presented a host of problems, to be sure, but there was something else at play—my self-respect. It felt like *that* was on the line as well. I needed to make this right.

I let the negative feelings course through my body and dissipate before I put pen to paper. Twenty minutes later, I had sketched a path forward.

Possible Motives:
- *Irena posed some kind of threat to her handlers or was cheating them in some way. Who was behind the prostitution ring?*
- *A disgruntled john had her killed and blamed it on Dante Ellis, because he was jealous of him?*

- *Irena was involved in something else that got her killed. What?*

Witnesses to interview:
- *Irena's friends—Lara Novak and Anika*
- *"Weird little fucker"*
- *Owner and management of the Impromptu and other employees of that era*
- *Emile the enforcer*
- *Investigation team—Detectives Jimmy Ryerson and Aldo Moretti. Still at LAPD?*
- **Need access to the Krasnova Murder Book…*

After I finished the list, I went into the kitchen to make another coffee. It had cleared off, and the weather to the south seemed held at bay by a soft but persistent northerly breeze. Zoe looked up from her computer and made a face. I opened the sliding glass door to the deck, heard the drone of a lawn tractor over at Gertie's, and smelled the faint aroma of cut grass. "You look like you need another coffee."

She rolled her eyes. "Maybe that would help. Whose cockamamie idea was it to write a book, anyway?"

I smiled, resisting the urge to ask what was bothering her. I'd learned from experience not to probe about her writing, to respond only to direct questions, which came infrequently. After I delivered her coffee, I went back into the study and called the main number of the Los Angeles Police Department.

"Could you please connect me with Captain Todd Whipple?" I asked the switchboard operator. "He works in the Robbery-Homicide Division." The detectives who investigated the Krasnova murder reported to Whipple, who was one of the few contacts in the LAPD I'd maintained over the years, having burned most of my bridges when I left. We were close back then, and the friendship we had was based on mutual respect.

After a short pause. "I'm connecting you. For your information, I'm showing him in the Gang and Narcotics Division."

"Todd," I said when he picked up, "it's Cal Claxton. It's been a while." We went on to exchange pleasantries before I asked, "So you've got a new home at the LAPD?"

"Yeah, I'm working exclusively in Narcotics now. Let the young bucks take on the gang bangers. They're armed like combat soldiers these days." He paused for a moment. "I'm guessing this isn't just a social call, Cal. What's on your mind?"

I told him about the exoneration of Dante Ellis, which surprisingly he hadn't heard about, and went on to explain my involvement. In summary, I said, "I'm interested in talking to Jimmy Ryerson and Aldo Moretti, the team that investigated the Krasnova murder, but I didn't want to make it a cold call. What are they up to these days?"

"Well, Ryerson's dead. He got mugged in a parking lot, for Christ's sake. Not long after you left for Oregon."

I was stunned into silence for a few beats. "No! I hadn't heard."

"Some punk put a bullet in his heart and took his watch and wallet. We pulled out all the stops but never caught the bastard. Damn shame. Jimmy was a good cop." I agreed, and he went on, "Moretti's retired. Last I heard he'd moved up your way, southern Oregon, I think."

"When did he retire?"

"Oh, couldn't have been more than eighteen months after you left."

At this point I got to the real ask of the call. "I need access to the Krasnova murder book, Todd. Any chance you could facilitate that? For old time's sake?"

The line went quiet for a while. "Jeez, Cal. That's against regs. We don't encourage retirees to do that sort of shit."

"I know. Pretty ballsy of me to ask, right?"

"You haven't changed a bit, have you?"

"This will be between you and me and nobody else," I said. "And I'll abide by any ground rules you want to impose. You know I need it, Todd." That said, I was reminded of the numerous times I hit up my best contact in the Portland Police Bureau for favors. It was shameless behavior but, hey, the cause was always righteous.

Another long pause. Finally, Todd sighed into the phone. "You're a lawyer, for Christ's sake. What makes you think you can suddenly morph into a detective?"

"I've had some investigative experience up here in Oregon. Trust me, I can handle this. But I need the book."

"You know you're one of the few people on this planet I would stick my neck out for, Cal. Let me see what I can do. No promises, buddy."

"Of course."

"What the hell kind of investigating have you done up in Oregon, anyway?"

"Google me, Todd."

CHAPTER SEVEN

"WE FOUND NO MARRIAGE, TAX, OR CRIMINAL RECORDS for Jamare Hakeem Ellis in California," Nando told me over the phone later that day. "Esperanza is checking the national databases now. As you know, this process moves more slowly than a glacier."

"Well, if anyone can find him it would be Esperanza," I said, speaking of Nando's office manager, probably the only human capable of keeping Nando's affairs straight.

"I take it the second meeting with the father proceeded peacefully."

"Yeah, it did. We're not exactly buddies, but he gave me no reason to worry. And he's bonded with Archie big time."

"Good. Keep Archie close at hand. Did you extract any useful information?"

I described the conversation and took him through the preliminary list I'd come up with and my discussion with Todd Whipple. "So, we may have a shot if we can locate some of the witnesses, and they're willing to talk. I'll know more once I get down there."

"When are you leaving?"

"As soon as I can clear my schedule. I'll drive and, on the way down, stop in to see one of the detectives who worked the case. He's retired and living in southern Oregon."

"What's Dante planning to do?"

"I assume he's going back to LA, but I'm not sure when. I've got a call in to him. I told him I have some more questions. He seems committed to the project, but we'll see."

"Indeed," Nando said. "He probably has no idea how difficult and time consuming an investigation like this will be. You need to be honest with the man, Calvin. Our chances of succeeding are minimal."

"O ye of little faith, Nando."

Dante called soon after that and said he was at a bar called the Lucky Labrador on Hawthorne in southeast Portland. "They play chess here, and I'm trying to arrange a game," he told me. "Can you come? We can have a beer, talk. I'm heading back to LA tomorrow."

I said I could, left Archie on the deck with Zoe, and arrived at the bar forty minutes later. I brought my briefcase along, figuring it would make me look more lawyerly in Dante's eyes, since I never dressed the part except in court.

A popular neighborhood joint, the Lucky Labrador was a big, high-ceilinged structure with exposed pillars and beams, hanging lights, and a bar that stretched the entire length of one side of the building. Patrons sat at the bar and at long, communal tables that filled most of the room. Toward the back, a crowd was gathered around two men facing each other over a chessboard. Dante Ellis was one of the players. He was focused on the game and didn't see me approach.

I slipped into the crowd and began to watch and listen. Dante's opponent, a thin, bookish-looking man with a Van Dyke goatee had his hand on one of his pieces—a black knight. He had a pained look of indecision on his face.

"He's hoisted with his own petard," a man next to me

whispered to his companion, a woman who nodded in agreement. The player finally moved his knight, and Dante responded immediately with one of his bishops. A low murmur went up from the crowd.

"Checkmate," Dante said in a voice I could barely hear.

As the crowd clapped, Dante's opponent stood and shook his hand. The man next to me said to his companion, "Damn, that took all of what, eight or nine moves? And Paul's a solid player. This guy's the real deal."

A young man stepped forward with the intention of being Dante's next opponent, but Dante saw me, excused himself, and came over to me. "I figured I had time to squeeze one game in before you showed up," he said with a deadpan expression.

"Your timing was perfect," I said. "I arrived just as you checkmated your opponent. The crowd seemed impressed."

He showed a modest smile. "I thought I was rusty, but that felt pretty good. That guy's an okay player, but he made some early mistakes. Half the players in San Quentin could take him."

We found seats at the end of one of the tables, well away from the other customers, and after we ordered the in-house IPA I said, "It must've hurt when they curtailed your chess games inside."

A slight nod. "Yeah, the damn virus really screwed things up. Chess was my island of sanity, you know, something rational with rules and structure, predictability." He grimaced and I could see pain clouding his eyes. "Sure, there were plenty of rules at Quentin, but they were all bullshit."

"What did you do to keep your mind occupied then?"

"Quentin has a good library. I read a lot. Books on chess strategy, mathematics, shit like that." He looked at me, his eyes registering something close to disbelief. "I almost gave all that up, what I love, because of the hatred I carried in my heart for you." He shook his head and studied the tabletop in front of him. "Messed up," he mumbled. "Really messed up."

"You didn't go through with it, Dante" I offered. "That's what counts."

He raised his eyes as if to speak, but our beers came. When the waitress walked away, he took a long pull on his IPA. "So, you got more questions?"

"I just want to make sure I've got the whole picture." I took a notepad and a copy of the list I'd made from my briefcase and slid one across the table to him. After walking him through it I said, "Does this look complete, or does it spark anything you hadn't thought of?"

He studied it for a while. "There was a woman, the madam of the escort service. She looked after the health of the girls, too. She wasn't around much, and I never saw her, but the girls talked about her a lot." A thin smile creased his lips. "I can't tell you her name, but her girls called her the Bitch Queen. She had the girls' respect, but she was feared, too. She's gotta know some shit."

"Not a very flattering nickname," I said, jotting down more notes. "Any idea where she worked? Hospital? Doctor's office?"

Dante took another pull on his beer and wiped his mouth with the back of his hand. "Nope. Never heard much about her except that she was tough and demanding. The girls respected her, but they feared her, too."

"I need her name, Dante."

"I'll try," he said and went on, "One thing I remembered about the Weird Little Fucker—had a driver and bodyguard named Alec, Alec Macleod. He wasn't a bad guy, really, never liked his boss much. Maybe he'd talk to you. Drivers always know a lot."

I jotted the name down. "Excellent. Anything else?" He shook his head, and I added, "We've run a preliminary search for Jamare. We—"

"Already?" he said, his head jerking back, his eyes registering something more than surprise.

"We haven't found him, but it's early days."

He dropped his gaze, pulled at his beard, then looked up at me. "Stop looking for him. I've been thinking about it. Don't want to barge into his life." He shook his head and pressed his lips together. "Not gonna do it."

"Why don't you let Jamare make that call?" I offered.

His eyes turned steely. "No. No searching for him. That's final."

—/—

"And he's apparently a damn good chess player," I said to Zoe. We were out on the side porch after dinner, huddled around a blazing propane fire pit as the sun sank behind the Coast Range. I'd been filling her in on my meeting with Dante. "He dispatched some Portland hotshot in a half dozen moves or so."

"Impressive," she said, "and he reads books on chess theory and math for fun." She took a sip of her Rémy Martin. "I can understand his reticence about reuniting with his son. He probably figures the boy has established a life without him, that his appearance could complicate things with his friends and with whoever brought him up."

"Yeah, that's the way I read it," I said. "Prison crushed the man's sense of self-worth. I told Nando to table the search for now, but I'm not going to let him give up on his son."

She showed the hint of a smile. "This quest you and Dante are on might restore some of that self-worth? Is that what you're thinking?"

"I suppose, but Nando thinks it's an exercise in futility, so who knows?"

She drained her Rémy and gave me a look, the one that always melts me. "Well, I think we should go to bed now. If you're going to be off jousting at windmills, I want you to miss me. A lot."

It was an offer I couldn't refuse.

CHAPTER EIGHT

A BAND OF REDDISH-GOLD FADING TO VIOLET SILHOU-
etted the Cascade Mountains as dawn broke. It was the
following Wednesday, and Archie and I were heading for
Los Angeles on the I-5. The view of the sunrise in all its
timeless beauty that morning was a reminder of why I loved
Oregon so much. Postponing a meeting here and promising
a Zoom call there, I'd managed to clear most of my calendar
in Dundee and Portland for at least the next month. Nando
was on standby. He would come south only if my preliminary probing turned up something worthy of follow-up.

Gertrude Johnson had greeted my plans with stunned
disbelief. "You're not serious," she replied, but, of course,
she knew I was. "You need billable hours, not a trip down to
Sodom and Gomorrah (She hated LA with a passion.) I just
did your taxes and you're not getting a refund. Far from it."

"I know, I know," I said with hands hiked up and open
in surrender. "This is just a fact-finding trip. If I turn up
something, Nando has agreed to help me investigate the
case pro bono."

Another incredulous look. "Well, that's a first. That
might soften the blow a bit. What got into him?"

I smiled. "He had an attack of conscience, Gertie."

—/—

Two hours into the trip, I turned off at the small town of Creswell to give Arch a break and get some breakfast at the local cafe known by insiders for its exquisite, made-from-scratch baked goods. Archie got a quick walk and after I wolfed down a ham brioche breakfast pocket and picked up an almond croissant and coffee to go, we were back on the road.

I had just taken the final bite of my croissant when a call came in. "Hey, Dad, it's me," a voice I loved to hear chirped from my car speakers. "What's goin' on?"

"Hi Claire," I said. "Arch and I are driving down to LA on a quick business trip." No way I was telling her why I was really heading to LA. "Where are you?"

"I'm in DC at a climate change conference, you know, trying to save the planet from frying itself."

"It's going to be up to your generation, I'm afraid," I said, then instantly regretted sounding too fatherly. She hated that. Armed with a Ph.D. in environmental science from UC Berkeley and as smart and independent as they come, she was the kind of warrior we needed for that battle.

With concern in her voice, she said, "Oh, Dad, are you going to be okay down there, with all the bad memories and stuff?"

"Yeah. I'll be fine. It's a short trip. No big deal."

We went on to catch each other up, and after we disconnected, I listened to John Coltrane's *Blue Train.* The music brought back some of the good memories of that time and place. I thought of Nancy and our house in Griffith Park, a small ranch with two bedrooms and the third converted into a studio for her artwork. She taught art at Occidental College and painted—mostly still life, landscapes, and stunning portraits. Those paintings, at least the ones she hadn't sold or Claire hadn't claimed, were stored in my attic in Dundee. And there they stayed, despite my daughter's urging that I hang them at the Aerie.

I wasn't ready for that and felt I never would be.

An abrupt lane change by an eighteen-wheeler jerked me out of my reverie, and a few minutes later I turned off at Gold Hill and took Old Stage Road past Medford to the small town of Jacksonville. I'd managed to reach Aldo Moretti—the surviving detective who'd worked the Krasnova case—earlier that week. He'd retired there and agreed to meet with me.

"This is a blast from the past, Cal," he said when I called. "Sure, it'll be great to see you again. Why don't you come to my place?"

I'd never been there, but I knew Jacksonville was on the historic register as an early Gold Rush site and was high on the charm scale. Following my GPS, I cruised through the center of town and wound up on the southwest outskirts. Wedged between a small vineyard and a large lavender farm, Moretti's place lay at the end of a long, tree-lined drive.

I rounded a curve, and the house came into view—a flat-roofed, stone and glass contemporary that seemed at odds with the historic environs. We parked, and when Archie hopped out of the backseat I watched in horror as he left a gift on my host's manicured lawn. I managed to bag it and stash it in the trunk, just before Moretti came around the side of the house.

"A fellow Oregonian," he said, cracking a big, welcoming smile. "Who knew we'd both end up here in the north country?" Moretti was heavier than I remembered, his dark hair was going to gray, and his hooded eyes seemed as hard to read as ever. He was dressed for comfort in a golf shirt, jeans, and expensive loafers with no socks. "Come on around back. I set some beers out. We got some sun today, so we can sit by the pool." He hesitated slightly before nodding at Archie. "Bring your pooch."

Arch and I followed him to a tastefully landscaped backyard, which included a swimming pool rimmed in natural stone with a waterfall at one end and a vanishing edge at the other. Strains of an Adele song floated from a set of outdoor speakers. I looked around admiringly. "Living the dream, Aldo."

He smiled with pride as we took our seats at a wrought iron table. "Yeah, twenty-eight years in the traces was enough, man, and I couldn't get far enough away from LA. How about you? How's lawyering up in the wine country?"

"It's good. Different. Now that I'm a defense attorney I realize how much firepower I had as a prosecutor. Hard to see it when you're part of it."

He rolled his eyes but kept the smile friendly. "Don't tell me you've gone all liberal on me?"

I laughed, remembering good-natured arguments about politics. But I didn't take the bait. "How's Donna?"

"She's fine, far as I know. We divorced, what, nine years ago now? I'm happily remarried."

"Oh, sorry to hear that, but glad you found someone." Before he could ask about my marital status, I said, "The exoneration of Dante Ellis was a shocker, huh?"

"You're not kidding. About all I remember about that case is that it was cut and dried."

"We put him at the scene, for sure," I said, "but we never

proved the gun we found in his car was the actual murder weapon. And we made his motive up out of whole cloth. I think we suffered from tunnel vision, to tell you the truth."

He waved off the comment. "Hell, Cal, you went to trial with a lot less." He smiled with a gleam in his eye. "And we knew you could sell it. You were our best prosecutor in those days. Everybody knew that."

"We got it wrong. That's the bottom line."

"And now you want to right that wrong?" He shook his head. "That's admirable, and I respect you for it. But from where I sit life's too short to go sifting through the past. We investigated the case and prosecuted it in good faith. Shit happens."

Tell that to Dante Ellis, I thought. But instead, I said, "Irena Krasnova was trafficked to LA from Eastern Europe and was part of a prostitute ring aimed at high rollers. What do you remember about that part of the investigation?"

"Like I said, not much. As I recall, her coworkers were uncooperative, and we never found out who was running the ring. Whoever it was ran a tight ship. *Nobody* was talking. And we weren't working Vice, for Christ's sake."

"Does the name Bitch Queen ring any bells?"

"Hmm, wasn't she the madam?"

"Apparently," I said. "What about jealous johns? As I remember it, Dante's counsel raised that possibility at trial but never revealed a name. Did we check that out? I'm drawing a blank on that, too."

"I couldn't tell you, but once we had the video of Ellis going in and coming out of her apartment, I doubt we beat the bushes all that hard."

Tunnel vision, I repeated to myself. We worked our way through several more questions, but it was clear I wasn't going to learn anything useful. Apparently, his memory was as bad as mine or maybe worse. We'd each had a beer when I got up and walked over to the pool to inspect the vanishing edge. "That's how they do it," I said, looking at the trough that caught and recirculated the water flowing over the edge. "Clever."

Aldo grinned. "Love my pool. Took a month to bring the rocks in and lay them, but it was worth it. Did a lot of the work myself."

"What else do you do to stay busy these days?"

"I grow cannabis. I have two-hundred and fifty acres under cultivation just south of here. All legal, of course. I got in early and scored one of the first licenses from the Liquor Control Commission. I think my background in law enforcement helped." He smiled with that gleam in his eye again. "If you can't beat 'em, join 'em, right?"

I laughed. "Looks like you landed on your feet, Aldo. Good luck with the business."

"Thanks, Cal. Sorry I wasn't more help, but when I retired that was it. I was finished with chasing bad guys and all the grief that came with it. Put that all in the past." He eyed me. "I'm surprised you want to revisit those days, given what happened to your wife and all."

I hid a flash of annoyance at the inappropriate comment but forced a smile. "Yeah, well, we do-gooders have to keep doing good, right?"

I turned to go, and behind Aldo, Archie lifted his leg and peed on one of his blooming begonia plants. I averted my gaze and didn't say anything. Sometimes I wondered just how perceptive this dog of mine really was.

Once underway, I thought about the encounter. I didn't learn a damn thing relative to the case. Had Aldo really put it all behind him, or did he simply not want to rehash what was, at least in retrospect, a shoddy investigation? I was pretty sure it was the latter, and given that, it was no surprise he was less than encouraging about my plans.

I laughed out loud thinking about his new business venture. LA cop retires to Oregon and buys a pot farm? The times had changed, for sure. But as I worked my way back to the I-5, anxiety settled on me like a cold fog. Sure, it was just the beginning of the investigation, but the enormity of the task I'd taken on so cavalierly suddenly hit me with full force. Was Nando right? Did I run the risk of raising false hopes in Dante Ellis? And that brought its own set of risks. Would he get disillusioned? Decide again to shoot me? I said that last piece to myself as a joke, but it really wasn't funny.

I floored the gas pedal to merge onto the 5 ahead of a tanker truck. There was no turning back now.

CHAPTER NINE

"MY KNUCKLES REALLY ARE WHITE," I QUIPPED TO Archie. It was the next day, and we were halfway up the Grapevine, that notorious stretch of I-5 that ascends four thousand feet from the floor of the Central Valley to the top of Tejon Pass, the northern gateway to Los Angeles. Monster trucks, two sometimes three abreast, lumbered along while cars wove in and out at twice the speed, like contestants in the Indy 500.

Welcome back to the City of Angels.

Just past Santa Clarita, I took the 405 towards Santa Monica, where I'd scored pet friendly Airbnb accommodations that didn't threaten to bankrupt me. Traffic was cheek to jowl but somehow managed to flow at eighty-plus miles an hour without a hitch. We arrived a bit early for check-in, so I parked in the designated spot in front of the apartment on Colorado Avenue. My new neighborhood had a friendly vibe with a mix of small apartment buildings and modest homes, most of which had well-tended yards. But in a sign of the times, I noticed security cameras here and there, including one mounted in the eaves of the house directly across the street.

I leashed up Archie and headed for the beach, a mile or so straight down Colorado Avenue. The sky was overcast—a late spring marine layer that Angelenos coined June Gloom—but that didn't seem to discourage the throngs on the beach, many of whom already had tans that made me look like Casper the ghost.

I slipped off my shoes when we hit the sand, and Archie whined and tugged at his leash. "Easy, Big Boy," I told him. "Not sure I can let you run free here." A cool breeze came off the water, the sand felt good on my bare feet, and it wasn't long until my freeway-induced tenseness fell away.

That's when I called Dante Ellis. "You're here," he said with a note of surprise in his voice. "I got back yesterday. The old F-150 ran like a clock. Tell you the truth, I didn't expect you to show up. We're really going to do this, huh?"

"We're going to give it a shot, Dante. The case is thirteen years old, so there are no guarantees, understood?"

"Yeah, I get that, but you told me you were a hotshot," he said with no hint of a tease in his voice.

"I was trying to persuade you not to blow my head off," I said in an attempt at humor.

He didn't laugh. "So, what's the game plan?"

"For openers, I need the names and any contact information for the witnesses we discussed—the Bitch Queen, Weird Little Fucker, Emile the Enforcer, and the last name of Irena's friend Anika. Also, any of the Impromptu staff at that time who'd be willing to talk to me."

"I've already made some calls."

"You have? Uh, you didn't disclose what we're up to, did you?"

The line went quiet for a few beats. "I might've said something to a couple of people, but I told them to keep it to themselves."

I could've kicked myself for not saying something sooner,

but Dante moved faster than I anticipated. "Good. Look, going forward, just say you're thinking about suing the city for more than your wrongful conviction compensation. Tell them I'm your attorney, that I'm down here fact-finding, okay? Word will get out sooner or later, but the less people know what we're really about the better."

"Got it. One of the people I talked to was a regular at the bar, a good friend back in the day. She told me she never believed I killed Irena. Didn't know Weird Little Fucker's name, either, but she told me his driver, Alec Macleod, might still be in LA. Said he was out of the life, doing some kind of religious mission work. She's going to get back to me with an address or a cell number."

"Excellent. I definitely want to talk to him."

"I also talked to a waitress who still works at the Impromptu, Sherri Haller. She said she'd be willing to talk to you as long as it's just between you and her. I'll text you her contact information. She also told me the owner's still around, a guy named Imhoff, Harry Imhoff. He was kind of a dick."

We exchanged addresses and disconnected after agreeing to meet the following evening. Archie and I walked for another mile or so along the beach. By that time, I had my pantlegs rolled up like a tourist and Archie was straining at his leash, barking at the gulls, and dashing in and out of the shore break like a little kid. The fresh sea air had swept my mind clean, and I had a sense that Dante and I had achieved liftoff, inauspicious as it was.

The apartment on Colorado was an add-on to a renovated bungalow. It had a gated back entrance leading to a small brick patio with some wrought iron furniture and a Weber barbeque. A hose next to the apartment door allowed

Archie and me to wash off the sand. I'd been told a spare key hung on a nail on the far side of the front windowsill. I found the key well out of sight and deemed the location reasonably secure. That, it turned out, was a mistake.

Our indoor accommodations were borderline claustrophobic—a living room with a Murphy bed, a kitchen alcove, and an adjoining bathroom accessible by a pocket door. The saving grace was the espresso machine in the kitchen. A one-pound bag of Lavazza Italian roast coffee stood next to the machine, a testament to Angelino hospitality. All the comforts of home.

I unpacked, showered, and then poured myself a glass of Carabella pinot noir from one of the half dozen bottles of Oregon wine I'd brought along. I swirled and sniffed it from a fluted wine glass that I'd wrapped in a couple of tee shirts for the trip. A little bit of home, I figured, wouldn't hurt.

I called Zoe next, and when I told her what I was drinking she said, "Hang on, I'll pour myself a glass." When she returned, we virtually clinked glasses and brought each other up to date. "I got a half chapter done and then hit a brick wall," she told me. "Who was I kidding, thinking I could write a novel?"

"Hey," I said, "no trash talk. Take a long jog. That always works for you."

"Easy for you to say down there in the sunshine. It's coming straight down here." We shared a laugh, and then she said, "So Dante hit the track running. That's a good sign, I think."

"Yeah. You know, I think he may turn out to be an asset. He's not real fond of me, but he seems committed to the task."

Zoe paused before answering. "Well, don't rely too

heavily on him until you're sure. He's been through a lot of trauma, Cal. There's a name for it—post-incarceration syndrome, and it can severely impact mental health. He could be unpredictable, even unreliable. Trust but verify."

I told her I would, adding, "Your plan worked the other night."

"How's that?"

I miss you, Zoe. A lot."

CHAPTER TEN

MY FIRST MORNING IN LA STARTED WITH A RUN ON THE beach, followed by a cold cereal breakfast and two double cappuccinos. I called Todd Whipple next and suggested lunch. "Sounds good," he said. "There's a little deli on Los Angeles Street called—"

"The Trimana," I said. "You're a creature of habit, Todd. Do they still have that great hot pastrami sandwich?"

"They do. The menu's chiseled in stone, you know. Meet me there at 11:30. If you arrive first, grab a booth in the back where we can talk."

I did arrive first. Like its menu, the deli hadn't changed—a throwback to mid-century soda shops with a menu on the wall, a row of red-topped stools at the counter, and a half dozen high-backed booths in the back. Todd Whipple hadn't changed much either. I watched as he entered the shop, his dark hair cut short and his body still trim, like he must've looked as an All-American wrestler at UCLA. His college nickname The Whip had stuck at LAPD.

I was disappointed, though. He was empty-handed.

I stood to greet him, and there was the usual moment of hesitation about whether to shake hands or bump fists. We did the former. "Love the 'stache, Cal," he said with a wry smile, "and the casual attire. Last time I saw you, you were wearing three pieces."

"Yeah, I had a suit-burning when I arrived in Oregon. The vests went in first." We talked and kidded each other for a while, and after we ordered our lunches, I got down to business. "So, the murder book?"

He rolled his eyes. "It's missing at the moment."

"*Missing?* How can that be?"

"All our murder books, past and present, were moved into the new Homicide Library, like better than 5,000 boxes. The Krasnova book isn't the first to go missing, believe me. We're also scanning them right now, so the books are getting moved around even more. I put maximum heat on the library team. It'll turn up. Sorry, I know you're counting on it."

I breathed a little easier but not much. It was generally conceded that the LAPD had developed the most comprehensive, well-organized murder book system in the country. Surely, they wouldn't lose the one I desperately needed. Surely Murphy's law wasn't unfolding here.

"Okay" I said. "Any idea on timing?"

"Soon."

Normal soon or LAPD-bureaucracy soon? I thought but didn't say. I was already asking too much. Our orders came up, and after we sat back down and began eating—a hot pastrami for me and a salami and Swiss for Todd—I said between bites, "Any chance LAPD will open a cold case investigation of who hired the Krasnova hit man?"

Todd swallowed a bite and shook his head. "The exoneration will eventually come up for review, but I don't think there'll be much appetite to do what you're attempting." He smiled at me. "Besides, you'll have the case cracked by then. I did google you, Cal. Damn, you didn't let any grass grow under your feet in Oregon, that's for sure."

Ignoring the compliment, I said, "Ryerson and Moretti reported to you during the Krasnova investigation. I—"

"They were one of eight teams I had at that time. Don't expect me to know all the details," he said, his tone borderline defensive.

I opened my hands. "No worries. I spoke to Moretti on the way down here, but he wasn't much help. What about Ryerson? Do you remember much about his involvement in the investigation? You know, the guy usually had a unique take on a case, and he was a worrier."

"Right. We used to call him Sixth Sense. He'd interview a witness and know right away whether they were telling the truth or not. And he could come up with a profile of the perp just by looking at the crime scene. Okay, he was a pain in the ass sometimes, but we always listened to him."

"Can you remember anything about his take on this case?"

"Yeah, I do remember that he and Aldo didn't always see eye to eye on it, although I'm a little foggy on what the hell the issues were. I mean, it was a slam dunk, right?"

"Except it wasn't. Can you think of anything else?"

Todd held a hand up while he chewed and swallowed a bite of sandwich. "Oh, yeah, one thing—he said Ellis showed what he thought was genuine remorse over the death of Krasnova. We all had a good laugh at that. How many murderers have we seen who can shed crocodile tears on demand? Too many." He looked at me. "You know it, and I know it."

"Did Ryerson open any other lines of investigation or

have any leads?" I asked. "You know, something I didn't hear about when we were reviewing the case back then?"

"Not that I remember." Todd raised his eyes to mine. Did I see a hint of, if not shame then at least regret? "I sure as hell didn't encourage it," he went on. "I thought we had enough to convict Ellis. Besides, we didn't need airtight cases when *you* were prosecuting. It's all about getting the conviction, right?"

"That's more or less what Aldo told me. I could make a case that I was being used, but that's bullshit. I lusted after the convictions as much as you did."

"And nothing's changed," Todd said. "It's the nature of the beast, Cal."

"Aldo also told me to let it be, that shit happens. What do *you* think?"

"You're stirring the muck up, that's what I think. It won't reflect well on any of us. I'm with Aldo. Let it go, my friend."

I nodded slowly and felt my face grow hot. "I expected something better from you, Todd. Does this explain the missing murder book?"

He shot me a look. "I'm going to let that question slide. You're on a fool's errand, Cal, but I won't stand in your way. If the book turns up, you can have a look at it. But this ain't Oregon. Watch yourself."

Don't hold your breath on seeing the murder book, I said to myself as I walked out of the deli. The man said "if" not "when."

CHAPTER ELEVEN

"I FILED A FORM CALLED AN ERRONEOUSLY CONVICTED Person Claim today with the help of my Innocence Project attorney," Dante said as we sat in the enclosed yard at my Airbnb that afternoon. He looked ripped in a tight tee shirt and had trimmed his beard, but his brown eyes had a pinkish tinge, and I caught a whiff of alcohol on his breath. Archie had greeted him with friendly butt wags and picked a spot next to his chair to lie down. He seemed glad to see my dog, but his reaction to me was icy, as if I were a necessary evil.

"Since I was found factually innocent of the conviction by a judge," he went on, his speech faintly slurred, "I don't need a hearing or nothing. Just the claim form, and then I'm eligible for compensation."

"Is it still $110 for every day you spent incarcerated?" I asked, referring to the compensation in place when I was a prosecutor.

"Nope. It's $140 now." He looked at me, and his eyes widened. "That's over three-quarters of a million dollars." He scratched his brow. "You know, I didn't think I was going to be around, so I didn't pay much attention to the money. That's more than I ever dreamed of having."

"You deserve every penny of it, Dante." I paused,

figuring this was a good time for a gut check. "Do you still want to go ahead with the investigation?"

"Damn straight," he said without hesitation. "The money's nice, but it doesn't change anything. I still want to know who the hell set me up and why." He looked pensive for a few moments before adding, "I don't want to be a charity case, either. I can pay you now."

"No. This is on my dime. It's not charity, it's what we agreed."

He cocked his head before nodding. "Okay, I'm cool with that. You got your reasons just like me." He pulled at his beard. "Been thinking about Jamare, too. I know I told you not to look for him, but a young man like him could use some of this money. Maybe you could arrange an anonymous donation from me?"

"Sure, I can do that. I'll tell my private detective to reinstate the search. You realize your son will want to know where the money came from."

"Anonymous donation, that's what I want," he said with finality. Then, changing the subject, he added, "My friend got back to me about the driver and bodyguard, Alec Macleod. Dude works at a mission in Skid Row, the Rock of Hope. It's on South San Pedro. She couldn't come up with a cell number. You'll have to go there and ask for him."

"Good," I said. "I'll look him up tomorrow. By the way, I called your waitress friend, Sherri Haller, and left a message for her to get back to me."

"Yeah, she told me you called. Said she gets off tonight at ten and could meet you, but she's nervous about getting dragged into something. She has a great job, makes really good tips. I told her you could be trusted." He bent down and scratched Archie behind the ears then looked up at me. "You can, right?"

The question annoyed me, but I pushed the feeling down. After all, Dante didn't know me any better than I knew him. "I'm a lawyer, Dante. Confidentiality is in my DNA."

A curt nod. "I'll reassure her, try to get her to meet you tonight. Stay tuned." He looked at his watch and stood up. "I'm going to a rapid chess tournament over in Garden Grove. Gotta beat the traffic."

"Rapid chess? What's that?"

"Instead of thirty seconds per move, it's ten, typically. It's like a sprint versus running a mile. Good for skill building."

I whistled softly. "You gotta have the game down cold to play that fast."

He puffed a dismissive breath. "Nobody has chess down cold, even the grand masters." With that, Dante turned to leave and swayed a little in the effort.

"Are you okay to drive?"

He turned back to me, his eyes flashing anger. "Fuck you, Claxton. Mind your own business."

—/—

I met Sherri Haller at an all-night diner on Rosecrans later that night. Late thirties or early forties, she was tall and angular with a pixie haircut and thick, enhanced eyelashes that gave her an edgy look. "Dante said I could trust you to keep me out of this," she said after I introduced myself and invited her to sit down. Her gaze was direct and her demeanor about as friendly as Dante's.

I reassured her, adding, "Do you mind my asking why you're so worried about speaking to me?"

She flashed a that-was-a-dumb-question look. "Whoever put that contract on Irena Krasnova is still out there, right? I'm single with a kid to raise. I don't want to wind up with a bullet in my head like her."

"You think whoever's responsible is still in LA?"

She shrugged a shoulder. "Does anybody ever leave this town?"

The waitress approached, poured us each a coffee, and we ordered. I said, "Do you have any thoughts on who could've set up Dante?"

Her face clouded over. "God, I hate going there. Irena was such a beautiful kid, you know? And despite her profession, she had a soul as pure as the driven snow." Sherri focused on something behind me for a few moments. "You have to suspect her traffickers, but she was their crown jewel. Why would they kill her? I mean, she had millionaires, A-list movie actors, politicians, all of them forking out big bucks to spend an evening with her. Makes no sense."

"What can you tell me about her traffickers?"

"Not much, except I heard a woman ran the show back then."

"The Bitch Queen?"

Sherri's eyes flashed. "I hate that term, but, yeah, that's what the girls called her. But Emile was her eyes and ears at the Impromptu." She anticipated my next question. "His last name's Szabo. He was upset by Irena's death." She smiled bitterly. "Not grief, you understand, but the emotion that follows a financial setback. At least, that was my take."

"Is he still in LA?"

"Nope. He died of a heart attack about a year after Irena was murdered."

I asked several more questions, and then our food arrived—a slice of pie for me and ham and eggs for Sherri. "This is my dinner," she explained between bites. "The life of a waitress."

After we ate in silence for a while, I said, "How did Irena's death impact the scene at the Impromptu?"

"Well, the girls were sad and freaked out at the same time, but, you know, business is business. Then the owner of the restaurant, a guy named Harry Imhoff, bought the escort service, at least the rumor was he bought it. Anyway, the scene changed after that."

"How?"

"The Slovenian girls began to leave, and a new group came in over time. The new girls tended to be local recruits." She made a face. "They were coarser, more streetwise."

"What happened to the Slovenian girls?"

"They drifted off, searching for the American dream, I guess." A wistful smile. "Most of them were survivors, you know? Not heavy into drugs and partying. They were vulnerable, because they were undocumented. The new girls are locked in because they have serious drug habits to feed. The clientele's gone down a notch or two, for sure—no more politicos and Hollywood types, at least no A-listers— but, you know, demand for the world's oldest profession's always strong."

"When did the escort service change hands?"

She gave me the dumb question look again. "It's not like there was some announcement. Maybe a few months after Irena's murder."

"Dante mentioned a man who was strongly attracted

to Irena back then, a regular at the bar. Tucker something. Dante didn't remember his last name. Do you remember him?"

"Oh, yeah. I was coming to him. Name's Tucker Bivens. The story was he moved a lot of hard drugs in those days. Yeah, he was *obsessed* with Irena. Tried to monopolize her, have her all to himself. She didn't like him all that much, and I think Emile got involved several times to tell him to back off."

"How did he take that?"

"Not well, but he never directly challenged Emile. Nobody messed with that guy."

"Was Tucker jealous of Dante's friendship with Irena?"

"To the extreme. Of course, Tucker was jealous of all men who had access to Irena. Dante wasn't sleeping with her, but they had something special, something intimate, almost like Dante was her big brother. Tucker *hated* that intimacy, and he probably figured Dante was a friend with benefits, too."

"Was he jealous enough to have her killed and lay it on Dante?"

"I wouldn't rule it out. He was soft spoken, the kind of man who doesn't need to act tough to be feared." Her thickly lashed eyes narrowed down, and the skin on her cheekbones tightened. "And men are capable of *anything* when scorned by a woman, right? If the traffickers didn't have her killed, he'd be my next guess."

"Dante mentioned that Irena was doing some modeling on the side. Do you know anything about that?"

Sherri sighed and looked wistful for a moment. "In a just world, Irena would have been a supermodel. She was thin, graceful, and her face, my God, could stop traffic. I did hear some rumors about her modeling but no details. Her friend, Lara Novak, might know more about that."

"Is Lara still around?"

"Yeah, I think so. I heard she became a masseuse. Works at some swanky wellness center in Beverly Hills—the Arlington, I think." Sherri smiled sardonically. "The American dream lives on."

"Irena had another friend named Anika. Do you know her whereabouts or her last name?"

Sherri's face clouded over a second time. "Molnar, Anika Molnar. She's dead, too. Opioid overdose. It wasn't long after Emile died. It was ruled an accident, but a lot of the girls suspected suicide. Anika was angry and despondent over Irena's death." Sherri wrung her hands. "It was like the Impromptu was cursed or something."

"I thought you said the Slovenian girls weren't into drugs."

She paused for a moment. "Yeah, that's a little weird, come to think of it. But, you know, drugs are always readily available, and newbies don't have the tolerance of an addict."

The conversation wound down from there. I picked up the check and walked her to her car. When she got in, she rolled down the window, looked directly at me and said, "Just so we're clear, Dante told me who you are. The only reason I came was because he asked me to. Maybe he can forgive you, but I can't. What you and the LAPD did to him was really rotten. You should all be ashamed." She rolled up the window and drove off.

The comment stung like a slap in the face, but I had to admit she had a point.

CHAPTER TWELVE

A SIZEABLE NORTH SWELL MATERIALIZED OVERNIGHT, unleashing a horde of local surfers clamoring to take advantage of Santa Monica's legendary surf spots. After our early morning beach jog, Archie and I sat on the sand and watched the action for a while. Every wave was jammed with surfers—vintage long boarders making sweeping turns, short board hot-doggers slashing back and forth across the steep faces, and every surf stylist in between. I marveled at the chaos, the scene reminding me of the situation I'd encountered on the Grapevine coming in.

There was no escaping traffic in LA, it seemed.

Nando called as we headed back to our apartment. "Have you secured the murder book?" he began.

"Not yet. I was told by the captain who supervised the Krasnova investigation that it's missing, but I'm not to be concerned, of course."

"Ha!" Nando blurted. "I was worried that would happen. Who at the LAPD would want you poring over a book that is a testament to their incompetence?"

"This cop's a good guy, but I was probably naïve to think he would go out of his way to help me. We'll see if he comes through."

I went on to describe my conversation with Sherri Haller.

When I finished, Nando said, "So, we have lost two more potential witnesses, but at least the death of Szabo appears unrelated to the matter at hand. Still, the unsolved shooting of one of the investigating detectives and now these two deaths set a tone, Calvin." I imagined my friend shaking his head. "You must use an abundance of caution down there."

"Of course," I said, adding, "I googled Tucker Bivens last night. He's CEO of a bitcoin trading company here in LA called CryptoNerds. Apparently, he's moved on from being an illicit drug distributor back when Dante was tending bar at the Impromptu. I can contact him at his company, but I'd like you to find out everything you can about him first. The same goes for the hitman, Ferris Spielman. Did their paths cross prior to the murder?"

"Consider it done. What about the victim's friend, Lara Novak?"

"She's a masseuse at a clinic in Beverly Hills. I've got an appointment for a massage next Tuesday. Two hundred and fifty bucks for an hour. Used another name."

I imagined the smart-ass look on Nando's face when he said, "Ah, the sacrifices we make for our work."

We ended the call on that note. Nando was right about the murder book—despite the tunnel-vision aspect of the investigation, there were undoubtedly details in the book that would save us time and effort at the very least. And he was right about the risks, too. Of course, we had no evidence the deaths of Jimmy Ryerson and Anika Molnar were related to the murder of Irena Krasnova, but there was no reason to believe they couldn't be.

—/ /—

It was mid-morning when Archie and I arrived at the Rock of Hope mission. Located in the heart of LA's Skid Row district, the one-story building had narrow vertical windows and an arched marble entry with the word BANK still visible above the door.

"He's making his morning rounds," a middle-aged woman with tired eyes and a no-nonsense demeanor told me when I asked for Alec Macleod at the check-in station. "Reverend Alec is a busy man. Do you mind my asking what your business is with him?"

I handed her a business card. "My client's seeking redress after having been unjustly incarcerated for thirteen years. The Reverend knew my client and may have information bearing on the situation." I smiled reassuringly. "They were friends. I'm sure he'll want to help."

She tossed the card on the counter without reading it, looked at Arch, then back at me. "Most lawyers who come around here wear suits and don't bring their dogs," she said with a deadpan expression.

"It's casual Saturday, and he's my service dog," I said with a straight face.

That drew a thin smile. "Sure he is."

I smiled back. "I'm parked in the sun."

That drew another smile. "I'm a dog lover. Bless you for not leaving him in the car." She used the landline on her desk to call Macleod and after a brief conversation said, "He'll meet you at the northwest corner of San Julian and 6th in fifteen minutes." She gave me directions. "It's a ten-minute walk. Folks around here call him The Rev."

With an office in Portland and having worked here in LA, I was no stranger to homeless encampments. But Skid Row's fifty square blocks—the city's notorious repository of its most downtrodden and broken residents—still managed to shock me. Archie and I wound our way through block upon block of tents, tarps, and makeshift lean-tos pitched on the sidewalks. The area teemed with people, some cooking breakfast on braziers, others wandering aimlessly while talking to themselves, and still others engaged in all manner of commerce, legal and illegal. There was a pervasive smell, too—a perceptible stench of human waste that seemed baked into sidewalks and trash-littered streets by the relentless California sun. I tried to ignore it.

When Archie and I reached the intersection of San Julian and 6th, we encountered a group of bystanders gathered around a young woman sprawled on the sidewalk next to a tent. A man knelt beside her, and as we approached, I heard him say, "She's barely breathing." He looked up, scanned the group, and when our eyes met, he said, "Call 911."

I nodded and did what he asked.

The man stripped off his backpack, extracted a small, sealed package and after peeling off the cover and removing a blunt syringe, proceeded to squirt its contents into one of the woman's nostrils. He then closed his eyes as if offering a prayer.

An older, street-worn woman who'd been softly sobbing on the inner edge of the group said to her companion in a low voice, "Thank God for the Rev." Her companion placed his arm around her and nodded.

Must be Narcan, I said to myself. Hope it works.

The young woman had gnarled, dirty blond hair but an angelic face that life on the street hadn't yet hardened. The assembled crowd waited in silence, as if this wasn't the first overdose rescue they'd witnessed. The three or four minutes that elapsed felt like an eternity. The woman swallowed, opened her eyes, and coughed. The crowd murmured its approval and went on its way.

"I'm guessing you're Mr. Claxton," the man said as we waited for the ambulance to arrive. "Audrey mentioned you had a handsome dog."

"And you must be Alec Macleod," I said, showing a smile and offering my hand.

He was a big man with black, brush cut hair, thick eyebrows, and a full beard. He looked back at me with intense, slate gray eyes. "Thanks for making that call. You looked like you'd be quick with your cell phone."

"Glad I could help. I've heard about Narcan, but that was amazing."

"Yeah," he answered, nodding. "It's the world's most underrated drug. Problem is, it has to be in the right hands at the right time." He glanced over at the woman, who was groggy but sitting up by this time. "The good Lord must have other plans for her."

After the ambulance left with the woman, Macleod led me to a small coffeehouse. We ordered at the counter and found a table in an outdoor area behind the shop. Archie lay down next to him and got his back stroked for the trouble. Sensing I could trust this man, I explained why I came to LA and why I sought him out.

When I finished, he sighed deeply. "Good Lord, you're asking me to go back to a very dark time in my life. I remember Dante Ellis as a decent enough man, and I'm ashamed to say I didn't question his arrest. I was a different person then. Irena Krasnova had the kind of beauty a pure heart gives a person, an inner light you can't miss. Her death was an obscenity."

"Your boss at that time, Tucker Bivens—did he see that inner light?"

His face stiffened, and his eyes became slits, giving me a glimpse of what bodyguard Alec Macleod must have looked like. The transformation was unnerving. "His attraction to Irena was"—he paused as if searching for the right words—"unnatural, obsessive."

"I understand she spurned his advances. What can you tell me about that?"

He blew on his coffee, took a sip, and gazed at the Formica tabletop for a few moments. "Well, Tuck was a regular customer of Irena's, but one night he couldn't wait for the motel, tried to have sex with her in the back of the limo. Rape, basically. She screamed for me to stop, and when I did, she smacked him in the face, jumped out, and took off. Tuck told me to go get her, but I refused."

"How did he react?"

"He was furious. It was the beginning of the end of my bodyguarding career. Best thing that ever happened to me."

"How did Irena fare that night?"

"I heard later that she called her handler and had him pick her up."

"A man named Emile Szabo?"

"Yeah, that's the guy." He smiled wistfully and scratched his beard. "Courage and resourcefulness can come in surprising packages, you know?"

"Could Tucker Bivens have had her killed out of spite?"

He set his coffee mug down and looked straight at me. "At the time I didn't connect those dots. I was a lost soul. But thinking back on it, yeah, Tuck was capable of anything, provided he didn't have to get his hands dirty."

"Does the name Ferris Spielman mean anything to you?"

"No. Was he the hitman, the man who died in prison?"

I nodded and moved on to questions about the business Tucker Bivens was in, but Alec said that was an area he was reluctant to talk about. So I shifted gears. "That was a big career change for you—going from the driver-bodyguard of a drug dealer to a man of God."

He smiled wistfully. "Let's just say I didn't come from a nurturing family. My dad beat my mom until the day I broke his jaw and gave him a concussion. I did some petty crime in my youth, and word got around that I was a tough guy. That's when I became Tuck's driver. A year later he gave me a gun—a 9mm Walther—and I became his body-guard, too." A bitter smile. "He liked having a bodyguard. It was status for him."

I waited, unsure if he was going to continue.

"Corny as it sounds," he said after a long pause, "my road to Damascus moment came when my dying mother implored me to change my ways." He looked at me and blinked rapidly to ward off tears. "She made me promise."

"Moms will do that."

He smiled wistfully. "Well, a failed relationship at that time didn't help, either. Anyway, I was brought up Baptist, so I talked my way into Bethany Christian Seminary. But I dropped out during my second year. The religious dogma they were serving up just didn't sit well with me. The mis-sion hired me anyway. Skid Row's the seminary of hard knocks. Been here twelve years."

"You're a reverend in the true sense of the word."

He shook his head and smiled. "People started calling me The Rev, and I kept saying I wasn't a member of the clergy, but it didn't matter to them. The name just stuck." He paused and eyed me for a moment. "I admire what you're trying to do here, Cal. We're all hopeless sinners, so for those of us trying to live righteously, it's always about seeking redemption."

I smiled and nodded. "I suppose that's true."

He held my gaze, his eyes wide, unblinking. "You've stirred up things I've been trying to forget. I feel ashamed, like I should have known a good man like Dante Ellis couldn't have killed Irena. I should have spoken out." His face grew hard, and I saw the bodyguard again. "I still know some people. I'm going to make some inquiries. You're right to suspect Tucker Bivens."

"What's he doing now?"

"I heard he's gone legit, but I find that hard to believe. The Holy Spirit can cleanse the darkest heart, but I think it's unlikely in his case."

"Getting back to Irena's handlers," I said, "what can you tell me about the woman called the Bitch Queen?"

He frowned as if he were being dragged back in time again. "She was the Madam. She ran the whole escort service operation, but no, I don't know anything about her except that she had some kind of medical background. The operation put a premium on the health of their girls, you know, since their clientele was the well-heeled in LA and Hollywood."

"Did she own the operation?"

"I don't know. I never heard."

"Can you inquire about her as well? Try to get a name?"

He smiled. "You're asking a lot, but I'll do my best." Then something crossed his face. Not fear so much as concern. "These are ruthless people, Mr. Claxton. You and Dante need to proceed with caution."

"I get that a lot," I said and then thanked him, gave him a card, and waited while he showed Archie some attention.

"I'll be in touch," he promised as he stood up and crunched my hand in his.

It was a brief encounter, but I came away feeling a connection with this man and a sense of admiration I reserved only for people who truly walk their talk. *And he still has some underworld contacts*, I said to myself. This could get interesting.

CHAPTER THIRTEEN

I'M ALWAYS HOPING FOR THAT BREAKTHROUGH MOMENT, a flash of insight that cracks a case wide open, but in my experience it rarely happens. I'm more likely to get to the finish line by doggedly connecting a myriad of smallish dots until a recognizable pattern emerges. But even in this scenario, there's usually a point in the investigation when the momentum seems to shift ever so slightly in my favor. I sensed that shift following a call I received as I was heading back to Santa Monica after meeting with Alec Macleod.

"Cal?" a vaguely familiar voice said. "It's Mimi Ryerson."

"Mimi!" I said, connecting the voice to the wife of Jimmy Ryerson, one of the detectives who'd investigated the Krasnova case—the one who was killed in a mugging. "How are you?" She went on to tell me that she'd never remarried, that her kids were in college, and she was working in real estate. After I sketched in my situation in Oregon, including the fact that I was in a serious relationship, I said something that should have been said a long time ago. "Look Mimi, I'm sorry I didn't offer my condolences after Jimmy's passing. The truth is, I cut all my ties when I left LA and didn't hear about it until Aldo Moretti told me just the other day."

"Oh, God, Cal, I understand," she said. "I know what a

blow it was losing Nancy. If I'd had a place to go, I would've left LA, too." She paused for a moment. "Speaking of Aldo, he called out of the blue and told me about your interest in that case he and Jimmy were investigating, and what you're doing to help that poor man who was exonerated." She paused again, and I waited for her to continue. "To be honest, Aldo pissed me off."

"In what way?"

"He said that if you contact me, I shouldn't cooperate, that it wouldn't be a good idea to stir up the past." She puffed her breath out in disgust. "That thin-blue-line crap doesn't wash with me."

"Understood," I said. "I heard Jimmy took a contrarian view of the case against Dante Ellis. No excuse, but that sentiment didn't reach my desk at the time I prosecuted the case. Do you remember anything more specific than that, something Jimmy might've said?"

"Nothing beyond the fact that he was frustrated, but that wasn't anything new with Jimmy." She paused for a moment. "Even after the trial, I know he was bothered about the conviction. He might've kept dabbling, you know, he did that sometimes with cases that interested him."

"Did he document any of that?"

"Maybe. He kept journals, kind of separate from whatever went into their murder book." She sighed. "He planned to write a book someday about how to go about investigating major crimes."

A tingling pulse snaked down my spine. "It would've been a good book. They didn't call him Sixth Sense for nothing. Do you happen to have the journals?"

"They're somewhere. I packed most of Jimmy's stuff

from his study into a chest and put it in the attic several years ago."

"Would it be possible to find the journals? I'd be interested in his comments about the case. I could help you search...."

"I'll give it a try and call you back." She sighed again. "Aldo really came on strong, Cal. I guess he doesn't want to be reminded that he screwed up and arrested the wrong man."

"Did Jimmy talk about the case?"

"Gee, that was a long time ago. He was very guarded, you know? He didn't want to expose me and the kids to the dark things he was involved in." Her voice grew husky. "He was always looking out for us." She paused, adding, "There was some tension between Jimmy and Aldo at that time, I do remember that. You know, Aldo had just been promoted into the job from Narcotics, so I figured Jimmy was probably expecting too much of him." She sighed wistfully. "You know how Jimmy was."

I said I did, repeated my offer to help, and we reminisced for a while. Mimi was generous in her praise of my late wife. "Nancy was a wonderful person and such a talented artist," she said at one point. "I hope you saved her work, particularly her portraits." I told her I had, without admitting they, too, were stored in an attic.

After the call ended, I was left with a sense of anticipation. If I couldn't get the official murder book, maybe Ryerson's journals would provide something to go on. And at the same time, I found it interesting that he was still bothered by something, even *after* Dante Ellis had been convicted. But my excitement was tempered by an ache in my heart for a past that was never to be again.

—/—

At the last minute I decided to pop in on Dante to catch him up and get a sense of how he was coping now that he was back in his old stomping grounds. There were a lot of ghosts in this city for me. I could only imagine what it was like for him. His motel was on Washington Boulevard in Culver City, just down from the Sony Pictures Studio.

"Jesus, what the hell time is it?" he said as he opened the door to his second-floor room. He was in boxers and a tee shirt and shading his eyes against bright sunlight.

"It's nearly noon. How about we get a late breakfast or an early lunch? I've got some news."

"Coffee. I need coffee."

"We can manage that."

He stepped aside. "Give me a minute to shower." He grabbed pants and a shirt and ducked into the bathroom.

I took a seat next to a small table on which a chess board and pieces rested. It looked like a game in progress with maybe half the pieces still in play and the others, the vanquished, arrayed on either end of the board. A digital timer with two screens sat next to the game, and next to that a stack of books on chess theory with a few books on mathematics mixed in. And on the nightstand next to his disheveled bed was a half full quart of vodka and an empty glass.

I picked up the book on the top of the stack—*The Shereshevsky Method to Improve in Chess*—and thumbed through page after page of diagrams, chess board configurations, and detailed text. A bookmark was placed two-thirds of the way through the tome. Dense reading, very dense.

I put it down and picked up one of the math books with

an intriguing title—*Is God a Mathematician?* The back cover blurb said it was a philosophical exploration of the questions surrounding math's ability to explain the physical universe. Another dense read. I was skimming through it when Dante emerged from the bathroom.

I set the book back on the stack and nodded toward the chess board. "Who's winning?"

He nearly smiled. "I'm working my way through Shereshevsky. Not a bad chess book. I just finished Livio's book," he added, with a nod toward the one I'd been skimming.

"How could God be a mathematician?" I asked.

His eyes lit up. "The question revolves around whether we humans *invented* math to help explain physical reality or whether math has always existed, a structure that we've been *discovering* over the centuries, a structure that could've been put in place by God."

"Fascinating. What's your view?"

"I'm with Einstein. He believed math's a product of human thought." He looked at me. "You want to borrow the book?"

"No time right now," I said, smiling. "You should consider going back to school to study math. You seem to have an aptitude for it."

He dropped his eyes and shook his head. "Too late for that. Who would have me? I'm thirty-nine, man, never finished high school."

"People your age do it all the time," I said. "Come on. We can discuss it on the way to breakfast."

Dante knew a little diner on Durango, not far from his motel. "There's a shaded parking area, so your dog will be okay," he said, surprising me with his thoughtfulness. By the time we got there, I'd given up trying to convince him of the feasibility of getting a GED and then moving on to college. "In prison you learn the things you want the most, the things you dream of, are the things to stay away from," he said at one point in our conversation. Zoe was right—Incarceration Syndrome was real, and Dante seemed to have a severe case of it.

Don't push too hard, I told myself. Time is on your side.

At the diner, we both ordered coffee and full breakfasts.

"So, Macleod's street name is The Rev? Really?" Dante said after I described my Skid Row visit. "I always figured he was okay, even though he was working for the Weird Little Fucker. But now he's an honest to God preacher? Who knew?"

"He told me he felt ashamed he didn't speak up for you, Dante."

"What did he say about his boss?"

"In so many words, he thought he could've done it, said it was Bivens' style to hire someone to do his dirty work. And his emotional attachment to her could have easily led to violence. It's a common pattern."

"How you gonna prove it? Thirteen years is a long time."

You're not kidding, I thought. "Not sure yet. I'm looking at his background. We need a break, a way to get inside this."

A malicious grin spread across his face. "Maybe I'll just kill him."

"Don't kid around like that," I said, although I wasn't sure he was kidding. "If Bivens did it, death is too good for him."

Dante nodded grimly. "You're right. Rotting in prison's a lot worse. But we gotta catch him, first."

I went on to relate the conversation I had with Mimi

Ryerson. I also admitted that certain people in the LAPD might not be too happy that I was reopening the case.

"Figures," Dante said in response. "Cops make mistakes all the time, but they're really good at hiding them." He fixed my eyes. "Funny, the cop who thought I was innocent got blown away. You gonna look into that, too?"

"If it's relevant, I will. Right now, I'm more interested in the journal Ryerson kept."

Dante gave me an eye roll. "I'll believe it when I see it. Why does some dead cop's wife want to help me, anyway?"

I smiled back at him. "I admit it's rare, Dante, but some people want to do the right thing."

CHAPTER FOURTEEN

"LOOK, CAL, THE GODDAMN MURDER BOOK'S MISPLACED, that's all. This is the LAPD, for Christ's sake," Todd Whipple snapped back at me when I called the next morning for an update. "What, you think our bureaucracy has gotten any more efficient since you left? It'll turn up. Remember, I'm doing you a favor here," he added, his voice ringing with annoyance.

I thanked him and signed off, wondering if I was getting stonewalled. I hadn't heard back from Nando about Tucker Bivens and couldn't talk to Lara Novak at the Arlington Wellness Center until the next week. So, without the book I was all dressed up with no place to go on the investigation. I didn't share the news about Ryerson's journal with Todd. I trusted the man, but at that point he didn't need to know I might gain access to what Jimmy Ryerson—aka Sixth Sense—really thought about the investigation.

After stopping at a florist in Santa Monica later that morning, I fought my way across town to Forest Lawn Memorial Park in the Hollywood Hills, where Nancy was buried. Located on a stretch of rolling hills between the LA Zoo, Griffith Park and Warner Brothers Studios, the cemetery was immense and dazzlingly green. The sight always made me I wonder how much water and chemicals were required to keep it looking that way.

To be honest, I was dreading the visit, but it was something I had to do. The cemetery covered hundreds of acres, but I found a cool, shady parking space and lowered the car windows for Arch. I had no difficulty finding Nancy's grave, which, I recalled, was just down an eastern slope from the resting places of Ozzie and Harriet Nelson of 1950s television fame. This was Hollywood, after all.

It was a still, cloudless day, not unlike the last time I visited more than a decade earlier, and as I laid a dozen yellow roses on the stone, I knew the petals would soon begin to curl and discolor. An apt, if unintended, metaphor for the impermanence of life, I thought. I was also struck by the absurdity of this burial custom—expecting a slab of granite with a few inscribed words to somehow preserve the memory of someone who was once a living, loving human being. That stone bearing the inscription would last, of course, but at the same time, it seemed so inadequate, so utterly impersonal, an insult to Nancy's memory.

My heart shrank in my chest.

But despite my qualms, as I sat on the grass next to the grave, memories began to flow—memories I hadn't allowed in my head for a long time. Our chance meeting at the Berkeley campus. The night we stole a rowboat and rowed halfway to Alcatraz in the moonlight. Her first art exhibit at that small gallery in Pasadena. Clair's birth and all the milestones that followed. It was a good life, but I could only venture down that path so far without being reminded of how it all ended and the role I played.

The mood broke, and as I started to leave, a solitary seagull circled Nancy's grave and landed on a headstone across from us. The bird stood silent, examining the scene with one round eye turned toward me, its snow-white breast gleaming in the sunlight. I sat still, watching the bird, and suddenly found myself thinking of Zoe Bennett, her compassion, her creative drive as a writer, the steadfastness that grounded her character. And I smiled thinking of her independent nature, her stubbornness, her feistiness.

"You'd like Zoe," I said out loud, as if I were speaking to Nancy. "She's an awful lot like you. I guess that's why I love her."

The seagull tilted its head, as if acknowledging my comment.

As I was leaving, I turned at the top of the rise. The bird was gone.

—⫠—

The rest of the day passed without incident, and after a late dinner and a long conversation with Zoe, Archie and I headed down to the north side of the pier for a run along the beach. It was a dark, moonless night, and as we ran I could hear the sharp staccato of the breaking surf, but I couldn't see the waves. This run was needed to help me deal with my frustration at the rate of progress on the case. I began to worry I might have to return to Oregon empty-handed. I knew deep down Zoe wasn't crazy about what I was doing here, but she was too supportive to criticize.

The last thing she said to me that night was, "You know what Nelson Mandela said, Cal—'It always seems impossible until it's done.'"

Back at the apartment, a black Lexus sat parked in front

bearing a vanity plate with *Impromptu* written on it. As Arch and I approached, a smoldering cigarette butt arced out of an open front window and landed with a shower of sparks on the sidewalk in front of us. I kicked the butt to the curb and glared at two shadowy figures sitting in the front seat of the car. Neither one spoke as the car window retracted. They both took up a lot of space in the front seats, I noted.

The gate leading to my apartment patio was ajar. I pushed it open, and a high-pitched male voice said, "Is that you, Cal Claxton? I figured you'd show up eventually."

Archie went into the patio first and answered for me with a low, warning growl. I tensed up and moved through the gate cautiously, and after telling my dog to chill, said, "Who the hell are you?"

"Harry Imhoff. At your service."

It took me a moment to place the name. "You're the owner of the Impromptu, right?" I said as I switched on a low wattage patio light.

"It's a burden I must bear, yes." Imhoff was seated, a mountain of a man, at least three-hundred pounds. The mass of rounded flesh was housed in stretch jeans, a tent-sized linen shirt, and pull-on sneakers with thick, white-edged soles. He remained seated and didn't offer his hand. I worried about the chair collapsing.

"You're just the man I wanted to see," I said, as Archie sat on his haunches next to me and assessed the situation.

Imhoff's close-shaved, pinkish cheeks and full lips gave him a boyish aspect, although his thinning hair was graying at the temples. "Well," he said in a voice that mimicked escaping helium, "if it pleases you, it tickles me to death. Why don't you go first?"

I set aside the question of how he found me and what

he was really after and gave him a vague spiel about how I was representing Dante Ellis in potential civil litigation. Then I said, "I'm looking for context here, Harry, you know, trying to get a sense of what was going on at the Impromptu at that time. For example, what relationships did Irena Krasnova have back then that should have been more thoroughly probed by the police?"

He cleared his throat and smiled without mirth. "Let me preface my remarks by saying how much I admire your willingness to help Dante. He's a good man. But to your question, I'm sure you understand that being a businessman in LA is *very* difficult, and the pandemic made it even worse. State and city taxes, burdensome regulations, lazy, unreliable workers, unfair competition...it's a wonder any small business can make a go of it in this city. I prefer to look forward rather than worry about the past."

He looked at me for a reaction. I returned his gaze but didn't say anything.

He scowled, and his fleshy face seemed to harden a bit. "I worry that your efforts might cause me great harm, Mr. Claxton."

"How could that be?"

He sighed dramatically. "I own a fine restaurant, but, alas, it barely breaks even some months. Good Company, my escort business, keeps me afloat, and the secret to any escort business is discretion. I'm sure you understand that."

I didn't respond but thought, *well, that answers the question of who owns the escort service now.*

He flashed the counterfeit smile again. "You force me to be blunt, Mr. Claxton. I don't need someone like you snooping around, asking my staff questions about something that happened a long time ago, tragic as it was."

"I have a job to do."

He went on as if he hadn't heard me. "This city is fueled by rumors and innuendo, and your actions are going to do nothing but fan those flames. Pretty soon the police will start coming around and asking questions again, maybe even the media, God forbid. I can't have that. Do you understand me?"

A seed of anger sprouted in my gut. "I'm not a big fan of prostitution rings, but it's not my intent to cause you any harm. And I can assure you that any investigations I undertake are carried out with the utmost discretion. But that said, you need to know that I always put the needs of my client first."

His face tightened further, his pulpy lips now a straight line. "This isn't Podunk Oregon, my friend, and my request isn't optional. Stay the fuck away from my business, my people, and my past. Am I clear?"

I felt my face get hot, but this was clearly not the time or place to start something. "I don't respond to threats," I said in a calm voice. "We're done here. You can show yourself out." I turned and let myself into the apartment, Archie followed, and I locked the door. A few moments later I heard the Lexus drive off.

I stood in the middle of the room, going back over what just happened, and then called Dante. After describing the encounter, I said, "How the hell did Imhoff know where I'm staying? You're the only one who has that information."

The phone went silent for several seconds. "Yeah, well, Sherri Haller asked me for it," he said in a slow, slightly slurred voice. "She told me Imhoff wanted to talk to you. I didn't think he'd threaten you like that."

"So, you just gave her my address? *Really?*"

"She, uh, she said Imhoff found out she met with you and told her to get your address, or he'd fire her ass."

"How did he know she talked to me?"

"She didn't say. There aren't a lot of secrets at the Impromptu, I guess. Just like when I was there."

"You should've told me about this," I said, "We're not going to get anywhere unless there's absolute trust between us. You asked me a while back if I could be trusted. What about you, Dante? Can I trust you?"

Another silence ensued. "Yeah, you can. Sorry, man. That was stupid not telling you. I didn't want Sherri getting hurt on my account, so I gave her your address without thinking it through. Then I was embarrassed to tell you. I really fucked up."

"Just don't let it happen again, okay? I've got your back and you need to have mine."

"Yeah, I get it. But don't worry. Imhoff's small time. He's probably bluffing."

I raised my eyebrows at the last remark. "Judging from the muscle he brought with him, I'm not so sure about that."

That's where I left it with Dante. I wanted to be reassured by his words, but I wasn't all the way there. His drinking added another layer of uncertainty. Should I have confronted him about it? I wasn't sure.

I looked at Archie, who lay watching me from the corner. "Nando was right, Big Boy. What could possibly go wrong?"

CHAPTER FIFTEEN

MIMI RYERSON CALLED FIRST THING THE NEXT MORNING, giving me renewed hope my investigation wasn't going to wither on the vine. "The good news is I found Jimmy's crime journals," she said after we exchanged greetings. "The bad news is the one you're interested in is in terrible shape. We had this freak downpour, oh, months ago now, and there must have been a leak in the roof right above the box the journal was stored in."

"Downpour in LA? You've got to be kidding me," I said. "Do you mind if I take a look, anyway?"

"Of course not, Cal. What's left of it is sitting on my kitchen table."

Mimi lived in Topanga, a small village on the western edge of the Santa Monica Mountains. It was a far cry from Huntington Park, where she and Jimmy lived in a three-bedroom tract home thirteen years earlier. Nancy and I hadn't been tight friends with the Ryersons, but we'd attended numerous barbeques in their backyard. They were way more social than we were back in those halcyon days.

Mimi's new place had the spacious front porch of a ranch house but with an added second story. It was set back from the road in a grove of mature live oaks. She met me at the door with a warm smile. I'd forgotten how attractive she was, with blond hair framing cornflower blue eyes and a smile that seemed to light up her face. "My," she said, holding me at arm's length after we hugged, "Oregon appears to agree with you, Cal. You look great." Her expression turned impish. "Kinda outdoorsy. I like the look."

"And you haven't changed a bit, Mimi." I looked around and smiled. "You gave up living in the burbs, huh?"

She laughed. "Oh, yeah. A cul-de-sac was Jimmy's idea of paradise. I like my privacy out here. And, you know, there's a great bohemian vibe in Topanga. Lots of artists, filmmakers, and musicians live out this way."

She led me into her dining room, where a pot of coffee and a couple of croissants were waiting. I was keyed up, anxious to get the journal and get on the road, but it was clear Mini wanted to talk. We reminisced about the good old days for as long as I could stand it, then I purposefully broke the mood. "Would you mind if I asked a few questions about Jimmy's mugging?"

Her mouth fell open for a moment, and I felt a twinge of shame at my lack of couth. "Um, there isn't a lot to tell. Jimmy went to a liquor store over on 6th to get some tequila. It was a Friday night." She smiled wistfully and focused on something over my shoulder for a moment. "We were really into margaritas in those days. Anyway, he came out of the store and had just gotten to our car when someone walked up, shot him, and took his wallet and Rolex. He died instantly."

"Nobody saw the shooter?"

"No one. It was dark. The liquor store clerk heard a pop but didn't realize it was a gun discharging. LAPD must've brought in every known mugger in the city for questioning, but nothing ever materialized. The only physical evidence they had was a single bullet, but they weren't able to trace it." She opened her hands. "That's about all I remember."

"Who caught the case?"

Something crossed her face before she answered. "Aldo Moretti. Whipple didn't want him investigating his partner's murder, but he insisted. He was broken up about it." She paused and eyed me. "Why the questions, Cal?"

I flinched inwardly. "It was boorish of me to bring it up so abruptly, Mimi. I apologize. I was just trying to fill in some blanks." I forced a smile. "I'm a detail guy."

Her eyes had filled, and she nodded, reaching out for my hand. "It's okay. I understand," she said with a faint smile. "I'm a cop's wife." She led me into the kitchen and stopped at the table, where a moldy, paper-bound journal rested in a shallow dish. "It was so damp and fragile I put it in a casserole dish." She reached in and gently eased the cover open. "It's the right journal, see?"

I leaned in and could barely make out the letters IR NA KRASNO MUR ER printed by a steady hand at the top of the first page. The missing letters were masked by fuzzy patches of yellowish mold and gray mildew spots. "That's got to be it. Great!"

She ran her thumb along the edge of the pages to show me that they were stuck together. "You'll have to dry it out before having any chance of reading it, I'm afraid. I hope it's useful, Cal."

I thanked her profusely and picked up the dish. At her front door, she put a hand on my forearm and rested her eyes on me. "It was great seeing you, Cal," she said. "Call me if you have any more questions or, better yet, if you just want to talk." Then she smiled and winked. "And I want my casserole dish back, so don't you dare be a stranger."

—/—

Nando called as I was heading back to Santa Monica. "Hold on," I told him, "I'm on the freeway, and I've got to get across four lanes in a quarter of a mile to make an exit ramp on the left side. And everybody's going eighty." He wished me luck and when I cleared the off ramp, I said, "So, what've you got?"

"You were right. Tucker Bivens has moved away from being a heroin and fentanyl distributor, at least that's the story I got from some PI contacts in LA. He was clever enough to avoid the feds and LAPD over many years, and the word is he is a man of great ambitions. He wishes to be rich like the man who made my Tesla and wants to colonize Mars."

"Yeah," I said, "that might explain his interest in cryptocurrency. Drugs weren't profitable enough."

"I don't get this crazy crypto business," Nando said, and I could just see my friend rolling his eyes. "I am from the old school. I like money I can hold in my hand and put in my wallet."

"And there it stays," I said in jest. "So that's it? No rap sheet?

"He had one relatively minor indiscretion—he spent eighteen months at the state prison at Corcoran for check kiting when he was twenty-seven years old."

"Okay, so he's using his ill-gotten gains to become a legit businessman."

"Perhaps, but you know as well as I, Calvin, that the drug trade has sticky tentacles. I have a few more sources to tap, so bear with me. Meanwhile, I was able to obtain

Bivens' personal cell phone number for one hundred dollars. I will text it to you in case you want to call him directly. I am sure he will be delighted to hear from you."

—//—

When we got back to the apartment, I booted up my computer and did some research. Forty minutes later, I bought a handheld UV light source online (promised one-day delivery) and then went back out to secure a small house fan, a soft-bristle brush, a pint of denatured alcohol, absorbent washcloths, and a roll of paper towels.

When I returned from my shopping tour, I stood the moldy journal upright in the casserole dish with the front cover opened wide. I positioned the fan to blow at the exposed front pages at the lowest setting . This was the first step in gaining access to Jimmy Ryerson's insights into the murder of Irena Krasnova. I had no idea how long the drying process would take, and judging from the way the pages in the bulk of the journal were fused together, success looked like a long shot at best.

I had a conference call scheduled with a judge in Oregon that day, one of the obligations I wasn't able to postpone. Preparation for the call shot the better part of the afternoon, and the call itself droned on for more than an hour. Just as I finished up, another call came in from a number my phone didn't recognize.

"Mr. Claxton?" the voice began, a voice I immediately recognized. "It's Alec Macleod. I have some information that might be of interest to you. Do you have time to talk?"

I hesitated for a moment. I wanted another chance

to pick Macleod's brain in person. "I'd rather not do this over the phone. How about this evening? I can meet you somewhere."

"Of course," he said, and we agreed to meet in his apartment at around seven. "Bring your handsome dog," he added. "I live in a dog-friendly building."

When we disconnected, I turned to Archie and gave him a thumbs-up. "What we have here is a cooperating witness. And you're invited."

CHAPTER SIXTEEN

ALEC MACLEOD'S APARTMENT BUILDING WAS ON THE corner of 6ᵗʰ and Maple in the heart of Skid Row. The streets teemed with humanity that evening, the going was slow, and the smell I associated with the area hung over the scene like an invisible cloud. Parking was tight, and when I spotted a single slot in a narrow alleyway next to a reeking, stuffed-to-the-brim dumpster, I grabbed it. The black SUV that had been following me for several miles cruised on by and then turned onto 7ᵗʰ. I assumed it kept going.

As Arch and I approached Alec's building, I stopped dead and gazed up at the structure, which reminded me of something a three-year-old playing with blocks might build. The façade consisted of stacks of cubical pods, which, judging by the single window in each one, were small living spaces. Some stacks were three, others four pods high, and all were four pods deep. The varying heights rendered the roofline staggeringly unsymmetrical.

The effect was whimsical and totally unexpected. I loved it.

"Welcome to Star Apartments," Alec said when he appeared in the lobby after I buzzed his second-floor unit.

"Amazing building," I said as we took the stairs. "Last

thing in the world I expected to see here or anywhere, for that matter."

"Yep, totally prefabricated, shipped here from Idaho in small pieces and put together with a couple of cranes. A hundred and three units. Rent's on a sliding scale. Wraparound services for the lucky tenants. I was given an apartment here because I work part-time counseling residents in the building—my night job." He shook his head with an apologetic look. "I hate to take up a space, but it made sense for me to be on site. There's a lot of trauma recovery going on here."

"They're lucky to have you," I said. "Seeing a building like this gives me some hope."

He clapped me on the back. "Good. Hope nourishes the soul, you know."

His apartment door opened directly into a tiny living room furnished with a worn loveseat, a wooden rocker, a small writing desk, and a straight-back chair. A single, shaded window faced the street. As Archie circled the room to select a place to observe the proceedings, my eyes were drawn to the art lining the living room walls, an eclectic collection of portraits, urban landscapes, and abstracts, some framed, others not.

Noticing my interest, he made a sweeping gesture. "Pardon the clutter. People on the street know I love art, and they give me stuff they've done. I hang the ones I really like."

I looked around the room again. "*Clutter?* I don't think so. I like your taste."

He smiled, mostly with his eyes. "Thanks. They give me a lot of solace."

I felt so comfortable with this man that without thinking I said, "My wife was an artist, mainly portraits."

The moment the words left my mouth I regretted it. I hadn't gone there to discuss my personal life, after all, and my use of the past tense begged a question.

He looked at me. "A good portrait says as much about the artist as it does the subject. She no longer paints?"

Archie watched from a corner as I squirmed inwardly. "She, uh, she passed away several years ago."

He held my eyes with a look that said he now understood something about me, something I hadn't intended to reveal. "Oh. I'm sorry to hear that, Cal. Losing a loved one is the hardest thing life puts us through."

I shifted in my seat and desperate to change the subject said, "So you have information for me?"

He leaned back in the rocker and slid his thick fingers into the knuckle grooves of his opposing hand. His face darkened. "I do. Let's deal with Harry Imhoff first. He knows about you and your investigation, and he doesn't like it."

"I know," I said, wondering whether I should mention the CRV that might have followed me. I decided not to. "He's already paid me a visit with a couple of heavyweights waiting in the wings to emphasize his point. He's worried my investigation might bring the cops sniffing around his escort business at the restaurant."

Macleod nodded. "He's a dangerous man, and it's not just the Impromptu that you threaten. He has other operations in LA, some escort and others just plain old prostitution rings. And I'm told it's not just women for hire, that drugs are also being pushed. It has grown to be a very lucrative business."

"Okay, I detest that, but it's not what I'm focused on. Tell me more about Imhoff. Did you pick up anything that would suggest he had a motive for killing Irena Krasnova?"

He shrugged. "He wasn't enamored with her if that's what you mean. He prefers young men, I understand."

I nodded. "I think he took over the escort business after the murder. Could Irena have stood in his way somehow?"

"It doesn't seem likely, but I just don't know. I did sense there was a side to Irena she kept well hidden."

"A dark side?" I said with a look of surprise. "I thought you said she was pure of heart?"

He opened his hands and smiled. "She *was* pure of heart, but she was human as well, and a survivor above all else. It's hard to say how that might manifest itself."

I felt a little crestfallen, but then Imhoff wasn't on my target list to begin with. "What about Tucker Bivens?"

Alec got up. "I need a drink first. You? I have some pre-teen Glenlivet."

I chuckled. "Twelve years old, huh? Sure."

He returned from his tiny kitchen with the drinks, handed me a glass of the amber liquid, and raised his. "*Slainte.*" I repeated the toast, and after we drank he gave Archie a Milk-Bone. "There're probably more dogs than people in Skid Row, so I try to keep dog treats handy."

Archie wolfed the treat down, and when he looked up for more, Alec gave him another one before my dog went back to his corner.

"As you probably know from your own research, Tucker Bivens now owns some kind of digital money business, a seemingly legitimate operation."

I nodded. "A bitcoin company called CryptoNerds."

"Yes, that's the name. Only one of my contacts was willing to talk about Tucker, and he had little to say about his new occupation. That could indicate it's not completely on the up-and-up."

"Any thoughts on what he's up to besides trading bitcoin?"

"Nope, but we're all creatures of habit and he made his fortune in the drug trade." His face clouded over. "The disturbing thing is that he has been making inquiries about *you*. Like Harry Imhoff, Tucker has heard about your investigation and is apparently not happy about it."

I had to laugh. "My hometown welcomes me back. Is Bivens worried I might nail him for Irena's murder, or does he share Imhoff's fear of collateral damage?"

"I don't know, but the threat's real, Cal."

My stomach did a half twist, but I didn't let it show. "No worries. What about the Madam they called the Bitch Queen? Did your contacts have any idea who she is?"

"They said this woman was adept at hiding her identity, but they mentioned a wellness center she might've been associated with—"

"The Arlington in Beverly Hills?".

"Yes, that's the place. You seem to know a lot already. My contacts didn't know much else, except she worked there during the period you're interested in."

I felt a jolt of encouragement. "Excellent. That's where one of Irena's girlfriends works now. That gives me something to go on."

We had a second glass of Scotch and combed back through the information, scant as it was, and kicked around the various scenarios without anything else of note surfacing. I thanked him and said I could find my way out. The sun had set, but it was still warm, and the dumpster I'd parked next to was ripe. I let Arch into the back seat on the passenger side, shut the door, and as I rounded the front of the car, two men stepped out from behind the smelly receptacle.

They were both in the shadows, but I got a sense of

their sizes—one was taller than me and other was wider, much wider than me.

"Thanks for putting the dog in the car. Makes our job easier," Wide One said.

Tall One pointed a finger at me. "We got a message for you, asshole."

"What would that be?" I said as the spit in my mouth began to dry, and the adrenaline started to flow.

"Get the fuck out of LA"

CHAPTER SEVENTEEN

NO WAY I WAS LEAVING ARCHIE TO THESE TWO, SO I stood my ground. Wide One moved to my left to cut off my only escape route. Tall One took a couple of steps toward me. I had enough spit left in my mouth to say, "Tell your boss that if he wasn't involved in the Krasnova murder, he has nothing to worry about." I knew it was probably a waste of breath, but it was worth a try.

Tall One laughed. "I'm not telling my boss nothin', he's telling *you*—go hug some trees in Oregon or whatever, but stop poking your nose into other people's business." He squared his shoulders, took another step forward, and launched a fist at me the size of a Christmas ham.

He was big, but a half-beat slow, and when I ducked the Christmas ham grazed the side of my head instead of removing it. But I lost my balance and crashed back against the front of the car. Archie started barking at the commotion.

I didn't like the odds, but I had no choice but to fight. I pushed off the hood, and as Tall One came toward me with his armed cocked, I kicked him hard in his kneecap. His eyes bulged, he grunted, and when he buckled and dropped his hands, I threw a punch that caught him flush in the face. We both cried out as pain seared my hand and cartilage shattered in his nose.

He went down, but Wide One reacted quicker than I expected, tackling me like an NFL linebacker. I fell with him on top of me, and when my head cracked against the pavement, a meteor shower exploded behind my eyes. He began to pummel me with blows to the face that I fended off with a free left hand but with only partial success. I tried to roll over to protect my face, but he had me pinned to the ground as he spewed epithets and continued to pound me.

I heard the frantic barking of my dog, and the last thing I thought of before blacking out was what would become of him?

When I came to, I found myself propped against the dumpster with Archie anxiously licking my face and Alec Macleod gazing at me with a concerned look. "Welcome back. You okay?"

I spit some blood and patted Arch on the head. "I think so." I looked around. "Where are my friends?"

"I sent them on their way"—he hoisted a baseball bat and wagged it— "with this. It's an authentic Louisville Slugger."

Smiling hurt my cut lip. "Thanks. I owe you for my teeth and my good looks at the very least. They were trying to convince me to go back to Oregon. Your timing was impeccable."

"I heard a dog barking and figured it had to be Archie. I knew that meant trouble. I got down here as fast as I could."

I nodded toward the Louisville Slugger. "Does that baseball bat help you do the Lord's work around here?"

He smiled with a hint of sheepishness. "The Lord makes allowances for tough neighborhoods. I've never had to use it, just brandish it occasionally. But God forgive me, I would've whacked the guy who was on top of you if he hadn't bolted when I yelled at him. The other one was in no shape to fight. You must've had something to do with that."

I raised my right hand to eye level and flexed it a couple of times. It was swollen and sore. "I did manage to land one punch. They weren't armed?"

"If they had been, you'd be dead now. They were sent to work you over, not kill you. Come back up to the apartment. I've got a first aid kit." After pulling me up by my left hand, he added, "I take it you're not going to call the police."

"Nah. It'd be a waste of my time. I got a fairly good look at them, but it would be their word against mine. Did you see them?"

"Yeah, but just a fleeting impression."

Since my balance was okay going up the stairs and I wasn't nauseous, the chance I'd suffered a concussion was low, I decided, and my hand, which continued to throb with pain, was probably just sprained. We talked while he applied antiseptic and bandaged my wounds. He was nearly done when he said, "You're sure they didn't tip who they work for? Think about it."

"Probably the two who accompanied Imhoff the other night, but I'm not sure. They didn't drop a name, just 'boss.'"

"So, either Imhoff or Bivens sent them."

"Looks that way. Lucky me."

He drew back to inspect his work. "Your lip should heal without a bandage, and the two gashes on your face closed nicely with butterflies, so no need for stitches." He paused and studied me for a moment. "You're not going to back down despite the risks, are you." It wasn't a question. "Why is that?"

I managed another smile that stung. "Stubbornness. It trumps my fear, I guess. I don't like to be told what to do.

Well, that and the fact that I feel personally responsible for what happened to Dante. I can never right that wrong. The investigation's the only way I can see to make meaningful amends."

He stroked his beard. "I didn't catch up with all my old contacts, so stay tuned."

"No. You've done enough. This isn't going to get any friendlier." He waved off my comment, which didn't surprise me. I said, "What about you? Promises to your mother aside, what's driving you to devote yourself to serving the Skid Row population?"

He smiled with a hint of resignation. "I'd like to say it's my burning faith, but the truth is half the time I'm not sure I believe in God. Sure, there's original sin or whatever you want to call our fall from grace, but humans also have the capacity to do good things, to make things better. Is that the spirit of God within us? I don't really know, and I'm not sure the question matters all that much."

"What does matter, then?"

He met my gaze and held it, his lips drawn tight. "Making things right in the here and now. That's what counts."

The conversation lingered on that philosophical plane for a while, and by the time Archie and I left our friendship was cemented. And God knows I needed a friend in LA.

I drove straight to Dante's motel, calling him along the way without any response. His F-150 was parked in the slot in front of his first-floor room, but when I knocked nobody answered. I tried the door. It was unlocked. I opened it, called his name, and scanned the room. No sign of a struggle, I noted with some relief.

Compared to my last visit, the room was more orderly, and another chess game was in progress. A different chess tome—*Bobby Fisher Teaches Chess*—sat atop the bookstack, and another quart of cheap vodka sat on his nightstand next to his motel key. The bottle hadn't been opened, and the glass next to it didn't smell of alcohol.

I let myself out and put a card in the door with a note to call me ASAP. He was okay, I told myself. Probably out for a walk, but uneasiness lingered.

When I got back to my apartment, the first thing I did was examine Ryerson's journal. The good news was that the first couple of pages had separated from each other. The bad news was that the rest of the pages were still an unyielding block. That, and the fact that the kitchen smelled like wet sweat socks left to dry on a rotting log.

I switched off the fan, eased the journal out of the dish, and scrutinized the first page. Although the ink was badly smeared, I could just make out a few words Ryerson had penned. Most of his handwriting was obscured by a layer of yellowish-green mold of some kind. I hoped it wasn't a toxic strain.

I tried brushing the moldy areas with the brush I'd bought, but that only smeared the spores without revealing the writing beneath. I next tried a cloth wetted with dena-tured alcohol, and that worked a little better. After several painstaking minutes, I'd uncovered maybe twenty percent of Ryerson's words on the front of that first page.

He began the journal with the following remarks dated one day after the murder:

> *This journal records some of my observations concerning the*
> *investigation of the murder of Irena Krasnova. She was an*
> *undocumented female (country of origin unknown at this*
> *point) working for an escort service called Good Company*
> *that operates out of a restaurant and cocktail lounge called*
> *The Impromptu on W. Pico. Krasnova died of a gunshot*
> *wound to the...*

The rest of that paragraph was not recoverable.

On the back of the first page, I was able restore this snippet:

> *...Every once in a while we catch a break, and this was one*
> *of those times. My partner and I reviewed security camera*
> *footage from Krasnova's apartment building, which resulted*
> *in identification of a suspect, a black male named Dante*
> *Ellis, who works as a bartender at the Impromptu. We have*
> *placed Ellis in custody and are in the process of obtaining a*
> *search warrant for his car and ...*

After reading the segments, I sat back in my chair as memories of Jimmy Ryerson flooded back to me. A tall man, almost gangly but always a sharp dresser, he had a joke or a comeback for every situation and a counterargument for every person's most cherished beliefs and opinions. He was a good father, too, proud of his kids, and he was crazy about his wife, Mimi. I shook my head and let my breath out slowly. Is there anything useful in the journal, Jimmy? I asked myself. Were you forced into consensus when you knew better?

I picked at the edge of the stuck pages with a fingernail. I wasn't sure I'd be able to recover enough of his comments to draw any conclusions or to find any new leads. But a feeling came over me at that moment, a vague perception that I might just be working on behalf of Jimmy Ryerson as well as Dante Ellis and Irena Krasnova.

Maybe I'd breathed in too many mold spores, but I couldn't shake the feeling.

I placed the journal back in the casserole dish and turned the fan back on. After feeding Archie, I made a salad with a wedge of iceberg lettuce dressed with olive oil, bleu cheese, and a squeeze of lemon, put a couple of small red potatoes in the microwave, and plopped three brats on the Weber out on the patio. Getting one's butt kicked works up quite an appetite.

The brats were sizzling when the gate swung open and Dante sauntered in.

"Saw your note and decided to stop by. My cell was..." He stopped in mid-sentence when he saw my face in the low light. His eyes widened. "What the hell happened?" I described the confrontation, and his expression morphed from surprise to worry. "You're not gonna cut and run, are you?"

The question pissed me off. I glared at him. "What do you think?"

He paused for a moment, then shook his head. "Probably not, right?"

I chose not to answer. "They might target you as well. They're driving a black Honda CRV. Keep an eye out. One of them, a tall guy, maybe six two or three, might have a bandaged nose."

That drew a sly smile. "You popped one of 'em?"

I raised my swollen right hand. "Broke his nose and nearly broke my hand."

"Damn, you're tougher than you look, dude. And the

Rev chased them off with a baseball bat? Man, wish I coulda seen that. Macleod's a good man to have on your side."

"*Our* side, I said. "I was in deep shit until he arrived."

"That close, huh?" Dante's nostrils flared, and his eyes grew hard and flinty. "Fucking Imhoff. Maybe his story that he's worried you might attract the cops to his escort business is bullshit. Maybe he had a thing about Irena nobody knew about. Maybe *he* had her killed for some sick reason."

"According to Macleod he's gay. Find us another motive," I said.

"I'll work on it.

"Do it discreetly," I said, then, "There's another angle. Alec warned me that Tucker Bivens is also unhappy that I'm asking questions about Irena. Bivens could've sent those two goons to scare me off."

Dante raised his eyebrows. "Whoa, the jealous john wants to shut your investigation down? That's damn near an admission of guilt. What's next with him?"

"I've got my PI looking at his background. I'm looking for a connection to Ferris Spielman. In any case, I'm going to talk to him, see if I can get a read on him. It's interesting that he knows I'm in LA"

"Ain't no secrets in this town," Dante said.

"I got another tip from Alec," I went on. "Apparently, the Madam was somehow associated with that wellness center I told you about."

He looked at me. "The one where Lara Novak works?"

"Right. The Arlington in Beverly Hills."

"Yeah, well I was coming to that," he said. "Sherri Haller called me today. She said Lara called her, said she heard about you and the investigation and doesn't want to get involved."

I felt a stab of disappointment. "Would she talk to you? I could coach you on the questions."

He laughed. It was tinged with bitterness. "Not a chance. She never approved of me back when I was friends with Irena."

"Why?"

He rolled his eyes. "Only a white guy would ask that question."

I nodded, feeling a twinge of embarrassment. "Okay. I've got an appointment with her tomorrow under another name. Maybe she'll have a change of heart."

Dante eyed the brats as I struggled to turn them over with my left hand. I invited him to join me for dinner, and when he accepted, I tossed a couple more sausages on and made another salad wedge. When our conversation finally shifted off the case, I said, "By the way, do you always leave your apartment unlocked?"

He flinched as a wave of pain crossed his face. "I *hate* locks, man. I like doors that open whether I'm coming or going. Locks take your freedom away." He managed a bitter smile. "Besides, I got nothin' to steal except some plastic chess pieces."

"And some good books," I added. "How's the chess going?"

His face brightened as he raised his chin. "Undefeated in LA but, you know, just pick-up games so far." He paused for a moment and changed the subject. "What about Jamare? You gonna find him or what?"

With all that was going on, I realized I hadn't asked Nando the status of his search. "Haven't heard yet, but we'll find him, I promise."

"I'm countin' on that."

We tucked into our food with enthusiasm, and after Dante left later that evening, I realized he never expressed any concern for the attack on me other than whether it might deter me from continuing the investigation. But that was okay. I didn't expect any thanks. And, frankly, the beating felt a little like unintended penance.

On the bright side, Dante had shown up sober. I took that as a good sign.

CHAPTER EIGHTEEN

ALIENS OBSERVING LOS ANGELES FROM SPACE WOULD definitely conclude the dominant life form is the automobile. I dwelled on that thought as I sat immobile on the 10 Freeway the next morning. A warm day was promised, so after a long run on the beach, I left a pouting Archie at the apartment. When at last the traffic began to move again, I found myself aggressively tailgating the car ahead of me until I came to my senses and backed off, like any self-respecting Oregonian would. Of course, my retreat caused a cherry red Ferrari adjacent to me to fill the one-car-length space I'd created.

In a typical cross-LA jaunt, I took the 10 to the 405 and the 405 to the 2 before finally exiting onto a surface street—the fabled Rodeo Drive in Beverly Hills. I headed south between rows of majestic palms, early blooming spring flowers, and high-end shops—a Ralph Lauren, a Louis Vuitton, a Cartier—before turning at Brighton Way. The contrast between this neighborhood and where I'd been assaulted the night before was jarring, to say the least.

Set back from the street, the Arlington Wellness Center was housed in a whitewashed Spanish style building with a tile roof and a graceful, colonnaded walkway that led past a bubbling fountain to the entrance. According to their website, the Arlington did it all—holistic primary care, acupuncture, chiropractic, natural medicine, and massage. It was costing me dearly for a ninety-minute session with Lara Novak, and as I entered the reception area, I wasn't at all confident the visit would be worth it. But I was stiff and sore from the beating I'd taken, and it struck me that a good massage might be just what I needed.

I checked in, and a few minutes later Lara appeared, introduced herself, and escorted me to a private room. She was trim and graceful, with raven hair—lots of it—pulled back into a tight ponytail and dark, tapering eyes that sat atop well-sculpted cheek bones. There was no warmth in her smile, and her demeanor was all business when she asked about my face, and I explained that I'd been in a fender-bender that caused my airbag to go off.

When she returned, I'd stripped down to my boxers, was facedown under a sheet listening to piped-in music with flutes, strings, and gently breaking waves, and trying not to laugh at the absurdity of the situation—the investigator has no clothes! She folded back the sheet to expose my bare back, applied a fragrant oil, and began the massage.

"Oh," she said as she expertly kneaded my muscles with surprisingly strong hands, "your upper back feels like a box of rocks."

"Yeah, well, I took quite a jolt." The massage felt so good I nearly forgot why I came. I stopped speaking while she worked her magic, shocked by the amount of tension she was releasing from my body. Finally, when she'd worked herself halfway down my back, I said, "I understand you used to work for Good Company at the Impromptu back in the day."

Her hands froze, and her fingers stopped kneading.

"This isn't that kind of place, if that's what you're wondering," she said in a cautious voice.

"No, Lara, that's not what I'm wondering. I want to know if you're willing to honor the memory of your friend, Irena Krasnova, by helping me find the person who had her killed."

"Oh, shit," she said as she stepped back from the massage table. "You're that attorney from Oregon, aren't you." Her eyes narrowed. "You lying bastard. You need to get out of here right now."

I sat up on the table with the sheet draped over my lap and put my hands up. "Wait. Hear me out. Just a few questions. No one else needs to know we talked."

She crossed her arms with a defiant look. "I don't know anything."

"You know more than you think, Lara. Sometimes the smallest detail can be of great benefit. Think of your friendship with Irena. She deserves to have the truth known about what really happened to her."

She stood, immobile, with her arms remaining crossed. The room was quiet except for the strings, flutes, and waves. Finally, she said, "Nobody will know I talked to you?"

"Nobody except Dante Ellis and possibly my private investigator," I answered. I made sure I hadn't been followed this time.

She paused and studied my face for a few moments, then sat down in a chair across from me. "Ask your damn questions. And I'm still getting paid for this."

I began by asking her about the scene at the Impromptu thirteen years earlier and her living arrangements. When Anika Molnar's name came up, I said, "I understand she died of an overdose. Was that a surprise?"

Lara chewed her lip for a few moments. "Well, Anika was broken up over Irena's death, but, yeah, I couldn't believe it. For most of us Slovenian girls—and that included Anika—the escort business was a means to an end, not a lifestyle."

"What end?"

She raised her chin and looked straight at me. "A real life here in America."

"Did anyone suspect foul play at the time?"

She shook her head with a disgusted look. "To the cops it was just another whore who overdosed. There was no real investigation that I heard anything about."

I nodded. "So, Irena's modeling was her ticket to a real life?"

She looked at me with surprise. "Oh, so you've been doing your homework."

I nodded. "What can you tell me about the modeling?"

"Not much. We were close, but she guarded that part of her life." Lara looked away as her eyes filled and a couple of tears broke loose. "It was her escape route." She looked back at me. "She, uh, she was secretive about something at that time, a scheme of some kind—"

"*Scheme?* Did she say what it was?"

"No. I could just tell something was up." Lara sniffed, wiped her cheek, and smiled wistfully. "When I asked her about it, she said that if she told me she'd have to kill me."

"Did the scheme have anything to do with her modeling gig?"

She nodded tentatively. "That's what I thought at the time, but I can't say for sure."

"Did you tell the detectives about this?"

"No. They hardly questioned any of us, and when they

did it was like they were just going through the motions. It would've been a waste of breath."

I asked several more questions about Irena's behavior prior to her murder but didn't learn anything else of consequence. "What can you tell me about the relationship between Irena and Harry Imhoff?" I said, moving on.

Her face stiffened. "Not much to tell. He was an ass, acting like he was doing us a big favor by letting us work in his restaurant."

"Would he have had any reason to hurt Irena?"

"Harry considered her a bit of a bad influence. You know, she was outspoken and made it clear her aim was to get out of the life."

"Would that have been reason enough to have her killed?"

She lost a bit of color and drew her lips into a straight line. "I'm not going there. I know nothing about that."

I nodded. "Okay. What about Tucker Bivens?"

Her eyes flashed at me. "He crossed a line with Irena." Lara went on to describe the incident in the limo that Alec Macleod had told me about. The two accounts jibed. "I know for a fact," she continued, "that she told Tucker that if he didn't apologize and leave her alone, she would go to the narcs."

My pulse ticked up a notch. "Did he apologize?"

"If he did, I didn't hear about it, and she died not long after that."

"You think Bivens had her killed?"

She froze again. "I will say that he was crazy about her, smitten to the core."

"Crazy *jealous*, maybe?"

She studied her powder blue Asics for a couple of beats

before answering. "I don't know, but I saw him cry at Irena's funeral. Would a killer do that?"

I couldn't think of a subtle way to broach my last subject, so I just blurted it out. "The woman you and your colleagues called the Bitch Queen was in the middle of all this. What can you tell me about her?"

Lara's face tightened. "There's nothing to tell. She was the boss. End of story."

"Come on, Lara. Who is she? Where is she now? I need to talk to her."

She glowered at me and shook her head.

I opened my hands. "Why are you protecting her?"

"Because I'm not stupid."

"She got you this job here, didn't she?"

Her eyes registered surprise. "And she got me out of Slovenia. She's not all bad, you know, She didn't make her girls stay in the life, at least the ones with ambition. There were always younger, more beautiful girls to replace us."

"Okay. I get your loyalty. She owned the escort business, right?" Lara nodded once. "She sold it to Imhoff after the murder?"

Another nod. "I think the murder spooked her."

A motive for Imhoff, I thought but didn't say. "Does she still work here at the Wellness Center?"

"No. I think she's retired or something."

I leaned forward. "Look, Lara. Do me one favor. Tell her I want to talk to her, that I'll keep the conversation confidential. Tell her she owes that to Irena. Will you do that for me?"

She paused, brought her eyes back to mine, and sighed with resignation. "Okay, I'll try, but I don't think she'll come forward." She looked at her watch and added, "You're still on the clock. Lie back down and I'll finish your massage."

I left the Arlington that day with a spring in my step. I had a lot to digest from the discussion and hoped that Lara would deliver the business card I'd left for the Madam. Several possible scenarios for Irena Krasnova's murder were forming in mind, and input from the Queen herself might help. Except, of course, if she was implicated. I couldn't rule that out.

It turned out that Lara Novak was one helluva good masseuse. Thanks to her magic fingers, I felt like, if not a new man then only slightly used.

CHAPTER NINETEEN

I STOPPED AT A TACO TRUCK ON THE WAY BACK FROM the Arlington Wellness Center. Between a couple of tasty fish tacos, I called my accountant, Gertrude Johnson, to check in. "Well," she said after I greeted her, "I hope you're wrapping up down there."

"Come on, Gertie," I said, "I haven't even been here a week. Give me a break." I went on to sketch out the case and answer her questions, couched as they were in a highly skeptical tone.

But as we finished up, she said, her voice now warm and caring, "Stay safe, dear, and come home soon. We miss you and that dog of yours around here."

I called Tucker Bivens next, using the number Nando had given me. The call went to his voicemail, so I left a message saying that my name was Paul Smith, that I was an investment counselor interested in investing a *substantial* amount of money in cryptocurrency on behalf of a client. "Please don't have a salesman call me back," I said. "I want your personal perspective, Mr. Bivens." I hoped my having his personal cell phone number would either impress him or make him curious enough to call me back.

Zoe was next on my list, but just as I scrolled down to her number on my favorites list, my phone chirped, and her name came up. "Sorry I didn't return your call last night," she said when I answered, surprised. "I put my phone on mute and crashed early. Shitty day."

"What happened?"

"The son of one of my clients overdosed. She didn't have any transportation, so I took her to the hospital. The kid took a pill laced with fentanyl. He didn't make it. Just sixteen. God, what a waste, what a tragedy."

"I'm sorry to hear that. Reminds me of the incident I witnessed in Skid Row." I went on to describe Alec Macleod's rescue of the young woman.

"Yeah. It's a frightening epidemic," she said when I finished. "Chinese fentanyl courtesy of the cartels. It's dirt cheap, so all the street drugs are cut with it, and if the cutter doesn't get the ratios right, it's deadly." She sighed, and I imagined the pained look on her face. "I don't want to dwell on this. How are things going with the investigation?"

"We're gaining momentum, and there's no shortage of suspects." I gave her a helicopter-view of my massage session with Lara Novak, and when I finished she said, "So, the restaurateur who bought the escort business worried about her being a troublemaker, the drug dealer-cum- bitcoin trader was threatened with exposure to the narcs, and the madam known as the Bitch Queen had a front row seat to everything that was going on."

"Yeah, and apparently Irena was working some sort of *scheme*—at least that's the word Lara used. This was right before she died, and it might've involved her modeling job, but I have zilch on that."

"The Queen can shed some light?"

"If she'll talk to me. But I'm not even sure Lara will give her my contact information, let alone convince her to call."

"How about checking with the modeling agencies? Maybe somebody remembers Irena or read in the paper that she was murdered."

"Yeah, that's a possibility. I took a quick look online the other night and found a couple of dozen agencies that were around thirteen years ago. Hollywood's right next door, after all. I typed up a list but haven't found the time to make the calls."

"I know this is Nando's territory, but send me the list," Zoe said. "I'll have a crack at it."

"You sure you have the time?"

She laughed at that. There was a bitter ring to it. "Well, my client list is small, and I'm not getting any writing done, so what the hell."

"No writing?"

"My muse, if I ever had one, is MIA. Haven't written a word for five or six days. Nothing seems good enough to keep, let alone providing any impetus to move on to the next page."

She paused, and I felt obligated to offer some advice, although I knew I would be treading on thin ice. "I'm no writer, Zoe, but I believe in action, that doing is always better than sitting around. Maybe you should just keep writing, lower your standards if you have to, but get something on the page. Force that damn muse to come back."

She didn't respond, and I thought, uh-oh, I've done it now. But then she laughed with warmth not bitterness. "That was vintage Cal Claxton, but you know what? I think it's worth a try. I'm going to stop trying to write the perfect paragraph. Can't do any harm, that's for sure. But email me the list of the modeling agencies. I'll find a way to get it done."

And I knew she would. She said she had to go at that point, but I had something to own up to. "Uh, by the way, there's been an incident."

"*Incident?* What happened, Cal?" I described the attack on me without downplaying the severity. When I finished, she said, "I was afraid of that. You hurt one of them. They'll be back."

"Maybe. But I'm going to be on my toes from here on. And they surely know I'm a retired city attorney, so I don't think they're going to escalate the situation. They'd be foolish to do that."

Zoe wasn't convinced, of course, and we went back and forth for a while. But she knew the risks going in and understood why I was committed to seeing the investigation through. Finally, she said in a voice laced with resignation, "Send me a selfie. I want to see what you look like." I promised I would, and we ended the call after expressing our love to each other.

Afterwards, I sat there in the LA gloom and closed my eyes. I pictured Zoe out on her deck with freshly budded vineyards in the background, her face framed by ash blond hair carelessly blowing in the breeze, her deep blue eyes smiling at me. I missed her. And I missed Oregon, too.

—/ /—

I hadn't heard from Todd Whipple, and since the Police Administration Building wasn't that far away, I decided to pop in on him. The gamble paid off, and after checking in thirty minutes later at the Gang and Narcotics Division main desk, I worked my way through a warren of desks and cubicles to his office. For a division room, the place seemed quieter than I remembered, with most of the detectives and support personnel staring at computer screens or talking on cell phones. I hardly garnered a glance.

White shirts and ties were no longer required at LAPD, but Whipple wore a crisply pressed button-down and a tasteful paisley tie. "You found me," he said, looking up as I appeared at his open door. "Coffee?" I nodded, and he filled two cups from a coffee maker on a side counter—a perk of being a captain—and handed me one as I sat down. He asked about my face, and I gave him the same cover story I'd given Lara Novak. I didn't need any distractions or an I-told-you-so.

Whipple had an impressive vanity wall with framed citations, golf outing pictures, an All-America wrestling certificate, and even a small replica of a bull whip, a joke gift referring to his nickname. He sat down behind his cluttered desk, took a sip of coffee, and shook his head. "I don't have the Krasnova book, Cal. Damn thing's lost."

"Lost? Last time you said it was misplaced. Now it's *lost?*"

He raised a hand defensively. "Don't feel picked on. Over two dozen books are missing after we did a thorough audit. But no worries, it will surface." He opened his hands, palms up. "We've come to realize digitizing thousands of books ain't exactly LAPD's forte, you know? And we're trying to do it on a shoestring, because we're way the flying hell over budget on the library project. Bound to have a few hiccups."

"Okay, I get it. I know you're sticking your neck out for me, Todd. I appreciate it."

He nodded, took a sip of coffee, and leaned back. "Are you getting anywhere?"

I wasn't in a sharing mood, partly because I was embarrassed at not having made more progress and partly because Whipple still didn't need to know what I knew. I summarized the situation, mentioning both Harry Imhoff and Tucker Bivens as persons of interest, without revealing why I suspected them and leaving out the names of the witnesses I'd talked to.

Whipple didn't react to either name, so I added, "I'm not sure if or how this all fits together yet, but I have hearsay evidence that Imhoff may be mixing drugs and prostitution at the Impromptu. And Bivens, who was a dealer before a bitcoin trader, may still be dirty. I take it they're not on your radar?"

"LA has no shortage of drug dealers and pimps. But thanks for the tip, I'll run the names by my detectives. If something pops up that goes back thirteen years, I'll let you know. Anything else?"

I was tempted to say that Moretti and Ryerson had conducted a shoddy investigation but thought better of it. I said, "Aldo Moretti retired to his pot farm after all this went down. Was that a surprise?"

Whipple grinned. "The retirement or the pot farm?"

"Both."

He lost the grin. "Why the hell do you care?"

"Just me being curious. I'm not implying anything."

"Well, all I can tell you is that he was chomping at the bit to get out of law enforcement. Took an early retirement package like you did." The grin came back. "You gotta love the guy, right? A goddamn pot farmer."

"Yeah, who knew?" I said, then changed the subject. "What about the Department—is it likely to reopen the Krasnova case?"

"Haven't heard a thing. The wheels of justice turn slowly." He smiled. "But I don't have to tell you that." He leaned forward and met my eyes. "Look, Cal, I know I got a little chippy last time we talked, but I admire what you're doing"—he smiled again—"even if it might make me look bad. So keep me updated. I'll let you know when the murder book shows up, and if there's anything else I can help you with, anything at all, call me."

I left LAPD headquarters feeling disappointed about the murder book, but somewhat reassured it was, in fact, lost and not being withheld from me. And to tell the truth, I was surprised and grateful for the offer of unofficial help from my old colleague. The only thing I was left wondering about was how a cop taking an early retirement could afford to buy a marijuana farm? The question didn't appear to be on the critical path of my investigation, but it bothered me just the same.

CHAPTER TWENTY

THE MARINE LAYER HAD BURNED OFF, AND A NICE BREEZE was wafting in from the Pacific by the time I got back to the apartment in Santa Monica. To say that Archie was glad to see me would've been the understatement of the year. I can't rub my belly and tap my head at the same time, but he managed to bounce on all fours while spinning in circles, wagging his butt at hypersonic speeds, and squealing at eardrum-shattering frequencies.

We both craved exercise, so after he calmed down I changed into shorts and a tee shirt, leashed him up, and headed for the beach. It was a Tuesday afternoon, but there were plenty of sun worshipers soaking up the abundant solar radiation. Some had heard of skin cancer, others not, judging from the array of skin tones on display.

The tide was low, affording us a strip of firm, wet sand to run on. We headed north from the pier with the blue silhouette of the Santa Monica Mountains looming in the distance. It felt good to stride out as the surf crashed and the gulls scattered. But halfway to Will Rogers Park, my cell phone rang. I uttered a couple of four-letter favorites and pulled up as Archie whirled around with a pained look on his face.

"Calvin?" Nando's voice boomed, "how are things in paradise?"

"Paradise?"

"Yes. It has been raining off and on in Portland for the past three days." He paused for a moment. "Is that surf I hear breaking in the distance?"

I laughed. Nando was a Cuban emigrant who chafed from time to time at Oregon's weather. "You don't want to know. What've you got?"

"We checked arrest records, work histories, and residences of the hitman, Ferris Spielman. He was arrested for stealing drugs from his place of employment, but the charges were dropped. I don't have the name of the place, but I'll get it. Of more interest, I think, is that Spielman served three years for assault at the state prison at Corcoran."

My pulse kicked up a notch. "Did he overlap with Bivens?"

"He did, although it was nearly eight years before the Krasnova murder. Bivens arrived at Corcoran three months before Spielman and served eighteen months, but the prison had about four thousand inmates at that time, so no guarantee they bumped into each other."

"Excellent work, Nando. Anything else?"

"Your reverend friend may be right about Bivens' current activities. A good source in LA thinks he may be using his bitcoin operation to launder drug money. But when I pressed my source, he admitted it was speculation on his part."

"Noted," I said.

"Are you still planning to interview him?"

"If he agrees to talk to me, of course. Any thoughts?"

"My father used to say, '*No tires de la cola del león.*'"

"If *cola* means tail, I get your point. Look, Nando, if Bivens is our guy—which looks a lot more likely now—he already knows I'm investigating the case, so what's the difference? And besides, I like to see who I'm dealing with, up front and personal."

"Okay. Just be cautious, my friend," Nando said with a tinge of resignation. "I have more. Harry Imhoff, the restaurant owner, is a bad actor, too. The same source says he supplies his working girls with fentanyl free of charge. The ones who take him up on it become slaves, because a fentanyl addiction requires a fix every six hours or so." Nando paused before adding, "I would like five minutes in a dark alley with this man."

"Me, too," I said, grinding my teeth at the revelations. "I just learned that Imhoff may have seen Irena Krasnova as a troublemaker at the time he was interested in buying the escort business." I gave Nando a quick summary of the Lara Novak interview. "Novak stressed that money was everything to this guy."

Nando paused as if considering the statement. "A potential motive but not so strong, I am thinking. How could one undocumented woman stand in this man's way?"

"Good point. Any news on Jamare Ellis?"

"No, not so far. We did not find him in any national databases. Esperanza did locate records of him in middle school and high school in Watts, but no record of him graduating. Poof. He just disappeared after his sophomore year.

"That must have been when he ran away."

"That could explain it. Esperanza is thinking he is either living off the grid or changed his name when he turned eighteen. Stay in tune. We will find the young man. You cannot hide from Esperanza."

Nando had to meet a client, so we disconnected at that point. I stood there on the beach with Archie eyeing me impatiently. Finding a potential connection between Bivens and Spielman was a bombshell, and it certainly elevated the bitcoin trader to my number one suspect. As I reflected on it, though, I was less dismissive of Harry Imhoff as a suspect than Nando was. Imhoff was clearly the kind of man capable of any misdeed, including having a beautiful young woman murdered. And I knew from experience not to underrate greed as a motive.

By this time, Archie was whimpering and straining at his leash. As I fell into a steady rhythm behind him, I felt energized. Two solid suspects after a week's worth of work, I said to myself. Not bad. Not bad at all.

—/⊢—

When we got back to the apartment, I took a shower, made a double cappuccino, and took Ryerson's journal out of the casserole dish for another examination. I was encouraged to see that the fan's gentle air currents seemed to be working. Four more pages had become unstuck. Except for a word or phrase here and there, the first two pages were illegible on either side, the ink a smeared haze below a pebbly film of mold. The third page revealed this partial entry after some TLC with the denatured alcohol:

> *We are close to an arrest in this case. Waiting only for bal-*
> *listics to confirm the gun found in Ellis' car...*

Nothing else was salvageable until I reached page seven:

...*arrest of Dante Ellis, despite not being able to connect the gun to the murder. Everyone in the office is high fiving such quick closure of a capital murder case! I think Aldo Moretti is contemplating a run for mayor. Ha! I have misgivings, although I went along with the arrest in the interest of reaching consensus. Here are the reasons I remain skeptical:*

1. *The MO looked like a hired hit, and Dante Ellis is clearly no hitman*
2. *We can't prove the gun found in Ryerson's car is the murder weapon, only that it's consistent*
3. *Ellis cooperated initially (until he lawyered up) and my take is that he's way too smart to have committed such a stupid act*
4. *His remorse over the victim's death seemed*

The rest was obscured, but I remembered Todd Whipple mentioning that Ryerson thought Dante Ellis' remorse was genuine.

I stood the journal back up in the dish and trained the fan on it again, the free pages rustling gently in the wash of the blades. Ryerson's remarks so far revealed nothing new, but I was still hopeful something useful would surface.

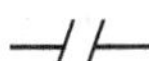

I was answering some emails when my cell went off an hour later. It was Tucker Bivens asking for my temporary alias, Paul Smith, investment counselor. I thanked him for the return call. "I'm a creature of habit, Paul, and tonight I'm having dinner at the club," he said, getting right to the point. "If you're free, we could meet there for a drink. It's the Jonathan Club over on Figueroa. Say six thirty. I can't wait to tell you the exciting story of cryptocurrency and the role my company plays."

I can't wait for the metaverse either, the sarcastic corner of my brain responded. But I told him I'd be there, and he went on to give me directions to the club's private parking lot. I knew the Jonathan Club by reputation, one of the most exclusive private clubs in LA, the type that uses five-figure annual fees and a velvet rope across the entry to keep out the riffraff.

I was relieved to be meeting Bivens there instead of at the CryptoNerd headquarters. If things go south when he finds out who I really am, better to be on neutral turf, I figured. Was it smart to conceal my identity going in? I wasn't so sure now. But if he talks to me, at least he won't have time to rehearse his answers.

I turned to Archie with a nervous smile. "Gonna need some luck on this one, Big Boy."

—/⊢—

Traffic was hellish that evening, but I managed to reach the Jonathan Club on time. The parking attendant at the adjacent lot was a smiling, blond-haired kid probably looking for a movie contract. When I told him who I was, he scanned a clipboard and nodded toward a Mercedes-Benz being maneuvered into a parking space by a chauffeur. "There's Mr. Bivens. He arrived just before you."

I parked near the Mercedes, and when Bivens walked by I introduced myself as that Paul Smith guy. He hesitated for a moment—probably because I wasn't dressed like an investment counselor—before offering a tepid fist bump. Despite being four inches shorter than me with a pronounced paunch, his squared-off jaw and fierce, avian eyes lent him a certain gravitas.

As I fell into step with him on Figueroa, he said, "Ever been to the Jonathan Club?" When I told him no, he looked up at the twelve-story building we were approaching with a measure of pride. "The club was founded in 1895 and has become the flagship private club of the west coast. Some of the most influential people in the country are—"

Pop pop, pop pop pop. Like many eyewitnesses, I initially thought the sounds were either a car backfiring or firecrackers. But when Tucker Bivens' blood and brain matter spattered on me, I knew differently.

CHAPTER TWENTY-ONE

THE HIGH-VELOCITY ROUNDS SLAMMED TUCKER BIVENS against an ornamental iron fence where he slid down and slumped forward like a rag doll. I gaped at him, frozen for an instant, before dropping flat on the sidewalk in case more shots were coming. But all I heard was the low growl of a powerful car speeding up Figueroa. I came up in a crouch and moved to the edge of the street just as two more cars passed by, blocking any possible view of the escaping vehicle.

"Holy shit, what happened?" the parking attendant said, his eyes the size of dinner plates as he surveyed the carnage that was once Tucker Bivens. "Is he, is he dead? Oh, man, he's got a hole in his...oh, man, are those brains?" He doubled over and emptied the contents of his stomach on the sidewalk.

I stepped around the vomit and checked Bivens for a pulse at his wrist and neck. He had none. I called 911 as passersby began to stop and gawk. "Send police and an ambulance to the Jonathan Club," I said. "There's been a drive-by shooting and a fatality." After I ended the call, my knees began to shake, and I felt a burning sensation on the side of my neck. I traced the tender area with a finger and realized it was a shallow furrow seeping blood, my own.

There was only one explanation for the wound—I'd been grazed by one of those hot rounds.

My knees shook even more as the realization sank in.

Two patrol cars arrived first and then an ambulance. After a paramedic applied a bandage to my neck and helped me clean the gore off my shirt, I gave a preliminary statement to one of the uniformed officers. I called Dante Ellis next, explained the situation as best I could, and asked him to take care of Archie for a bit. He said he could do that, and I told him where the spare key was hidden. "Keep your eyes open, Dante. I'm not sure what's going on. I'll come to the apartment as soon as I can."

"No, I didn't know the victim personally," I said to one of the two detectives who arrived ten minutes later. "We were going to have a drink here at the club." I went on to describe why I was in LA and that Tucker Bivens was one of the witnesses I needed to interview. I made sure to mention I was a retired city attorney to bolster my credibility and owned up to the fact that I'd arranged the meeting using the Paul Smith moniker.

The detective, a veteran named Charlie Banks, had thinning gray hair and a nose reddened by a web of broken capillaries. He raised an eyebrow. "Why the alias?"

"Bivens knew my name and probably wouldn't have agreed to meet with me."

Banks nodded, "You think this shooting is connected to your investigation?"

I absently touched the bandage on my neck. "I honestly don't know. I'd like to believe I happened to be at the wrong place at the wrong time. Bivens probably had some serious enemies in this town." Banks pressed me on that point, and I described what my PI had been told about his possible drug dealing background and money laundering. "But I've got no hard evidence of any of that," I said.

"What was your interest in Bivens?"

I paused for a moment. "To be honest, he was emerging as a suspect."

Banks gave me a skeptical look. "How do you know *Bivens* wasn't in the wrong place at the wrong time?"

I managed a smile, although my knees were still a little shaky. "Good question, but contract hits don't usually fail."

The detective eye-nodded toward my neck. "The shooter missed killing you by an inch or so. Maybe somebody wanted you *both* dead."

Harry Imhoff sprang to mind, of course, although I knew of no connection between him and Bivens except Irena Krasnova's murder thirteen years earlier. I went on to describe Imhoff's visit to my apartment and the threats he'd leveled at me that night, as well as the encounter with Tall One and Wide One in the Skid Row alleyway. "I should've reported the attack," I explained, a bit sheepishly, "but it was dark, and I didn't get a very good look at them. They were driving a late model Honda CRV, black."

"Did you see that car tonight?"

"No. I was watching for a tail, but it's hard to be certain in heavy traffic."

The interview went on for another half hour or so. When we finished, Banks told me not to leave town and that he would be back to me with follow-up questions. Finally, he looked me in the eyes and cracked a thin smile. "I remember you back in the day, Claxton," he said. "You were a rising star in the DA's office. Now you're in my line of work. How did that happen?"

"It's a long story," I said. "Too long." I was in no mood for chit-chat.

I was backing out of my parking space in the Jonathan Club lot when a text from Dante pinged in:

Archie fed and walked. We're just chillin at your place. No worries.

As I pulled out onto Figueroa, I wasn't particularly anxious to talk to Dante, given that my head was still spinning. I thought of Alec Macleod and realized I wasn't more than a couple of miles from his place in Skid Row.

Ten minutes later, I pulled into the alleyway next to the Star Apartments and scored the same parking spot in front of the overflowing dumpster. The smell made my eyes water.

After buzzing me in, Macleod met me on the first-floor landing. "What happened, Cal?" he asked as he stood staring at my bloodstained shirt.

"Give me a glass of Scotch and I'll tell you."

I followed him up to his apartment and waited while he poured us each three fingers and added ice. When he handed me my drink, I took a healthy swig before saying, "Tucker Bivens was shot to death in a drive-by in front of his private club on Figueroa. I was standing next to him."

Macleod stiffened in his seat at the news, his eyes widening with shock. I took him through the events and then placed a finger on the blood-stained bandage on my neck. "A bullet just grazed me. I didn't notice the wound until after I'd attended to Bivens and called 911." I drank some more Scotch, a tremor in my hand rattling the ice cubes slightly. "I'm lucky to be sitting here."

"Thank the Lord," Macleod said.

"If it was divine intervention, then by all means," I responded. "But to be honest, it felt like dumb luck. Two humans standing next to each other. One gets a scratch, one gets his brains blown out. Seems kind of arbitrary to me." I met his eyes and managed to smile. "And don't tell me the Lord has a plan for me, like that girl you saved the other day. I'm sure the Lord doesn't waste his time on skeptics like me."

Macleod laughed at that. "I'm a mere mortal who struggles with faith every day. True believers will tell you there's no luck, that God controls *everything* in the universe, including the fact that you lived, and Tucker Bivens died." He took a sip of Scotch and sighed deeply. "That's a bridge too far for me, despite what I said the other day. But I do believe that life isn't just a series of random events, that there are spiritual forces at work. King was right, I think. The arc of the universe is long, but it does seem to have a righteous bend to it." He paused and gazed past me. It's mysterious, but it's beautiful, too."

I took another drink. "In any case, I'm still standing, but my investigation just blew up in my face. I've established a probable link between Bivens and the hitman, Ferris Spielman, which is my firmest lead so far. But now that Bivens is dead, there's no chance of convicting him of hiring the hit on Irena."

"Why is that?"

"Simple. A dead man can't defend himself, and our justice system is based on equity between the state and the accused. If he did hire the hit," I went on, "he could've been killed tonight for some other reason, something related to

his current activities. Was my being there just a coincidence, as unlikely as that seems?"

"He swam with some mean sharks back in the day,"
Macleod offered.

"Right, and I also just learned he may still be in the
drug business." I paused for a moment, thinking of my
phone conversation with Bivens. "He told me he was a creature of habit, that he ate at the Jonathan every week on the
same day. If he has enemies, they could easily know that."

Macleod nodded. "On the other hand, *you* could've
been the intended target."

I rolled my eyes. "Of course. That's another possibility.
I told the police I'd been threatened by Harry Imhoff and
probably attacked by his men. Imhoff might want me out of
the way, either because he fears I threaten his prostitution
business, or *he* had Irena killed and thinks I'm closing in on
him." I opened my hands, palms up. "But I didn't tell anybody where I was going, and I don't think I was followed to
the Jonathan Club."

"You may have noticed that tail the other night," he
countered, "but if Imhoff wanted you followed again
without being detected, he could probably get that done."

I raised a hand to concede the point. "Okay, he could've
used two cars to follow me, which makes it tough to pick up.
I've done that myself. So, Imhoff is definitely still a suspect."

Macleod refreshed our drinks and sat back down.
"What are you going to do now?"

I chewed my lip for a moment. "My prime suspect is
dead, and I don't have any other solid leads. I guess an argu-
ment could be made to pack it in, to tell Dante Ellis I tried
and failed. To be honest, that course of action crossed my—"

"But you're not going to do that," he interjected with a knowing smile.

"That's right. I can't convict a corpse in a criminal court, but if I can prove Bivens did it, there's another option—I can sue his estate in *civil* court and take a chunk of his assets on behalf of Dante Ellis. That should help square it between Dante and me."

"If Bivens didn't do it?"

"Well, I'm back to square one. So, it's still full speed ahead as far as I'm concerned."

"What about your personal safety, Cal?"

"My gut says I wasn't a target tonight, but going forward I'm going to act like I was. And if I was a target, Imhoff probably ordered it. The cops are going to descend on him based on what I just told them, so I doubt he'd be stupid enough to come after me again."

"I'll pray for you," Macleod said, but then he clenched his jaw, and I glimpsed the bodyguard countenance once again. "Last time you were here, I promised to keep digging, but nothing's come of it. I'll see what the street says about this drive-by shooting. Stand by."

I left not long after that, anxious to get back to Archie and feeling better about facing Dante. It'd been a long night, and I struggled to stay alert on the freeway, where drivers kept things perilous in the lighter evening traffic by upping their speed accordingly. The ground had shifted under me, and despite my declaration to Macleod, I wondered if I had the staying power to see this investigation through.

I wasn't at all sure, but at least I had a somewhat reluctant man of God praying for me. It was better than nothing.

CHAPTER TWENTY-TWO

"YOU'RE GONNA STAY IN LA AFTER THIS SHIT?" DANTE said. I'd just finished telling him about the death of Tucker Bivens and the close call I had. His normally hard, unyielding eyes seemed to soften. "Man, I don't know what to say. I hated your guts for years, but when the time came, I couldn't kill you. Then I just hated you and never believed you were all that committed to helping me, that you had some agenda I didn't understand or know about." He actually smiled. "Now I'm starting to respect you, man. You got beat up the other night, now you almost took a bullet for me, and you're still hanging in? Who does that?"

We stood face to face in an awkward moment. I returned the smile. "Not gonna lie, Dante—I had no idea what I was getting myself into when I agreed to help you. And the honest-to-God truth is, this is more about me than you. Sure, I know I owe you, that it's the right thing to do, but the main reason I'm here is that I have to look myself in the mirror every day. You know what I mean?"

He nodded. "Yeah, I get it. It's cool, no matter what the reasons."

The tension between us broke. I stretched and yawned. "You hungry? I'm starved."

His face brightened. "Got any more of those brats?"

"No." I paused as I ran through the limited eat-in options. "I don't have any tortillas, but I do have some eggs and a jar of salsa, some potatoes, and a couple of tomatoes. I could make us something close to *huevos rancheros*."

He smiled, the kind that's unforced, and I caught a sense of the Dante Ellis before thirteen years of incarceration traumatized him. "I'm down for that," he said. "One of my favorite dishes back in the day."

After giving Archie a butcher bone, which he promptly took to a corner and started to work on, I gave Dante the task of peeling and chopping potatoes and frying them on one of the two galley stove burners. Meanwhile, I explained why I was drying Ryerson's journal on the kitchen table and then moved it and the fan to the living room. I prepared the eggs, sautéed the salsa with some extra tomatoes and onions, and toasted up some sourdough bread.

Given the meager ingredients, the meal came together nicely, and we ate for a while in the comfortable silence that hunger and good food creates. Finally, Dante said, "What if Bivens was our guy? What the hell do we do now?"

"Full speed ahead," I said and explained the civil suit option.

Dante threw his head back and laughed. "Damn. I could wind up richer than God."

"We've got to prove he hired Spielman first," I said.

"Then let's take a look at that journal."

"You read my mind," I said. "It looks like several more pages have dried out enough to allow them to be read. Ryerson kept this journal despite the evidence against you, because he had doubts about your guilt. He thought you were too smart to have done what you were charged with."

"Yeah, but if he believed in my innocence so much, why did he go along with the arrest?"

"He got overruled, Dante. It's no excuse for what happened to you, but the pressure on law enforcement to close cases is relentless, and with the video evidence you were low-hanging fruit."

A bitter smile. "Lucky me. I'm glad you're still digging, but it probably doesn't matter now with Bivens missing his brains. I mean, he was our guy, right?"

"It's probable, but we need proof. If Ryerson kept an interest in the case on the down low, we might learn something vital from his journal."

"That'd be cool," Dante said. "By the way, where were you when all this was going down? I don't remember you at my arraignment."

"Something personal came up. By the time I got involved, your case was pretty much a done deal as far as the investigation was concerned."

His eyes went flat, and he curled a lip. "Meanwhile, I was cooling my heels in the city jail. What happened, anyway?"

"My wife killed herself. I took some time off to bury her."

Dante recoiled at the words, and there was dead silence for a while. Finally, he said, "Aw, shit, man, I'm sorry. That's gotta hurt."

"Yeah. Still does."

"Is that why you left LA? I was wondering about that."

I nodded. "I wanted to start over somewhere that didn't remind me of my wife and the life we had here."

Dante rolled his eyes. "But you hung in for my trial. Lucky fucking me."

"I was numb. Working was all I knew. But I fell apart after the trial and was forced out."

Dante nodded. "Know that numb feeling. Did they fire your ass?"

"They probably should have. I had a pretty severe anger problem. The city offered me an early retirement. I took it."

Dante shook his head. "Man, that's some heavy shit."

I nodded, and then we both started clearing the kitchen table. After we loaded the dishwasher, I fetched the journal from the living room and got out my brushes, cloths, and alcohol. I counted sixteen pages that were now free of the fused mass, but nearly all the entries were smeared and indecipherable. Apparently, Ryerson used a ballpoint pen with blue ink that didn't hold up to the onslaught of mold and mildew that infected the journal.

But as luck would have it, Ryerson must have changed pens at some point. The last three pages were in black ink and looked somewhat more promising. `

With Dante looking over my shoulder, I moistened a cloth with alcohol and gently loosened a film of crusty mold from the first of those pages and brushed it off. It was dated three and a half weeks after Dante's arraignment and began with the entry:

> My partner and I got into a heated argument today about witnesses. He's arguing that since four of the vic's friends and associates described Ellis' relationship with Krasnova as close, we have enough to convince jurors they were having an affair. He reminded me that everyone's got a dirty mind. However, the two friends I interviewed would not confirm a sexual relationship, which is needed to strengthen alleged motive of jealousy, etc. I told Moretti I planned to dig deeper...

The rest of the entry was too smeared to read.

"Dude got that right," Dante remarked. "Anyone who really knew Irena and me knew we were just good friends."

On the next page Ryerson had entered a list of witnesses he still wanted to interview. None of the names were new to us except one, and it was the only name underlined. Only one problem—it was only a first name.

I pointed to the name. "Do you remember her?"

Dante stroked his beard. *"Gabby?* The name's vaguely familiar. Give me a minute."

We went on to the third page, which was intermittently legible, but nothing in Ryerson's comments caught our interest. I put the journal back in the casserole dish, realigned the fan, and just as I turned it back on, Dante yelled out. "Got it—*Gabriela!* She came to the bar a few times to have a drink with Irena. Worked at a gallery or studio or someplace like that. They always went off in a corner, kind of hush hush."

"Remember her last name?"

Dante shook his head. "Not sure I ever knew it."

"When was this?"

"Not long before the shit hit the fan, maybe a couple of months or so. Only saw her a couple of times."

"Can you remember anything else about her?"

"Nothing, except she was a little older, maybe thirty then, and she was almost as beautiful as Irena." He smiled. "I never forget a pretty face." He paused and eyed me. "Why do you think Ryerson underlined her name like that?"

"Good question," I said, thinking of Lara Novak's comment about Irena planning some sort of scheme. "We need to find Gabriela."

"Give me some time," Dante said. "Maybe something else

will come to me." He expelled a breath. "That period in my life's like thick fog, man."

By this time, Archie had parked himself next to our guest, who was absently scratching him behind the ears as we talked. Our conversation drifted away from the case. Dante said at one point, "I don't know about you, but the LA I came back to has changed. It's a lot meaner out there on the streets now. Not just addicts and lowlifes, but everyone. You know what I'm saying?"

"Yeah, I do. The friendliness I remember is gone. The city's like an anthill on steroids now." I shook my head. "But I'm probably remembering an LA that never really existed."

"Well, at least this city has a lot of good chess venues."

"How's the chess going, anyway? Still undefeated?"

Dante brought his chin up and squared his shoulders. "Yep, but I haven't played any ranked players, either. Got my sights set on a title, man, USCF Candidate Master."

"Impressive," I said. "What do you have to do to reach that level?"

He rolled his eyes. "The rating system's complex, but basically I have to play in sanctioned tournaments and beat ranked players to build my rating score. It's a steep climb— only about fifteen percent of players in the world reach CM level, and that's just a steppingstone to Grand Master. I'm registered for a USCF tournament next week in Venice Beach, my first."

"I've never been to a chess tournament. Mind if I come?"

He gave me a look. "It's not like a football game, but sure, knock yourself out."

After Dante left, the last drop of adrenaline I'd been

running on was consumed, and I felt an overwhelming desire to sleep. My conscience told me to call Zoe first, but I figured that would be counterproductive given the exhaustion I felt. I did manage to pull the bed down and crashed with my clothes on. Mercifully, I slept soundly despite having nearly taken a bullet in the neck.

The last thing that crossed my conscious mind that night was what Macleod had said about life. He was right about it being mysterious, but as images of Tucker Bivens' bloodied corpse flashed through my head, I wasn't all that sure how beautiful it was.

CHAPTER TWENTY-THREE

ARCHIE AND I WERE OUT ON THE BEACH THE NEXT morning when Detective Banks called and asked me to come in to sign my statement and answer some follow-up questions. That cut our run short, so I decided to take Archie with me, figuring a ride in the car would beat hanging out in our empty apartment. On the way there, I called Mimi Ryerson to see if I could drop by after my visit to Banks to discuss a few more details. She agreed and insisted I stay for lunch.

Dedicated a couple of years before I left town, LAPD Headquarters was a massive, multistoried building with mirrored windows that captured the complete reflection of its next-door neighbor, the iconic, ninety-six-year-old City Hall. It was a clear morning, and as I approached, its image shimmered in the sunlight like a mammoth mirage.

After I cleared security, Banks escorted me to an interview room, where I read over my statement from the night before. When I finished, he said, "Did you think of anything else to add to this?" I told him no, and he eyed me for a moment before continuing, "We think we've got one of the guys who jumped you."

"*What?* You picked him up already?" I said, astonished.

"We caught a break. We got a witness who saw two

men drop a car off a couple of miles from the scene last night and get into another." He shook his head. "The witness was pissed they parked the car in a space reserved for her palm reading business, so she got the plate of the car they drove off in. We picked the owner up this morning. Whataya know? He broke his nose a while back. Slipped in the shower."

"How tall is he?"

"Six three, give or take."

"That fits. The other car was used in the drive-by?"

Banks held up crossed figures. "It was stolen. We found it in Compton, based on the woman's description. Our techs are all over it as we speak. Powder residue, shell casings, prints of him and his accomplice, who knows? We're holding broken-nose on car theft at the moment. Here's his booking photo." He handed me a four by six, black and white print. "Look familiar?"

I looked at the photo, then back at Banks. "I don't know… hard to tell with his face all distorted."

Banks chuckled. "You shouldn't have hit him so damn hard. We won't chance a lineup, then, but we have a recording of his interrogation. Want to hear it?"

The detective led me to their media room, where I donned a headset, and after broken-nose had uttered several sentences, I said, "Maybe that's him, but I can't say for sure. That whole scene's kind of hazy."

Banks's smile vanished. "That's a shame, but, hey, 'maybe' is half the way there."

"What's his name?"

"Conway, Eddie Conway. He's got a lengthy rap sheet, including felony assault for which he did five at Quentin."

"Even if I was positive about his voice, you're going to

need more, of course," I cautioned. "Voice recognition evidence doesn't always hold up that well in court."

"Understood, but it's good to know we're on the right track," Banks said as his smile returned. "And I figure you'll make a pretty damn good witness."

I congratulated the detective on the fine police work, and as I was leaving, I saw two uniformed officers escorting Harry Imhoff through the security checkpoint. He wore a gigantic golf shirt and Bermuda shorts that displayed a set of pinkish, hairless legs the size of porch columns. He was not a happy camper. When he saw me, he bristled, his face high-blood-pressure red. "Is this your doing, Claxton?" He pointed a stubby finger at me. "You're going to regret this, you fucker."

I stopped and opened my hands. "Nice to see you, too, Harry, and there you go again, threatening me." I looked at the two officers. "You both witnessed that, gentlemen. My name's Calvin Claxton, and this man just threatened me. Please make sure Detective Banks learns about this. Thank you." With that I sauntered past the three of them without another look.

When I reached the street, my knees were a little shaky again. If Imhoff was that undisciplined in the presence of law enforcement, I asked myself, what the hell would he do next? I turned my head, and the bandage on my neck chafed at the skid mark left by a bullet. The possibilities were unsettling.

My only consolation was the knowledge that Charlie Banks was a damn good cop.

—/ /—

"Handsome dog," Mimi Ryerson called out to me from the front porch of her modest, two-story home. I was giving Archie a short walk before putting him back in the car, which I parked down from her house in the shade of a live oak. Mimi had apparently seen me arrive.

"Name's Archie. He tends to go where I go," I said.

"Well, bring Archie in. I love dogs." I didn't think it served any purpose to tell Mimi how I acquired the bruises and bandages or what just happened to Tucker Bivens, so I used the fender-bender excuse and kept mum about the shooting. Partially screened by an oak tree, I gambled she wouldn't notice my car was unscathed. She knelt in front of Archie once we were in her living room. "An Aussie tricolor," she said, stroking his broad back. "Wonderful breed. He's big for an Aussie, isn't he?"

"Yeah, seventy pounds, most Aussies are fifty. Doesn't slow him down much."

"Oh, look, his little eyebrows are the same coppery color as his eyes. What a love." Archie accepted Mimi's adoration with canine nonchalance, and when she finally stood, she looked at me and smiled. "I made us a light lunch, but there's plenty of it."

While Archie looked on, we lunched on avocado toast served with smoked salmon and capers, sliced tomatoes, crumbled blue cheese, and a chilled Chablis. The shared meal brought more reminiscing about our former lives, although we were both careful to keep the banter light, at least until Mimi looked at me over her wine glass and said, "Have you been able to recover anything useful from Jimmy's journal?"

"Yes, just yesterday I found the name of a witness who might've been overlooked in the original investigation. Jimmy had underlined her name in a list he'd made. We're trying to locate her now."

"The journal's still readable? I'm amazed."

"It takes some TLC." I went on to explain the slow drying process and the extensive damage from the mold. "It turns out the color of ink in Jimmy's pen made a huge difference. Blue ink is a disaster, but black's more mold resistant and gives me a shot at salvaging some of his comments. I'm hoping he used more black than blue pens."

"How far have you gotten?"

"Less than twenty pages, only a few of them legible. I did find some comments from Jimmy about being frustrated with Aldo Moretti. Apparently, Moretti figured they got their man so why bother with more legwork. Does that ring any bells?"

Mimi's face stiffened as if it were a chore to go back in time. "Nothing beyond what I told you before. Things seemed tense between them." She managed a wry smile. "But that wasn't all that unusual. I mean, Jimmy wasn't that easy to get along with, trust me."

"Does the name Gabby or Gabriela trigger any memories? I don't have a last name."

Mimi furrowed her brow for a moment. "No. Should it?"

"She's the witness I mentioned—about thirty then, very beautiful. She was a good friend of the victim, but she wasn't in the escort business. Not sure whether Jimmy ever questioned her."

Mimi cocked her head and closed her eyes for a moment. "I remember Jimmy saying something about the escort business, that the victim wanted out." Her eyes opened wider. "Something about a friend who was helping her get into modeling, I think it was. I remember because Jimmy was pissed that Aldo didn't want to bother questioning her." She raised her chin with a gleam in her eye. "Maybe Gabby was that friend. You said she was beautiful, after all."

"Yeah," I said, "that fits with some of what Dante Ellis remembers. Did Jimmy say anything else about her?"

Mimi shook her head, then smiled tentatively. "Hey, I was lucky to remember that. Like I said before, I don't like..." Her smile collapsed, and her eyes filled and spilled over. "Oh, damn, I promised myself I wouldn't..." She forced a smile above a trembling chin and looked at me with wet eyes. "I do this sometimes, out of the blue. I'm sorry."

"No, no," I said. "It's okay. I understand. I've been there, Mimi."

She looked at me, her eyes glistening in the light. "This woman you've met. Zoe. She must be special." I smiled, and she went on, "I can tell, Cal. You seem very, uh, I don't know, centered." She put an open hand to her chest. "I'm a mess. I lied about not remarrying. Tried it once for two years. It was a fucking disaster."

I winced at her words. "I'm sorry to hear that, Mimi. For years, I was the polar opposite of you, afraid to commit until I met Zoe."

"When was that?"

"We met at the beginning of the pandemic. Before that, my love life was a disaster, too."

She sniffed and dabbed her eyes with a napkin. "I'm happy for you, Cal." She sighed deeply. "You know, even now, sometimes when I'm reading or napping and hear a noise, I look up and expect to see Jimmy walk into the room." She rolled her eyes. "God, it's been thirteen years. I guess I'm just a one-man woman."

I smiled. "Jimmy's a hard act to follow."

She sighed. "That's for damn sure. The thing is, I feel detached, you know, no closure. Somebody killed Jimmy—just walked up and shot him—and they're still out there, free as a bird. It's something I can't seem to reconcile." She smiled bitterly. "I know it's crazy, that I should've moved on, but I haven't."

We stayed in this vein for a while, and when I finally got up to leave, she followed me to the door. I turned to say goodbye, and she fell into my arms and cried on my shoulder. I let her cry, sensing her need for emotional release. When she finished, the shoulder of my shirt was wet through. As I broke from her embrace, I surprised myself by saying, "I'm casting a broad net with this investigation. If I learn anything about Jimmy's murder, I promise you I'll follow up."

The moment the words left my mouth I could have kicked myself. Not because I didn't mean what I said, but because it was premature to have said anything that might kindle renewed hope.

She pulled her head back, her wet eyes suddenly open wide and fixed on mine. "You think there's a connection between the two murders?"

"I don't know, but I intend to find out." That was also more than I should have said, but I felt I owed her something after bringing the subject up. And the truth was, even though I hadn't admitted it until that moment, my gut told me something was off about Jimmy Ryerson's murder.

I left Mimi standing on her porch, and as Archie and I headed back to Santa Monica, the cynical corner of my brain kicked in with a vengeance. You don't have any good leads for the case that brought you here. Take on Ryerson's murder? You've got to be kidding.

I had no defense except for the feeling in my gut.

CHAPTER TWENTY-FOUR

I CALLED ZOE ON MY WAY BACK TO SANTA MONICA. "OH, my God, Cal, what have you gotten yourself into?" Zoe asked as I finished describing the Tucker Bivens shooting. She wanted to know if I was a witness or a target, and I had to admit I wasn't sure. And in a moment of weakness, I left out the part about one of the bullets grazing my neck. I would own up to that later, I rationalized. I was already treading on paper-thin ice where Zoe was concerned.

"The police have already made an arrest," I said, injecting a note of optimism into my tone, and after we sifted through what I knew at that point, I added, "The cops know Imhoff threatened me twice and that the man they arrested was one of the two who accosted me in Skid Row."

"So Imhoff wouldn't dare come after you?" Zoe asked.

"Right," I said, trying to hold the optimistic tone.

"Since Bivens was your prime suspect, I don't suppose you could drop..." her voice fell off, and she added more to herself than me, "No, of course not."

A troubling silence followed. Finally, I said, "How's the modeling agency search going?"

"Nothing yet, but I've assembled a complete list of all the agencies that were in business in LA and Hollywood at that time. There were thirty-eight, but twelve have gone out of business. I've contacted eight of the remaining ones so far. They've all been willing to talk once I explain what we're trying to do. Five said they had no records or recollection of working with Irena Krasnova. Three said they'd get back to me after talking to their staffs."

"That's a great start," I said. "There's another person I need to find." I went on to tell her about Gabriela. "I don't have a last name. She may have been Irena's link to the modeling business. She'd be in her early to mid-forties now."

"Without a last name I probably won't get very far," Zoe said. "But I'll give it a shot. Give me Dante's cell phone number. I'll keep him in the loop, too."

I read off the number. "That's a brilliant idea," I added, feeling slightly embarrassed I hadn't suggested their collaboration. Zoe was inclusive by nature.

Our conversation eventually turned to life in the Red Hills. They'd had a lot of rain, which boded well for the vineyards, Gertie was as feisty as ever, but Zoe's Spanish was not progressing as fast as she'd hoped. *"No hablo español con fluidez,"* she said, her voice ringing with frustration. "I suck at Spanish."

"No, you don't," I shot back. "Give it some time."

"Maybe this is a bad idea. Maybe I've got a white savior complex or something."

"You're a gifted psychologist, and you want to help people. Nothing complex about that. Look what you've done for Elena Fuentes. She's encouraging you to counsel in Spanish, right?"

"Yeah, and she's helping with my pronunciation, too."

"I don't think she's too worried about your skin tone."

"Okay, I'll give it another month" she said with finality.

"How's the book coming?" I asked, sensing it wise to change the subject.

"I got maybe a third drafted, mostly the setup. Everything's rosy, but my protagonist is going to suffer a devastating loss." She paused then sighed deeply. "Let's hope life doesn't imitate art."

The comment stung. "Not going to happen, Zoe. I don't want you to worry about me."

She sighed. "I'd hate you if I didn't love you so much. Come back to me in one piece, Cal. That's all I ask."

—⁄⊢—

It was a balmy eighty degrees, so I took my laptop and cell phone out to the fenced-in patio to get caught up on my Oregon law practice. A call to Timoteo told me he was holding down the fort in Dundee, but just barely. "All I can say," he remarked, "is that when you get back in three weeks you're going to be slammed. Half the people in Yamhill County want a piece of you."

I winced inwardly at the time frame. *Three weeks?* I'll be lucky to wrap this thing up that fast. "Look, Timoteo, I might've been a tad optimistic about my stay down here. Don't schedule any court appearances for at least the next four weeks. That'll give me some breathing room. I can handle client meetings on Zoom until I get back."

"Okay, I'll do my best," he replied in a voice decidedly lacking confidence. "We're probably going to lose some business, maybe a lot of business."

"We'll survive," I told him. When we disconnected, I looked over at Arch, who lay in the shade watching me for signs of a possible foray to the beach. "Now I know what stepping into quicksand feels like, Big Boy."

I was sitting there stewing about my situation when my cell phone rattled awake on the wrought iron table. It was Alec Macleod, who said he happened to be in the area. I gave him my address, and he said he'd be at my place in ten minutes.

I heard the deep bass rumble of a motorcycle out front and opened the gate just as Macleod was getting off a Harley Davidson. It was all black with wire spoke wheels, a chrome-framed windshield, and leather saddlebags. "Nice bike," I said.

He took off his helmet, ran a hand over his hair, and smiled a bit sheepishly. "Every man has his vanities," he said. "If there's a heaven, this is what they're driving."

I invited him into the courtyard. After fetching us each a long neck, we settled in around the table with Archie looking on. "So, what brings you to Santa Monica?"

He took a swig of beer, looked at the label, and said, "Mirror Pond Pale Ale. Not bad. You bring this from Oregon?"

"I never leave home without it," I answered, holding back a smile.

He took another pull on the beer. "I met an old acquaintance at a bar in Malibu earlier today. I knew him when I was in the life, the kind of guy who'll run his mouth if you buy him a few drinks. Anyway, he says LA's drug underworld is buzzing about the shooting. Word is Bivens was taken out because he was trying to corner the fentanyl trade in LA. Somebody either on the supply side or the distribution side took offense." He swung his eyes to me, his face grim. Guess whose name came up? Harry Imhoff."

"Surprise, surprise," I said and told him about the arrest of Tall One. "So maybe I wasn't a target," I concluded. "That's what my gut was telling me all along."

"Of course that won't matter to the cops," Macleod said. "They'll assume Imhoff was after you, based on that first attack in the alley and the fact that he threatened you." He threw his head back and laughed. "What did Lovecraft say? 'From even the greatest of horrors, irony is seldom absent.'"

That drew a smile from me. "So, Imhoff goes after Bivens, and I just happen to be there? If I wasn't on Imhoff's hit list, I probably am now. I told the cops everything, and they hauled him in immediately." I smiled. "I was coming out when they brought him in. He didn't appreciate the irony, believe me."

Macleod studied me for a few moments. "Still going to persevere, I take it."

"This doesn't change anything, but I'd be lying if I said the investigation's not taking a toll. My absence is starting to impact my law practice, and worst of all, I'm putting the woman I love through an emotional wringer." I went on to explain that Zoe's former husband was an adrenaline junky who died in a climbing accident. I looked at my friend. "I'm wondering if I'm just being stubborn and selfish."

Zoe didn't ask you to stop, did she?"

I shook my head. "Actually, she's doing some research on the case for me."

"Then I'm guessing she knows what she signed up for, Cal, that she accepts who you are."

"She has said those words, but I think the shooting unnerved her. And I didn't even tell her how close it really was. I feel like I'm hurting her, which is the last thing in the world I want to do."

He held my gaze, his slate gray eyes like steel marbles. "It's admirable for you to feel that way, but maybe you should give Zoe more credit. Maybe she's as committed as you are." He gave me a knowing smile. "Obviously, you would never fall for a shrinking violet."

We finished our beers, and then my friend announced he had to get back to Skid Row. Archie and I followed him out to the street, and after he mounted his bike, I said, "I don't know my Harleys. What model is this?"

He patted the gas tank. "FXS Low Rider, 1584 ccs. I've had it twenty-five years." He beamed a smile. "The only way to travel in LA"

I whistled. "Looks brand new."

He started the engine and put his helmet on. "Yeah, well, she's my baby." With that, he took off with a low, thrumming roar.

Archie and I stood and watched as he headed west on Colorado Avenue. It hit me that every time I talked to this man, I wound up feeling uplifted somehow. My return to LA wasn't necessarily going the way I hoped, but I'd made a friend, a good friend. That was something.

CHAPTER TWENTY-FIVE

THE NEXT AFTERNOON ARCH AND I HEADED TOWARD Venice Beach and its fabled boardwalk, which lay only two miles south of the Santa Monica Pier. The sky was gun-metal gray, and what little surf existed that day was obliterated by a stiff on-shore breeze. Only a handful of surfers, beginners no doubt, were out in the water. Once we hit the sand, I stowed my Tevas in my backpack and treaded a barefoot path along the shifting shoreline. Archie dashed in and out of the water, barking with delight but showing a healthy respect for the incoming waves, small as they were. He was a herding dog, not a water dog, after all.

The low rumble of a distant drumming circle and the pungent odor of cannabis were adrift in the air well before I could see anything of the boardwalk. The iconic strip hadn't changed much since the last time I was there over a decade earlier—still the same old freak show flea market vibe that put the place on the map.

A big blue tent between two sixty-foot palms just off the walkway marked the home of the Venice Beach Knights. A sign at the entry to the tent claimed it was "A Chess Club with No Walls." Another sign read "USCF Tournament this Week." We were fifteen minutes early for Dante's chess match, his first game with a ranked opponent. A small crowd had gathered around a chess board that sat perched on a card table. A woman wearing thick-lensed glasses, maybe late fifties, sat at one side of the table, an array of black chess pieces already neatly in place on the board in front of her. She seemed oblivious to her surroundings, her nose buried in a Stephen King paperback.

I found a seat towards the back, and Arch lay down next to me. I was reading my email and watching the time. The match was scheduled for 3 P.M., and at 3:10 I was relieved to see Dante coming down the boardwalk and surprised to see Lara Novak arm and arm with him. My surprise turned to concern when I noted he seemed to be walking a bit unsteadily. He sauntered up to the table, conferred with a tournament official, and then introduced himself to his opponent. Was there a hint of a slur in his voice? I wasn't certain, but the welcoming smile on his opponent's face died a slow death.

Dante turned to seat himself and lost his balance momentarily, catching the corner of the table with his thigh. "Whoops!" he cried out as the table tipped over, spilling the board and the black and white chess pieces into a heap on the canvas floor. His opponent stood watching in horror, as if the pieces had abandoned all chess-like decorum and were now engaged in hand-to-hand combat.

"Aw, shit! I'm sorry," Dante said as he dropped to his knees to begin picking up the pieces. "Don't leave," he implored the woman.

Her face hardened. "I don't play chess with drunks," she said before she spun on her heels and walked out of the tent.

The tournament official, a portly man with a white, flowing beard and ornately tattooed forearms said in a faltering voice, "I'm afraid I'm going to have to ask you to leave, Mr. Ellis." He turned to the small crowd. "Sorry, folks. The next match will be at 7:30."

Dante stood up, teetered unsteadily, and glared at the official through squinty eyes. "Okay, dude, but give me my registration money back. Twenty-five bucks." He stuck his hand out, palm up.

By that time, Lara had moved to one side of Dante, and I stood at the other. I said, "Don't worry about the fee right now, Dante. Let's get you back to your apartment." To the official, I said, "He's not drunk. He's reacting to a medication." I knew that wasn't true, of course, but I was hoping to minimize the damage to Dante's reputation with the chess community.

Dante stuck up an index finger. "Yeah, that's it. I'm taking a new fucking medication."

I had to suppress a smile. He may have been drunk, but he caught my drift in a hurry.

The official looked relieved. "Fine, Mr. Ellis. Come back for your money, but leave now, please."

Dante and Lara had come in her car, and she offered Archie and me a ride back to Santa Monica. As we crawled up Highway 1, Dante morphed from semi-belligerent to remorseful to sound asleep by the time we reached my place.

"Come to the patio for a minute," I said to Lara in a tone that barely hid my anger. "We need to talk."

"Hey," she said as I shut the gate, "this wasn't my fault, you know."

I turned to her. "I didn't say it was, but what the hell happened?"

"He'd been drinking when I picked him up. He said he wanted to get some lunch, so we stopped at a bar and grill on Venice Boulevard. She shook her head slowly. "He drank his lunch, said it would relax him, make him play better. I didn't say anything. I figured he knew what he was doing." She met my eyes and shook her head again. "Maybe I should've tried to stop him."

"How did you contact him?"

"Sherri Haller gave me his cell phone number."

"Why, Lara? Why did you call him?"

A shy smile. "I don't know. I always liked Dante, thought he was a nice guy. I wanted to tell him how happy I was that he got out of prison. I never thought he killed Irena for a second. I—"

The patio gate swung open, and Dante came in, grimacing and rubbing his forehead. "Got any coffee, Cal?" He turned to Lara. "Thanks for the ride. I need to talk to Cal now. I can get an Uber back to my place." He hesitated for a moment before adding, "I'll call you."

She forced a nervous smile. "Sure, Dante. I'm sorry you missed the match."

He shook his head and called out to her as she headed to her car, "Not as sorry as me."

Dante followed me into the apartment, slouched into a chair at the kitchen table, and put his head down. I was busy making coffee when he looked up at me, tears streaming down his cheeks. "I'm a worthless piece of shit. That was a sanctioned match I blew. The USCF will probably ban my ass now."

"You're not worthless, Dante. You're trying to recover from the traumatic shock of being unjustly incarcerated. Cut yourself some slack. And the chess federation won't ban you. That's not going to happen, trust me." His eyes were shiny with tears. "Want to talk about it?"

He closed his eyes and raked the fingers of both hands

through his beard. "I don't know. I lost my nerve, I guess. Woke up at five this morning thinking about the match. Everything I knew, all the theory, all the strategy, the moves, everything seemed jumbled, disorganized. I tried to relax and go back to sleep, but I couldn't shut my mind off."

"That's nothing unusual. Getting nervous is a natural reaction. I'll bet even Spassky and Fisher got butterflies ahead of big matches."

"Oh, please," he said, "spare me the pop psychology. I was totally intimidated."

"What about all the matches you've won? Your success at Quentin?"

"Doesn't matter. This was a *sanctioned* match. That woman today, she's ranked." He looked at me straight on. "You know what I did this morning? I got up and had a couple of belts of vodka. It worked. I fell back to sleep."

"When did Lara call you?"

"Midmorning. Said she just wanted to say hi. We talked for a while, and by then I had a pretty good buzz going, so I invited her to join me."

"I thought you told me she didn't like you?"

Dante shrugged.

"Did she ask you about the case?"

He blinked several times as if to clear his head. "Uh, yeah, she did. Now that you mention it, it seemed like it was more about that than me."

"What did you tell her?"

"Not that much, that our top suspect got taken out in a drug beef, but that we were still working the case, that we might sue Bivens' estate."

I made a face. "Did she mention the Madam? She's still in contact with her."

"Nah, we didn't get into that." He shook his head. "Blew it again, right? Instead of pumping her for information, I was running my mouth off, trying to impress her."

"Lara's a beautiful woman. Anyone would be flattered by attention from her. If you continue to see her, turn the tables—find out everything she remembers about the events leading up to Irena's murder, get the Madam's name if you can. And don't tell her anything else about what we're up to, okay?"

He nodded and fixed his eyes on mine. "Sure you want to continue to work with a fuck-up like me? I won't be pissed if you don't."

I held his gaze. "I'm going to hang in, Dante, but the truth is I did consider going back to Oregon today. I'm worried about your drinking. Booze puts your judgment in the crapper. We can't run an investigation like this without—"

He waved me off. "Okay, okay. Save the lecture. I know the drill. I fucked up. Give me another shot."

"I said I was going to hang in," I repeated.

—⊣⊢—

"Human beings weren't meant to be caged," Zoe told me at our check-in later that night. I had just described the scene at the chess club. "In prison, you shut down to survive day to day. Now Dante's starting to reconnect with himself, to feel his emotions. This can be overwhelming."

"So, no surprise he's using alcohol to numb himself."

"Exactly. Self-medication's a common response, Cal. He needs counseling to help his re-entry. He's out of San Quentin, but he can't get out of the prison in his head."

"I doubt he'd be open to counseling, but any suggestions?"

She paused for a moment. "He needs time. Keep him busy, push the chess, keep him away from alcohol if you can. Most of all, Cal, just be there for him."

"I'll do my best," I said, and after we disconnected, I was confronted with the fact that Dante's lengthy prison stay not only robbed him of that time but also left psychological scars as well. And I was the one who put him in prison. The implications of that act were almost unbearable.

Something else gnawed at me that night, too—what the hell was Lara Novak up to?

CHAPTER TWENTY-SIX

I WAS OUT ON THE PATIO LATER THAT EVENING SIPPING A Remy Martin and thinking about the case when Archie's low growl alerted me to visitors. "You in there, Claxton?" a familiar voice asked as feet shuffled and the latch on the gate rattled.

"Come on in, Todd," I answered.

Todd Whipple came through the gate, followed by Aldo Moretti.

"The thin blue line in the flesh," I said as we shook hands. "What's up?"

"What's up? Jesus, Cal, I just heard about the Bivens' shooting," Whipple said. "That was way too close, buddy."

I shrugged. "A miss is as good as a mile."

Whipple glanced at Moretti and then looked back at me. "Aldo's in town on business, so we thought we'd pop in to see how you're doing."

Moretti's rosy glow suggested he'd had a few. He nodded in agreement and raised his eyebrows. "That was a gnarly scene, Cal. Glad you're okay."

Archie kept my guests company while I went inside for glasses. When I returned, I poured us each three fingers of Remy. We clinked glasses and sipped the cognac. Whipple held his glass up, and light from an outdoor fixture set the amber liquid aglow. "Back in the day we didn't drink this pricey stuff," he said. "Your practice up in the wine country must be lucrative, Cal."

I shook my head, smiling. "Well, I do have low overhead and the pension from my early retirement, of course. Only problem—it was too damn early."

A round of laughter ushered in some reminiscing and storytelling. Finally, Whipple changed the subject. "I talked to Charlie Banks about the Bivens incident. He said they have one of the shooters already and have a BOLO out for the other. But you know that, right? Apparently, you had a run-in with the two of them the week before. I told you this isn't Portland, Cal."

I bristled at the condescension but managed to smile. "Point taken. Not feeling a lot of love from the City of Angels. On the bright side, I'm only here a week and I've got a suspect for who arranged the Krasnova hit."

"You mean the vic, Tucker Bivens?" Whipple said. "Banks told me about your theory."

Moretti said, "You got more on this guy?"

"Bivens was a jealous lover, obsessed with her," I said.

"So, if he can't have her, nobody can?" Moretti said.

"Exactly. It was common knowledge around the Impromptu that he was insanely jealous." *And you should've known that*, I thought. "He didn't want to get his hands dirty, so he hired Ferris Spielman to do the job. I just learned they did time together in Corcoran."

Moretti leaned in. "Well, he's dead now. Looks like you're shit out of luck to me."

I couldn't let that one pass. I swung my gaze to my ex-colleague. "You'd like that, wouldn't you, Aldo? Mimi Ryerson told me about your efforts to discourage her from cooperating with my investigation. What the hell's up with that? Dante Ellis spent thirteen years in San Quentin for a crime he didn't commit. And we put him there. You don't think it's worth getting at what really happened?"

"Your suspect's dead now. What else is there to do?" Whipple interjected in an obvious effort to lower the temperature.

"I'm going to prove Bivens killed her and sue his estate for damages. Ellis deserves more than the wrongful conviction money. He lost his wife and didn't get to see his son grow up. He's a traumatized mess now."

Moretti looked at Whipple before turning back to me with a gotcha expression. "Oh, so there's money in it for you?"

I felt my neck getting hot. "I'm working pro bono, Aldo."

He set his glass down and leaned in. "Jesus, Cal. We all fucked up on this case. It happens. You know that. Leave well enough—"

"Hey," Whipple cut in, "this isn't worth arguing about." He aimed a disarming smile at Moretti, then gestured in my direction. "The man's gonna do what he's gonna do. You know Cal as well as I do, Aldo."

Moretti glared at me. "Yeah, well you're showing more allegiance to some fucking, no-account bartender than to the organization you served. That's bullshit." He got up abruptly, tipping his chair over backwards. "Where's your head? I gotta take a leak."

"Second door on the right," I said.

"For Christ's sake, cool your jets, Aldo," Whipple chimed in.

"Fuck you, Whip," he said and then sauntered into the apartment, leaving the chair overturned on the bricks.

Whipple put the chair upright and turned to me. "Don't worry about Aldo. You know, blue runs in his veins. The thought of anyone slandering the LAPD makes him go ballistic." He sat back down and took a drink of his Remy. "He's already had a few, which never helps. Sorry, Cal."

"What's he doing in LA, anyway?"

"Pot business. He's running a high inventory right now, so he's looking for buyers. He's uptight. He bet the farm on the venture. Literally."

Circling back, I said, "What else did Banks have to say?"

"He likes Imhoff for the hit, thinks you were the target, not Bivens. But so far, he hasn't found a scrap of evidence linking the car to the shooting, and they don't have a murder weapon. The guy with the broken nose—the one whose voice you recognized—just made bail, too. Car theft's all we have on him."

"Shit," I said. "I was afraid of that." I eyed Whipple closely. "There's another scenario, you know."

Whipple smiled knowingly. "The hit was still set up by Imhoff, but Bivens was the target."

I nodded. "What does Banks think of that?"

"Not much. He's got a suspect with motive—you're messing around in Imhoff's sandbox—and he hopes to link the hitters to Imhoff and your previous attack. That's a strong beachhead. Bivens was collateral damage."

"What do *you* think? My sources tell me Imhoff and Bivens might've gotten crosswise over the fentanyl supply chain. And it's unlikely Imhoff knew I was going to be at the club, but it was a predictable, weekly event for Bivens."

The knowing smile again. "Interesting theory."

I rolled my eyes. "You know more than you're telling

me, Todd. Your narcotics team must be looking at this. Can't you give me—"

At that point, Moretti came out of the apartment. "I'll be in the car, Whip," he said, avoiding my eyes as he let himself out and slammed the gate shut.

Whipple shook his head and frowned. "He can be such an asshole when he drinks. I need to take him back to his hotel."

We both got up. "You have to be looking at the Bivens-Imhoff relationship," I persisted. "What can you tell me—"

"Look, Cal," he cut in, "you know I can't discuss anything ongoing with you. You know the goddamn drill as well as I do."

"Come on, give me a break here."

"Oh, so you're standing on principle, but I can't? Is that the way it works? I'm already crossing the line by trying to get you that damn murder book."

I opened my hands but didn't respond. He had a point.

"And why the hell do you care, anyway?" He went on. "It's what Bivens did thirteen years ago that should matter to you."

"It's a loose end, damn it. I detest them." I paused for a moment. "Since you brought it up, is there any news on the murder book?"

He let his breath out and frowned again. "Afraid not. Sorry about that." He got up. "I'd better get Aldo back to his hotel." When he got to the gate, he looked back at me. "Look, Cal, if I hear anything relevant to your probe, I'll get in touch. I don't particularly like what you're doing here, but I understand and respect you for it."

Archie, who had followed Whipple to the gate, turned

to me after it clicked shut. "You think he means it, Big Boy? You think he'll ever give me anything useful?"

My dog looked back at me, his coppery eyes unreadable.

CHAPTER TWENTY-SEVEN

SUNLIGHT STREAMING INTO AN EAST-FACING WINDOW awoke me the next morning. After feeding Arch and wolfing down a bagel loaded with cream cheese, smoked salmon, and capers, we headed for the beach. Archie's energy level was off scale that morning, a clear indication he needed some serious exercise, so I packed a couple of Frisbees in my backpack. Just the act of packing the discs caused my dog to bark and bounce around like he was on a pogo stick. Slobber ball was good but chasing down Frisbees even better. A brisk breeze blowing north to south that morning turbo-charged the discs, which Arch snapped out of the air with the grace of a gazelle and the skill of a major league center fielder. It wasn't long before his athletic prowess had drawn a small crowd, who began cheering *olé* every time he caught a disc.

What a showoff.

My cell phone buzzed just as we were leaving the beach. "Mr. Claxton? This is Natalia Pavlin. I understand you wish to talk to me." The accent was mild and possibly Slovakian, at least to my newly trained ear. I was pretty sure who it was, which gave me a buzz of excitement.

"Uh, yeah. Are you Lara Novak's friend, the woman who owned an escort service at the Impromptu thirteen years ago?"

"I have some free time this afternoon," she replied, ignoring my question. "Perhaps we could meet for a drink. I think it would be mutually beneficial."

"I can do that," I replied.

"Splendid. We could meet at the Maria Sol restaurant on the Santa Monica pier at, say, 2 PM. I understand you have a dog. I'll book an outdoor table so you can bring him if you wish."

I readily accepted.

Back at the apartment, I was gratified to see more pages had unstuck themselves from the bulk of Jimmy Ryerson's damaged journal. Ten or twelve pages—all written in black ink, thank God—and they looked legible. The rest of the journal was drying out nicely, too, promising more to come.

I sat down with a double cappuccino and scanned the pages. A week after Krasnova's murder, Ryerson made the following entry:

> *Who the hell is the "Bitch Queen"? A nickname for the madam of the prostitution ring Krasnova worked for. None of the girls claim to know her real name, which is BS. Harry Imhoff is playing dumb as well. Okay, we made a quick arrest, but I'm not satisfied we've cast a broad enough net.*
>
> *Discussed this with my partner. "Kick it over to Vice and let them worry about it," he says. "We've got our murderer. You've seen those beauties. Hell, the mayor and half the city*

council are probably customers at the Impromptu." I ignored his cynicism (laziness?) and said this was bad police work. We didn't have the complete picture yet. A partner is a partner, but I'm not going to stand by and let the integrity of this investigation go in the shitter.

I sipped my coffee and read on. I'd forgotten what a stickler Jimmy Ryerson was. Uncomfortable memories began bubbling up about how his colleagues sometimes laughed at his zealousness behind his back. Had I joined in? I had, on occasion, and the admission rekindled an all too familiar sense of guilt.

Further on, Ryerson wrote:

Finally received the cell tower data for Krasnova's cell phone. Moretti grumbled but finally agreed to split the follow-up on calls and texts prior to her death. I wanted six months prior, but we'd finally agreed to ask for four on the warrant. I took the last two months, which turned out to be a wash except for:

- *Three incoming calls, tightly spaced, from Tucker Bivens during the week prior to the murder. Bivens is a john who frequents the Impromptu. The defense will be all over this! We need to clear this guy!*
- *Three outgoing and one incoming with the suspect, Dante Ellis, during the two weeks prior. Good corroborating evidence of a relationship between Krasnova and Ellis!*
- *Four outgoing, three incoming from someone at the Jansen Modeling Agency in Beverly Hills. Who and why? Needs follow-up.*

After reading these entries, I immediately called Zoe. "Hmm," she said when I finished describing the Jansen Modeling Agency reference, "this might be where Gabriela worked?"

"Does the name of the agency ring a bell?"

"No, but let me check my notes." She came back after a short pause. "Afraid not, but I'll go back and see when they went out of business or if someone bought them who's still in Beverly Hills."

"Good," I said. "And I'll see if this helps Dante's memory."

"I'll do that," she said. "I've already talked to him. He sounded okay, by the way."

"Good." Next, I read back Ryerson's comments about his partner, Aldo Moretti, and then described my unexpected visit from Moretti and Whipple.

"Now you have insight into the origin of the rift between Ryerson and Moretti that Mimi told you about," Zoe said when I finished. "What do you make of that?"

"No surprise, now that I think about it. Ryerson was a by-the-book cop, and Moretti's veins may run blue, but he had a reputation for cutting corners back then."

Zoe puffed a dismissive breath. "And a general disdain for people caught in the criminal justice system, judging from his reference to Dante as a 'fucking, no-account bartender.' I mean, he doesn't show any remorse for helping convict an innocent man?"

"None that I can detect. And now I'm wondering why he's so threatened by my investigation. Was it simply that his and the LAPD's reputations might be damaged? After all, he's retired now and doesn't even live in California."

"It's not surprising that he's alarmed about how this will reflect on him," Zoe responded. "And you can bet it's more about him than the LAPD. Insecure, judgmental types never let their guard down. They fear anything that might reveal some unsavory truth about them."

"Unsavory truth?" I said. "I've had a few sips out of that cup."

"But you've admitted your mistakes, Cal, and you're trying to make them right. That's the difference between you and him, Cal. You're growing, he's not."

"Maybe so," I said. "Maybe he's just a narcissistic prick." In the back of my mind, however, I wondered if there could be other reasons for Moretti's behavior.

Our conversation eventually drifted to lighter topics. At one point I asked, "Is it bud break yet?" referring to the spectacular spring flowering of the grapevines up in the Red Hills where Zoe and I lived.

"Yes," she replied, "five days ago. They're in all their glory right now."

I pictured the vineyards below my old farmhouse, the orderly rows of vines now speckled with tiny white blossoms and emergent, lime-green leaves. An unexpected jolt of homesickness hit me like a Mack Truck. "Damn," I said, "hate to miss bud break. Sounds like a promising year."

"Hey," Zoe said in a soothing voice, "there'll be other bud breaks. And just think, you'll be tasting the wines those buds produced down the road, so nothing's lost."

She was right, of course. After we disconnected, I realized that, sure, I missed the bud break and I missed my Aerie, but it was being away from Zoe that really tugged at my heart. I looked over at Archie, who was curled up in a corner watching me. "I've got it bad, Big Boy," I told him.

CHAPTER TWENTY-EIGHT

BY THE TIME ARCHIE AND I SET OFF FOR THE SANTA Monica pier that afternoon, a brisk northerly breeze had transformed the gun-metal sky to a brilliant, crystalline blue. The breeze wrinkled but didn't whitecap the Pacific, which stretched out to join the sky with hardly the trace of a seam. The amusement park at the entry to the pier was jammed with regulars and tourists, and the line in front of the solar-powered Ferris wheel (the world's only) was the longest I'd seen yet. I was happy that Natalia Pavlin afforded me the opportunity to bring Archie along, because I'm always interested in how a subject reacts to my dog and vice versa.

Archie and I arrived first and scored a table with a view of the surfing action on the north side of the pier. The swell was strong, but the waves were choppy and ragged owing to the wind. But that didn't stop the dozen or so surfers—locals judging by their skill levels—from shredding the poorly shaped breakers. Archie settled in next to my chair. I ordered a Dos Equis and sat sipping it for maybe ten minutes before Pavlin arrived.

I had no idea what to expect, but I knew it was her the moment she entered the outdoor pavilion. Statuesque with silver highlights in her long black hair, she wore a body-hugging jumpsuit and clutched a Gucci bag. I stood and our eyes connected. She approached the table, her long, dangly earrings swaying with her stride, and offered her hand. Archie stood to greet her, but she ignored him.

"Thanks for coming," I said as she pulled out a chair and seated herself.

"Of course," she said as she studied me with probing eyes. Her countenance was stern, her face Botox-tight and heavily made up. She got right to the point. "I was so surprised to hear that Dante Ellis was released from prison. I didn't know the man, but people who did never believed he could have killed Irena Krasnova, even after he was convicted." She raised an eyebrow. "He is a free man now, but he wishes to stir up the past? I'm surprised at this."

"Well, personally," I said, "I can't blame the man for wanting to know who set him up. His incarceration had a terrible impact on his life."

An almost teasing smile spread across her face. "You're the man who prosecuted him, and now you're helping him? That seems rather odd."

I ignored the comment. "I was hoping you could answer a few questions Dante and I have." We were interrupted by a server, and after Pavlin ordered a Cadillac margarita, I pressed on. "I understand that at the time Irena Krasnova was murdered, you owned the Good Company escort service. Is that correct?"

She met and held my eyes, her expression all business. "Are you recording this?"

I opened my hands. "No, I'm not."

"Would you mind turning off your cell phone?"

"Of course," I said and pulled my phone from my

pocket, powered it down, and set it on the table. I raised both hands and smiled. "Not wearing a wire, either."

She nodded curtly. "The escort service—yes, I did own it at that time, but it's not anything I wish to be known for."

"Understood. What are you doing now?" I asked, more out of curiosity than anything else.

"I'm retired," she answered. "And I dabble in the stock market." Her margarita arrived in what looked like a fishbowl with a straw in it. She took a long drink and then dabbed her blood red lips with a napkin.

"You sold the business to Harry Imhoff some months after the murder," I went on. "Is that true?" She nodded. "At that time, Irena was having problems with one of your customers, a man named Tucker Bivens." I described the rape scene between Bivens and Irena that Macleod had told me about, adding, "She threatened to expose his narcotics dealings after that, right?"

"Yes, I did hear rumors to that effect." She smiled pensively. "Irena was—as you say in this country—a real pistol."

"Would Bivens have seen this as enough of a threat to have her killed?"

"You would have to ask him," she said, then covered her mouth with her hand momentarily. "Oh, you can't. He's dead."

I didn't smile. "So you know nothing about the man?"

She took another long, loving drink of her margarita. She was a drinker, no question. "He was a good customer. Paid cash. Do I think he could have had Irena killed? Definitely. Tucker Bivens was capable of any atrocity. Would I be willing to say this in court? No." I gave her a look, and she shot back, "Don't you dare judge me for not coming forward. It was you and your so-called justice system that sent the poor man to prison."

I raised my hands in mock surrender. "Okay. Message received." I asked her about Anika Molnar, Irena's friend who died of an overdose, but learned nothing new. "Does the name Gabriela or Gabby mean anything to you?" I asked next.

Pavlin's head retracted, and her eyes widened slightly, but she recovered in an instant. She pursed her lips. "No. It does not."

"During that time, did you hear or were you aware that Irena was planning something that might help her get out of the life? Modeling, perhaps, or a scheme of some kind?"

Her heavily lashed eyes narrowed, and she raised her chin with a hint of defiance. "No. Irena and I were close. She would have shared that with me. Who told you this nonsense?"

"I'm not at liberty to say," I answered. "Aside from Lara Novak and Alec Macleod, do you know of anyone else who might know something about the relationship between Bivens and Irena around the time of her murder?"

Pavlin laughed with contempt. "I'm not at liberty to say, either. Surely you understand why I can't name names, even now."

"Point taken," I said and then shifted focus. "What about Harry Imhoff? He would've been concerned about Irena's threats. Scrutiny by LAPD might've threatened business at the Impromptu, to say nothing of making it difficult to buy your escort service."

She smiled bitterly. "Oh, Harry was worried about losing the deal, no question. He even asked me to talk to Irena." She dabbed her lips after another pull on the margarita. By this time her napkin looked like a used bandage.

"Did you talk to her?"

"I did, but I didn't feel she listened to me."

"You just told me you two were close."

"She was headstrong. What can I say? And Harry Imhoff is a swine. He, too, is capable of anything."

I leaned in. "Tell me more."

Her jaw muscles flexed before she answered. "When he bought my business, he began replacing my girls with whores and addicts."

"Why?"

She shot me an incredulous look. "For money. Why else? He cut the take of the girls in half but made pills and cocaine freely available. Now he has nothing but a stable of addicts who are basically slaves. It is disgusting."

"What happened to the girls he forced out?"

She shook her head. "I was able to help some find work, others fell by the wayside, I'm afraid."

"All of your girls were Slovakian as I understand it. How did they get here in the first place?"

"There are ways, but I know nothing of that."

I shot her a skeptical look but opted not to press it.

"What I can tell you," she continued in a defensive tone, "is that they were all beautiful girls who had no future except dead-end marriages in Slovakia. Here, at least, they had a chance at something better."

"Like Lara Novak?"

"Yes, like Lara Novak," she answered, lifting her chin in a look of pride bordering on self-righteousness.

I wondered how many of the Slovakian girls had 'fallen by the wayside,' and why she chose to sell her business to a 'swine', but I knew asking would probably end the conversation. Instead, I said, "Do you know of anyone else who might've had a reason to harm Irena?"

She shook her head with finality. "It could only be

Bivens or Imhoff. Irena was so popular, almost saintly. And if I had to choose between the two, it would be Bivens. Such a nasty little man. I hope he's rotting in hell." She eyed me with what passed as a look of sympathy. "I am sorry that your best suspect is dead. That must make your investigation rather difficult."

"Not necessarily."

Her eyes stayed on me for a moment, and then she slurped up the last of her margarita and dabbed at her lips with a napkin. "You have other suspects?"

"The investigation's ongoing. I haven't reached any conclusions."

"I see." She glanced at her jeweled watch, then stood up. "Well, I need to go now. I hope I have been of some help."

"You have," I said, and as she turned to leave, I added, "When you called, you said our meeting would be mutually beneficial. Have I helped you in any way?"

She smiled. "Well, I feel less worried you will drag my name through the mud."

I smiled back but gave her a non-answer: "That's not my intention."

After she sashayed out of the pavilion, Archie got up from beside my chair, thrust his front legs forward and executed a perfect downward dog. I looked down at him and said, "Well, Big Boy, I guess not everyone finds you irresistible. So, what do you think? Is the Queen as innocent as she wanted us to believe? A sex trafficker with a heart?"

My dog looked at me, his eyes unblinking.

I laughed. "I didn't buy it, either."

I paid the check, and as we threaded our way off the pier, I wondered about Pavlin's fear that I might document our discussion. Was it her sex-trafficking past? Maybe she failed to pay taxes on the sale of her business? Or was it something else that had her so paranoid? Hard to say. But a couple of things did seem evident—first, Irena Krasnova's threat to expose Tucker Bivens' drug dealings was as much a motive for murder for Pavlin as it was for Tucker Bivens or Harry Imhoff. What's a high-end escort service sell for? A lot, judging from her early retirement and apparent affluence. Second, like Lara Novak's exchange with Dante the day before, Pavlin didn't tell me much I didn't already know, while showing a healthy interest in my investigation.

Were Novak and Pavlin a tag team?

CHAPTER TWENTY-NINE

ONCE ARCHIE AND I WERE HEADED UP COLORADO Avenue, I called Nando to bring him up to date. *"Aye yai yai,"* he exclaimed when I described the Tucker Bivens' shooting. *"Es una locura.* I knew LA was dangerous, but this is crazy, my friend."

"Yeah, but I'm not ready to fold here," I said. "If it was Bivens, I'm going to prove it and sue his estate into oblivion. If it was someone else, I'm going to catch them."

Nando laughed, his trademark basso profundo. "Of course you're staying. I already knew that. What do you need now besides a Kevlar vest and an armed detail?"

"I need you to do a deep background on Natalia Pavlin. She's Slovenian, the madam for the escort service I told you about.''" I spelled her last name and described our meeting on the pier.

"Ah, the Queen Bitch. You found her."

"I did. She's probably here on a green card or undocumented, I'm not sure which. She was pitching either Bivens or Imhoff for the hit, but I don't trust her. She had a motive, too, and she knows more than she's telling me."

"I am on it," Nando said, "and I have some news for you—Esperanza has found a lead on the Ellis boy—the record of a name change from Jamare Hakeem Ellis to

Jamare Gilpin recorded in Orange County. He dropped his middle name, apparently."

"Do you know where the name Gilpin came from?"

"Probably from foster parents he had, but we don't know for sure."

"Do you have an address?"

"Esperanza is working on it. He has a LinkedIn account with a good picture. He's a handsome young man. Teaches high school in Costa Mesa, a city south of Los Angeles."

"How about other social media?"

"He does not partake."

"That's great work, Nando. Thank Esperanza for me."

There was a long pause before Nando said, "I don't need to tell you to watch your back, do I, Calvin?"

"No, you don't," I said with a ring of harshness I hadn't intended. After we disconnected, I shook my head at my defensiveness. *Pride goeth before a fall,* I reminded myself.

Back at the apartment, I wasn't too concerned that the patio gate was ajar. But when the front door was, too, the hair on the back of my neck stood at attention. I distinctly remembered locking the door, which now had a key inserted into the doorknob. The spare key that hung on the far side of the windowsill, no doubt. Picking up on the vibe, Archie pushed the door open with his snout and started to go in. "No, Big Boy," I whispered as I clipped his leash back on. If someone was still in there, I didn't want my dog confronting them.

I stood stock-still and listened. Not a sound emanated from the apartment, and Archie's calm demeanor hinted that no one was inside. But just in case, as I backed away from the door, I spied a small garden spade stuck in the ground next to a row of geraniums along the fence line. I grabbed it, reapproached the door, and called into the apartment, "You're busted. If you come out now, you might miss the cops." I waited. Nothing. I shouted a second time, waited again, and then entered the apartment with the spade in my right hand and Archie on a tight leash in my left.

Sitting on the coffee table, my briefcase was open, and the papers it contained were scattered on the living area floor. In the bedroom, the lid to my laptop, which I always leave down, was up. I wasn't worried about the laptop—it was password protected—and there hadn't been anything sensitive in my briefcase. The small dresser had been gone through and socks, tee shirts and underwear were strewn across the floor, but my Glock 17, which I'd stashed in the top drawer, was still there.

As break-ins go—and God knows I'd had my share—this one, at least, hadn't completely trashed the apartment. I walked back into the living area and was in the process of expelling a breath of relief when the items on the kitchen table caught my eye. The fan sat in front of Mimi's casserole dish, where I'd left Jimmy Ryerson's journal. The fan blades obscured my view, so I walked over to have a closer look.

The journal was gone. *"Shit."*

I slumped down on a kitchen chair and let out a long, deep sigh. Archie came over to console me. I couldn't believe it. The process of drying out the journal pages was working so well, and I was just beginning to extract useful information. What else had Ryerson written about the Krasnova murder that would help me? I would never know, and that realization stung even more, because it was clear I was never gaining access to the LAPD murder book.

Like I said, *"Shit."*

Natalia Pavlin immediately came to mind. She had

called and arranged our meeting on the pier, so she knew where I would be and how long I would be gone. She also suggested I bring Archie, which made the break-in possible. Could she have arranged it? If so, why? The only reason could be she was somehow involved in Krasnova's murder.

Had a new investigative front just opened up? I wasn't sure, but it was a sobering thought.

I fetched a Mirror Pond out of the fridge, popped the cap off, and went out on the patio to think things through. Another possibility hit me—the visit from Todd Whipple and Aldo Moretti took place out here on the patio, but Moretti had used my bathroom that night. I was pretty sure the light had been on in the kitchen alcove. Could he have seen the journal and recognized it for what it was? Did he come back and take it out of spite? That possibility seemed in character. If so, he would've been watching my movements, but I hadn't noticed anything suspicious in the street when I left for the pier.

There was another possibility, of course. He could have taken the journal, not out of spite but because he feared what was in it. *That* possibility was as sobering as my new-found suspicion of Natalia Pavlin.

I thought about calling the Santa Monica police but decided it wouldn't serve any useful purpose. Nothing of monetary value had been taken from my apartment, and in any case, I wasn't keen to involve another jurisdiction in my investigation, which was growing more complicated by the minute.

I considered the break-in method next. I got up and checked where the spare key had been hidden. It was gone, indicating it was the same key left in the doorknob. Had the intruder known the hiding place? Probably not. It was more likely that he or she simply looked for a spare key before forcing the lock, which would've made some noise. Not the move of an amateur.

I drained my beer and looked at Archie with a sheepish smile. "Okay, maybe I should've hidden that damn key in a better place on day one, but look on the bright side—at least we won't have to repair the door or change the locks."

That's when I thought of the security camera I'd noticed on my neighbor's house. I bolted across the street and rang the doorbell.

"Yeah, my security camera covers your side of the street," the neighbor replied to my inquiry. Wearing a tie-dye bathrobe, he was an older gentleman with shoulder-length silver hair. "Why do you ask?"

"Any chance I could review your footage? I was just broken into an hour ago."

"Damn," he said, shaking his head, "the camera's in place, but the batteries need changing. My partner's been on me for weeks to fix it. Sorry about that."

I slunk back across the street and looked at my dog. "So much for technology."

CHAPTER THIRTY

AFTER STRAIGHTENING UP THE APARTMENT, I TOOK some time to jot down the key points I'd gleaned from Ryerson's now-missing journal. It was a short list. By the time I finished and took Archie out for a walk, the sun was getting low but hadn't yet touched the horizon. It felt like time to catch up with Dante, but when his phone went immediately to voicemail, I decided to pop in on him at his motel.

The 10 Freeway was jammed with impatient drivers that evening, some of whom had a death wish judging from their propensity to tailgate at eighty-five miles an hour. The blood finally flowed back into my knuckles when I exited at Overland Avenue in Culver City and scored a parking space right in front of Dante's motel.

"Yeah? Who is it?" Dante called out from inside his room when I knocked. I told him it was me, and he opened the door. He was shirtless in a pair of jeans, and he seemed, if not relaxed, at least unstressed. A first.

"Hey, Cal, come on in."

"I thought we could catch up at my place. I've got a couple of steaks that need devouring."

"Oh," he said, "I—"

"Dante?" a female voice called out from the bathroom. "Can you hand me my clothes?"

"Yeah, baby, just a minute," he called back. "We've got a visitor." He turned to me. "It's Lara Novak. She, uh, dropped by for a visit." Despite his effort to suppress it, he broke into a smile.

I smiled back. After all, what did I expect of a man forced into celibacy for over a decade?

He gathered up a bra, panties, shorts, and a top from the disheveled bed and passed them through the bathroom door, which had opened slightly. "It's Cal Claxton," he said before Lara pulled the door closed. He turned back to me. "She, uh, was just on her way out. A steak sounds pretty good."

Lara came out of the bathroom a few minutes later. Still tall in bare feet, her wet hair hung past her shoulders like a dark curtain, which had the effect of framing her lovely face. She was, indeed, a beautiful woman. After exchanging somewhat awkward greetings, I said, "I met with Natalia Pavlin earlier this afternoon. If you had something to do with that, thank you."

She smiled. "Well, I was able to find her and pass on your contact information. I'm glad she followed through. Did you learn anything?"

"Mainly that she wasn't about to name names, with the exception of Tucker Bivens and Harry Imhoff. She thought either one could have arranged Irena's murder."

Lara slipped on a pair of sandals, kissed Dante, and stepped to the door. "I agree. Could've been either one of those bastards."

I nodded. "I got the impression Pavlin is enjoying a very comfortable retirement. She must have made a bundle when she sold the escort service. Know anything about that?"

She paused at the door, and her face stiffened ever so slightly. "The only thing we working girls were told about

Good Company's finances was what to charge our clients. But I did hear something about Natalia being good at picking stocks." With that, she let herself out.

Her exit, I thought, had the earmarks of a hasty retreat.

—⊣⊢—

Back at my apartment, I fired up the Weber, coated a couple of Yukon Golds with olive oil

and sea salt, and because time was short, popped them in the microwave. While making a salad, I broke the news about the theft of Ryerson's journal.

"Son of a bitch," Dante said when I finished, his eyes wide. "You know what this means?"

I nodded, because I knew where he was going.

"Bivens didn't do it!" he said. "The fucker's dead, so he couldn't have taken the journal or had somebody take it for him." Dante raked his beard with the fingers of both hands. "That means we can't sue his estate."

"Most likely," I said. "You're back to just the compensation from the state. How does that make you feel?"

He waved a dismissive hand without hesitation. "Shit, I figured it was pie in the sky anyway. I'm still gonna get more money than I ever dreamed of having." He looked me straight in the eye. "I'm more committed than ever if that's what you're worried about."

"Good," I said as I sliced tomatoes and cucumbers for the salad and made an oil and vinegar dressing. "How did Lara wind up at your motel this afternoon?"

"She, uh, called and sort of invited herself over."

"When did she arrive?"

"Around two," he said, cocking his head slightly. "Why do you ask?"

"While my apartment was being broken into, Archie and I were tied up on the pier with Natalia Pavlin, and you were busy here in your room with Lara. That's an interesting coincidence."

Dante smacked his forehead with the heel of his hand. "Oh, fuck!"

"What?"

He studied his shoes for a few moments. "I, uh…I told Lara about the journal the morning of the chess match." He looked up at me, his eyes pleading. "Didn't tell her much, just that we had it and were getting some stuff from it. Bragging, I guess. I wanted to impress her."

"Whoops," I said with an expression that didn't hide my anger. "Why the hell didn't you tell me this?"

His eyes fluttered for a moment, and I thought he was going to tear up. "I was in a fog, man. It just came back to me, and I didn't think it was such a big deal then. I'm sorry, Cal. I didn't tell her squat about the investigation today."

"Did she ask?"

"Oh, yeah. We played twenty questions and no answers." He paused for a moment. "By the way, Lara just called the Queen by her first name, *Natalia*. Did you catch that?"

"I did," I said, as I placed the two thick rib-eyes on the grill. "It sounded like she's on a first name basis with her."

Dante leaned forward in his chair. "So, Lara and the Bitch Queen are playing us?"

"Maybe. Pavlin had as good a motive as either Bivens or Imhoff to silence Irena. She's apparently living the dream after selling her business."

Dante nodded. "That's an angle I hadn't thought of."

"But we don't know the real purpose of the break-in," I went on." Was it simply to see what I'd left lying around unsecured, so the theft of the journal was unplanned?"

"Or did someone go after it intentionally, because they feared what was in it?" Dante added.

"Exactly," I said.

Dante scratched his beard. "Anyone else know about the journal besides Lara and the cop's wife who gave it to you?"

I had to smile. "Good question. You might be off the hook. There is another person who may have known." I described the visit from Moretti and Whipple, including Moretti's anger at me and his foray into my apartment to use the bathroom.

Dante gave his forehead a faux swipe and smiled sheepishly. "Whew, I feel a little better. So, the dude could've copped it just to gum up our investigation?"

"I can't rule that out, but we just don't know at this point." The steaks hissed and flames flared when I turned them over.

"Nice grill marks," Dante said with a wistful look. "Takes me back, man. I did my steaks over charcoal, you know, white hot briquets. No offense. This is good, but..."

"I hear you," I said, smiling. "Grilling steaks over propane's a little like making instant coffee, but I'll bet we don't leave anything for Archie tonight." We had a good laugh, and then I said, "I've got some news about Jamare." Dante sat quietly and listened while I told him about the name change to Gilpin and that we were close to having an address. When I finished, I pulled up Jamare's picture on the LinkedIn account and handed Dante my cell phone. "Here's a picture of your son."

He cupped the phone in his hand and studied the

picture for a long time before looking up with a stunned expression, eyes brimming with unshed tears. "That's him? That's Jamare? He's a grown man now." He shook his head and broke into a broad smile. "I can't believe it."

"Kids tend to do that, grow up," I said, chuckling. "And he's handsome, too."

Tears broke loose from both eyes and streamed down Dante's cheeks. "Damn, he *is* handsome, isn't he?"

I said, "click on his profile."

Dante was unfamiliar with the app, but after a few moments he looked up at me with a beaming smile, like some proud new father in a maternity ward. "Jamare's a high school teacher. Chemistry. Graduated from UCLA magna cum laude. Likes to backpack and surf." Dante's smile was so broad I thought it might crack his face. "That's amazing, just amazing."

"Want to meet him?" I said, and the moment the words left my mouth I knew I'd made a mistake.

His smile crashed. "No, man. I told you I don't want him to know about me." He looked at my phone still clutched in his hand. "He's changed his name, has a good life goin' on. He doesn't need some ex-con barging in and screwing things up. No way I'm doing that. No way."

"He's an adult," I countered. "Maybe you should let him—"

Dante's eyes flashed a warning. "No, goddamn it. Just get his address like we agreed."

The microwave pinged, signaling the potatoes were done, and a few moments later I removed the steaks from the grill. I would've paired the meal with one of the pinots I brought from Oregon, but I didn't want to serve alcohol to Dante. We ate in silence for a while, and then he began talking about his son. As he spoke, his facial features softened, and his voice dropped to a lower register and took on a tone of reverence, as if he were sharing something precious.

He was, of course. At one point, he put his fork down, smiled, and said, "We were in a rental place then, but it had a big attic. I put a bar across a couple of rafters up there to do chin-ups. Jamare used to come up and watch, and then one day he asked for his own bar." Dante smiled and slowly shook his head. "I put one in for him, and he was up to ten chin-ups by the time I got arrested and thrown in jail."

I flinched inwardly, thinking the memory of his arrest might rekindle his anger, but the nostalgia of the moment held sway, and Dante went on without recrimination. "He graduated magna cum laude, and I'll bet he's strong as a bull."

"He's got half your genes. He's gotta be strong. And I'll bet he can play some chess, too."

He allowed a thin smile and looked past me with a faraway expression. "You know, I still have a bunch of letters I wrote him. The letters started coming back to me. Must have been when he got fostered out. Never got his new address, but I kept writing and sending them to the only address I had, our old place." He laughed, a single, sharp note. "I'm a stubborn fucker."

I was right about the steaks—they went fast and so did the rest of the meal. When we finished eating and reminiscing, Dante said, "So, where do we go from here?"

I paused to gather my thoughts. "It's complicated. Unless Tucker Bivens conspired with someone who's still out there, we're left with Harry Imhoff and Natalia Pavlin. Both had compelling financial motives to silence Irena. Bivens did time with the hitman, Spielman, but Corcoran is a big prison, and we know of no connection between

Imhoff and Spielman. Also, Imhoff's goons took Bivens off the board, but they could've been gunning for me."

Dante stroked his beard. "Maybe it's Imhoff. He likes using contractors."

"Maybe. As for the Queen," I went on, "my private investigator is running a deep background check on her. We'll see if anything turns up."

"What about your cop buddy who wants you to shut down the investigation?" Dante asked.

"Aldo Moretti could've taken Ryerson's journal. But if he did, it was probably to discourage me from continuing the investigation, because it might tarnish his service record."

Dante shot me a skeptical look. "You sure that was all he was worried about? Cops showing up out of the blue? I don't trust the bastards."

I nodded. "Like I said, Dante, it's complicated."

CHAPTER THIRTY-ONE

MY CELL PHONE BUZZED AT 1:35 THE NEXT MORNING, awakening me from a deep sleep. I reached for the phone, knocked it off the nightstand, and went down on my hands and knees to retrieve it from under the bed. After a couple of choice expletives, I mumbled, "H'lo?"

"Cal? It's Mimi. Sorry to bother you, but I was wondering if you could come pick me up?"

The weakness in her voice snapped me to attention. "Sure, Mimi. Where are you?"

"At the Topanga Medical Clinic on Route 27."

"What happened?"

"Someone was in my house. I came home and surprised them. They whacked me on the head."

"No! Are you okay?"

"I look a mess and have a headache, but, yeah, I'm okay."

"Did you get a look at them?"

"No. I couldn't even tell you if it was a man or a woman."

"I'm leaving right now."

—⧸⊢—

Two and a half hours later we were sitting at Mimi's kitchen table sipping coffee laced with bourbon. The police had interviewed her, and the crime scene techs were finished with their work. Her left eye was swollen shut with a purplish half-moon beneath it, and a welt the size of a walnut showed through her hair above her left ear. Archie, sensing Mimi's vulnerability, lay curled at her feet like a service dog.

We had thoroughly discussed the attack—which took place as she entered her second-floor bedroom—and were on to speculating about what was behind it. I sighed and shook my head. "I'm feeling guilty here, like I've brought my damn problems to your doorstep."

"How so?" she asked, her good eye fixed on me.

"My apartment was broken into yesterday afternoon. My stuff was gone through, and Jimmy's journal was taken."

Mimi's hand went to her face. "Oh God, that's scary."

"Yeah," I said. "I'm wondering if your prowler was looking for anything else Jimmy might've written, something damning."

She paused for a moment. "Maybe, but my office was rifled. And some jewelry in the bedroom was taken along with a set of old silverware in the dining room I seldom use."

"Are the rest of the journals up in the attic?"

"Yeah, in an old trunk. The police looked up there. They said that area appeared to be untouched."

"Let's take another look. You don't have a basement, and the water-damaged condition of the journal stolen from me could've suggested it had been stored in an attic. If not an attic, maybe a garage."

Access to the attic was through a pull-down ladder in the second-floor hallway. I went up first and then offered a hand to Mimi. Archie whined a bit, but after deciding he couldn't manage the ladder, plopped down next to it. The stale air smelled faintly of mold, and the space was cluttered with the detritus that accumulates in most attics—old furniture and toys, rolled-up rugs, and boxes whose contents had escaped Goodwill or the trash heap.

A stained, antique trunk sat off to one side, a skeleton key in the lock. I pointed at the trunk. "That's where you keep the journals, right?"

"You guessed it," she said. "The chest happened to be right below the one leak in the roof." She walked over to the trunk, turned the key, and the lid creaked when she lifted it. She looked up at me, shocked. "*Gone*. All the other journals are gone. You were right."

"How many were there?"

"Seven or eight. Jimmy only kept a journal on cases that really interested him."

A few minutes later we were back at the kitchen table with fresh coffee. Mimi blew some steam from her cup and took a sip. "The intruder was after the journals but took the jewelry and silver to make it look like a garden-variety burglary. Right?"

"That's my take," I said. "And the trunk was relocked, so you wouldn't notice they were gone, at least for a while."

She shuddered perceptibly. "Who could've done this, Cal?"

I added a little more bourbon to my coffee and told her about my meeting with Natalia Pavlin and my visit from Aldo Moretti and Todd Whipple. When I finished, she smirked and said, "So Aldo's in town and look what happens."

"You think it was him?"

Her eyes filled, and her lower lip quivered. "He hit me, Cal. His boy used to attend sleepovers at our place. Why would Aldo hit me?"

"If it was him, panic, probably. He only wanted to incapacitate you so he could get the hell out of the house."

"If?"

I opened my hands. "I can't rule out Natalia Pavlin, Mimi. The timing of her arrival on the scene is just as suspicious as Moretti's. And if someone she hired found the journal at my place, it wouldn't take Sherlock Holmes to figure out where the rest of them might be stored."

Mimi rolled her eyes. "Not likely. Aldo's got a thing about this case. He's worried about the part he played or something even worse. I just don't trust him."

"I know. Neither do I." I expelled a breath. "But there's more to this. Remember when I showed up here with the bruises?" She nodded. "I'm sorry, but I told you a fib. I wasn't in an accident. I was beaten up by two men hired by Harry Imhoff, the owner of the restaurant where Irena Krasnova worked."

She managed a wry smile. "I wondered about that. You're not the greatest liar, Cal Claxton."

"I was just trying to spare you the drama. Imhoff was trying to scare me off. Anyway, he's a suspect, too. Uh, there's something else. My best suspect at the time, a guy named Tucker Bivens, got his head blown off last week in a drive-by shooting. I witnessed it."

Mimi's mouth dropped open. "My God, Cal, you've kicked over a hornet's nest."

"Apparently. The cops think Imhoff hired the hit, but they don't have enough to arrest him or the goons that work for him." What I didn't mention was that I hadn't yet ruled out the possibility that I was the target of the attack.

Her mouth curled into a sly smile. "Well, at least you can cross the headless guy off your list of suspects."

I laughed. "It seems I've got a surplus of suspects but not much else. Bivens was the only one I could tie back to Ferris Spielman, the man who murdered Irena Krasnova. Now he's permanently off the board."

Mimi set her coffee cup down and leaned over the edge of the table. "Is Aldo at the top of your list?"

"You think he should be?"

She furrowed her brow. "I told you about the tension between Jimmy and Aldo during the Krasnova investigation. Maybe I underestimated how intense it was. Maybe it was more than just Aldo being Aldo, you know, trying to skate by with the minimum effort. Maybe Jimmy stumbled onto something Aldo was mixed up in? Something shady?"

"But Jimmy never said anything to you about that, right?"

"No, he never did, but he wouldn't unless he was absolutely sure. Aldo was his partner, after all, and besides, Jimmy always kept a space between his work and me and the kids."

I nodded. "I've had the same thoughts about Aldo."

"Yes, and remember that he told me not to cooperate in your investigation. Maybe that was a warning." Mimi's face hardened. "Could Jimmy's murder be somehow connected to all this?"

I shook my head. "I just don't know. Right now, everything's up in the air. Losing the journal was a blow."

The brow above her good eye arched. "You're not going back to Oregon, are you?"

"No, I'm not going back to Oregon, and I'm sorry as hell I got you tangled up in this mess. Are you going to feel safe in this house? I mean, you're very isolated out here."

She got up and extracted a Sig Sauer semiautomatic

from a top drawer next to the stove. "I keep this puppy right here in the kitchen. And Jimmy made sure I could shoot it," she said, holding the gun up. "And I've also got his Glock in my bedroom upstairs. I'm a cop's wife. I'll be fine."

We left it at that, and when Archie and I were at the door saying goodbye, Mimi smiled wistfully. "You know, Jimmy would've loved this case. I wish he was around to help you."

"Me, too," I answered. "He was a good man."

She grasped my collar, pulled my head forward, and, to my surprise, kissed me lightly on the cheek. "So are you, Cal," she said, then smiled and winked. "And don't forget, you still owe me a casserole dish."

CHAPTER THIRTY-TWO

ARCHIE AND I GOT BACK TO OUR APARTMENT IN SANTA Monica just as the sun was rising. By the time I fed him and collapsed on the bed, the cramped room was filled with bright sunlight. I got up muttering, pulled the shade, and managed to sleep until a little past eight. After a shower and a call to Zoe that went to voicemail, I was out on the patio munching a bowl of granola. I'd just gotten up to make another cappuccino when I heard the low rumble of a motorcycle. It sounded familiar.

"Top of the morning," Alec Macleod said as he opened the gate and walked in, holding his bike helmet. Archie went up to him, his butt in full wag, and Macleod dropped to one knee to embrace him. "I needed to get out of the city," he said, looking up at me. "You and Arch up for a walk on the beach?"

The swell that morning was coming from the northwest, three to four feet, which meant every serious surfer in the area was clustered on the north side of the Santa Monica pier. We watched the action for a while, and as we started up the beach Macleod sucked in a deep breath, spread his arms, and said, "God, I needed this. Thanks for joining me, Cal."

"Sure. Problems in Skid Row?"

"There're *always* problems in Skid Row. Too many desperate people, too few resources. But the fentanyl tsunami, that's changed the game." He shook his head. "Never thought I'd say this, but today's street scene makes the black tar heroin epidemic look like the good old days." He stopped and faced me, his face contorted with grief. "We've had four OD fatalities in the last three days, all young adults."

"Unimaginable." It was all I could think of to say.

He kicked at the sand. "In my profession, we refer to people as the children of God, you know, creatures capable of transcending their base instincts. But sometimes I think Darwin was right—we're just another species, one that's struggling to ascend the evolutionary ladder like our relatives in the animal kingdom. Oh, we're the clever apes, for sure. Hell, we've invented drugs so addicting they could've hooked Jesus himself. And for what end?" He kicked at the sand again. "It's *always* the same—for silver, goddamn pieces of silver."

"I'm in Darwin's camp," I said, "but I hope there's a special ring in hell for fentanyl purveyors."

Macleod laughed. "Oh, yeah, down low where the fire's hottest. Makes me want to believe in hell, which I don't."

We walked in silence for a long time. The surf rumbled, and an onshore breeze carried a strong, clean ocean scent. My mind turned to what Nando had reported about Harry Imhoff using fentanyl to keep his prostitutes in line. I told Macleod about that and brought him up to date on the break-ins, both at my place and Mimi Ryerson's, and we discussed the case. At one point I said, "There's a loose end I've been meaning to ask you about—do you remember a friend of Irena's named Gabriela? She went by Gabby. I don't know her last name."

Macleod stopped abruptly and studied his wet sandals. "Yeah, I knew her," he said in a voice I barely heard over the sound of the surf. He looked up at me, his eyes suddenly sad. "What about her?"

"Do you know her last name?"

"When I knew her, she was Gabriela Belmonte, but I later heard she got divorced and went back to her maiden name. I don't know what it is."

"What can you tell me about her?"

He heaved a sigh, and we started walking again to Archie's delight. "Like you said, she was Irena's friend. They were close. She worked at a modeling agency, like a talent scout, you know, in charge of recruiting beautiful women for modeling jobs."

"Do you remember the name of the agency?"

"Nope. Not sure I ever knew who she worked for."

"She ever say anything about what Irena was up to before her death?"

"Nah, that's not what we talked about."

I turned to my friend with a surprised look. "Oh, so you knew her well. What did you talk about?"

"I took her home several times at Irena's request," he said, avoiding my gaze. "That was back when Tucker was under Irena's thumb. Gabby was separated at the time. We used to talk about, you know, life, religion, what the hell we're all supposed to be doing here, that sort of thing. Sometimes we talked until dawn." He stopped and met my eyes. "I fell in love with her, and I know she had feelings for me. We were never intimate, but I certainly wanted to take our friendship to another level."

"What happened?"

"She suddenly ghosted me. It was after Irena's murder.

No explanation. I tried contacting her, but she moved. Haven't seen her since."

I held his gaze. "I'm sorry to hear that, Alec. Did that have anything to do with your decision to change professions?"

A faint nod. "It was a factor, yeah."

"Why didn't you tell me this earlier?"

"I don't know. It didn't seem that relevant. And she's not exactly a topic I want to dwell on."

"I understand. Know where I can find her?"

He shook his head. "It won't be easy. Her divorce records are sealed. I know because I checked. But I reached a dead end, since I don't know her maiden name or the name of the agency she worked for."

"Can you remember where she used to live?" I asked.

"Sure. It was a duplex over in Westwood."

"I've been craving a ride on your Harley. How about we take a spin over there?"

—⊣⊢—

I lied about craving a ride on Macleod's Harley Davidson, at least if it involved traveling on an LA freeway, which it did. We took the 10 to the 405 and got off on Wilshire Boulevard in Westwood. In a word, the trip was harrowing, although Macleod handled his bike with consummate skill. It wasn't him I was worried about.

Gabriela's former residence, an attractive Spanish-style duplex, was on Midvale Avenue near the National Cemetery. While Macleod waited on his bike, I knocked on doors until I found a neighbor who had known Gabriela.

"Who wouldn't remember Gabby?" quipped a fiftyish

man three doors down. "She was a handsome woman and a great neighbor."

He didn't recall anything useful about her, but his wife did. She told me Gabriela worked at an agency on Wilshire, DeBarge Model Management, which had either gone out of business or been sold, she wasn't sure which. She had no idea where Gabriela moved to. "She was just gone one day. Left without even saying goodbye," she told me.

Back at my place, I invited Macleod in for a drink, but he declined. "I've got a sermon to deliver tonight at the Rock," he said as he balanced the bike with outstretched legs while I got off. "I need some time. You know the drill— I'm supposed to come up with something uplifting."

"Think about our walk on the beach, and Archie chasing seagulls," I suggested half in jest. Then, in a more serious tone, I added, "If I find Gabriela, want me to say hello for you?"

He revved the engine of the Harley, a subconscious impulse, I think. "That ship has sailed. Just tell her I hope she found what she was looking for."

—⌁—

"I've had a great day," Zoe gushed when she called me back an hour later. "Just finished a chapter, and I think it's pretty damn good."

"Read it to me," I said, knowing what the response was likely to be.

She laughed, a sound that always endeared her to me. "Not on your life, Cal Claxton. Maybe you can be a first reader, but that's way down the road." I wanted to hear more about the story line, but she immediately shifted the focus to my investigation. I filled her in, ending with the news about finding Jamare Gilpin and Dante's response.

Zoe sighed. "Dante's reaction is textbook incarceration syndrome. He doesn't feel worthy of his successful son, and he'll probably need therapy to break out of it, so I wouldn't push it. Meanwhile, sex is *very* therapeutic. Tell him to have as much as possible with that woman as long as he doesn't give her any vital information."

"Roger that," I said, laughing. "There's something else—I've got a last name for Irena's modeling agency friend, Gabriela. It's Belmonte. She worked for DeBarge Model Management on Wilshire in Westwood. They're no longer in business."

"Great. I haven't found a trace of Irena Krasnova working anywhere in LA. This gives me something solid to go on. Stay tuned. I'll find her."

The conversation finally turned in the direction I feared. I'd been down in LA for ten days, and although I'd managed to kick up some dust, I really had very little to show for my efforts. Zoe began in a tentative voice, "I know this may not be a fair question, but given what you have right now, what's your sense of timing to wrap this up? I'm missing you and Archie, Cal."

I didn't react defensively, because it was, in fact, a fair question. "I can't say for sure," I said. "What I do know is that whoever was behind the murder is still out there, and by now they know I'm serious about this. My gut says that's going to cause things to accelerate." As soon as the words left my mouth, I knew I'd phrased that badly.

"Oh, Jesus," Zoe said, "that's what I was afraid of. It sounds even more dangerous."

"I'm on full alert. Trust me, I want to get back to Oregon as soon as possible… But I can't leave until I see this through."

"Or die trying," she said, so softly I barely heard it.

The words hung in the space between us for too long. Finally, I said, "That's not going to happen, Zoe."

"That was a childish reaction," she said in a tone suggesting she'd caught herself. "I gave you my blessing on this, Cal, but the thought of losing you is…well, unthinkable. Maybe I'm not as strong as I thought I was."

"Of course you are," I blurted out and then cringed at the mansplaining sound of it. I had no right to make that judgment.

But instead of lambasting me, she ignored my clumsiness. "Glad you think so. Look, don't mind me. I'm going to focus on finding Gabriela Belmonte for you. All I ask is that you focus on keeping your butt out of harm's way. A deal?"

"A deal," I said, and that ended the call. I sat back and thought about what had just transpired. I understood her reaction completely. After all, Zoe had lost her second husband to a mountain climbing accident. "An adrenaline junkie," she'd characterized him in a moment of candor. Was I an adrenaline junkie, too? Was that how she saw me? I didn't think so, but if she did, I could see her point.

I looked over at Archie, who lay in the corner with his chin on his paws, watching me intently. "Whose idea was it to come back to LA, anyway?" I asked him.

He raised his chin and looked back at me, as if to say *if you want to go back to Oregon, I'm all in.*

CHAPTER THIRTY-THREE

LIKE A LOG IN THE SURF, I ROLLED OVER AND OVER THAT night, and when dawn broke I awoke feeling depressed. As I sat out on the patio sipping my usual cappuccino, I began arguing with myself. You've found Jamare, the practical side of me pointed out. Why not focus on reuniting father and son? Isn't that enough to assuage your guilty conscience and avoid the possibly of having Zoe sour on you? But the answer from my stubborn side came back the way it always did—it might be enough for Dante and surely enough for Zoe, but it's not enough for you. This is an act of redemption.

Around nine, a call came in from Detective Banks that shook me out of my lethargy. "I've got a body here," he began after a brief greeting. "It's Eddie Conway, the guy whose nose you rearranged. I'm over at the morgue at LA General in Lincoln Park. Can you come over? I'll grease the skids for you."

The term 'rush hour,' of course, is a misnomer, particularly in LA, where nothing rushes on the freeways between seven and ten in the morning. A case in point: the fifteen-mile trip to the morgue took fifty minutes. But I was lucky enough to snag a parking space a half-block down on Mission Road. I sat there in my car, gazing at the building, frozen, as dark memories poured over me. This is where they brought Nancy after her suicide thirteen years ago. Even though I was the one who discovered her body, after they took her away I came to the morgue to see her one last time.

Memories of that day—the echoey sound of gurney wheels on tile as her covered body was wheeled in, the pungent smell of disinfectant and formaldehyde, and the heart-shattering, utter stillness of her face—came on like a bad dream. Todd Whipple had pulled some strings to avoid an autopsy, at least. He was right. The thought of someone sawing and slicing on Nancy was out of the question.

Pulling myself back to the present, I gained control of my emotions enough to enter the building. Banks was waiting at the check-in desk, slouched in a chair. He had a two-day growth, but his eyes were clear and alert. "I've already signed you in, Claxton," he said as he got up. "Just come on through."

"Where did you find the body?" I asked as we walked down a long, narrow corridor.

"Access road to a bike path on the LA River below Compton. He was shot somewhere else and dumped there like a bag of trash."

"Any leads?"

"Zilch so far. The bullet's still in his head, so we're hoping we can at least get a read from the ballistics."

"What about his partner, the one built like a Mack Truck?"

The detective shook his head. "We've chased down dozens of leads, but the guy's in the wind."

"Wonderful," I said under my breath. "Let's get this over with. No guarantee I can identify him."

"Understood. Just do the best you can."

The cold-storage room was larger than I remembered, with double rows of refrigerated lockers on three of the four walls. Banks led me over to locker 32-A, pulled out the steel tray holding the body, and folded down the cover sheet. Except for a bullet hole above his right eye, the cadaver looked like he'd just dozed off. His face was the color of putty, his eyes were gently closed, and the bridge of his nose was straight but slightly discolored.

This time I recognized him immediately.

"Yes, that's one of the men who attacked me in Skid Row, the one you told me was named Eddie Conway," I said. "His nose was bent and swollen in the booking photo you showed me last week. Now that it's straight I'm positive he was one of my attackers."

"Excellent," Banks said. "That ties him back to Harry Imhoff, because he and his accomplice more or less told you Imhoff sent them to beat you up. Right?"

I nodded. "Like I said in my statement, Imhoff threatened me first, and then Conway and his buddy jumped me. They didn't use Imhoff's name, but it was obvious who sent them."

Banks studied me for a moment. "What do you think went down here?"

"Looks like Conway got fired with extreme prejudice. Maybe this is what happens when a hitman bungles a job and gets picked up for car theft. My guess is his partner killed him at the behest of their client."

Banks nodded "And the client would be Harry Imhoff?"

"That's my story, and I'm sticking to it," I answered, which drew a smile from Banks. "Have you found any other evidence linking Imhoff to the Bivens shooting?"

"We lifted a single print on the seat adjustment lever

of the stolen Volvo we think they used for the hit. The rest of the car was clean as a hospital room. Print's not Conway's or anyone in the car owner's family, and it isn't in the system. We're hoping it belongs to his accomplice." Banks settled his cop eyes on me. "By the way, I assume you can account for your whereabouts between noon and four yesterday afternoon, the time of Conway's demise. You have a pretty good motive for seeing him dead, after all."

"Believe it or not, I was with a man of God yesterday afternoon," I said, and gave the detective Alec Macleod's cell phone number. "He'll vouch for me."

"How about *your* investigation? Bivens still your favorite for the Krasnova hit?"

I shook my head. "Not anymore. I'm looking hard at Harry Imhoff now, but I'm about as far along as you are."

"*Whoa,*" he said, "so Imhoff isn't just worried about you messing up his escort business, he's scared you'll pin a murder on him?"

"Possibly. I'm curious—has Narcotics shown any interest in your case?"

Banks blew his breath out. "You know Todd Whipple, keeps his cards in tight. I've briefed him. That's about it."

With that, Banks covered Conway's head, and when he pushed the steel tray back into its slot, the door snapped shut with a loud click that seemed to underscore the finality of his death. The detective's parting words were something along the lines of us sharing information, but I was sure that what he had in mind was more of a one-way street in his direction.

—⊣⊢—

"How are things in the City of Angels?" a voice boomed in my ear just as I reached my car. It was Nando Mendoza, and his voice was so cheery it irritated me.

"Don't ask," I said and proceeded to fill him in.

"Hmm," Nando said when I finished, "it seems you have made Señor Imhoff very nervous. Does he now rise to the top of your suspect list?"

"He's certainly at the top of LAPD's list for the murders of Bivens and Conway, but I'm also interested in Natalia Pavlin." I didn't mention Aldo Moretti. The retired detective was still just a question in my mind rather than a suspect.

"Then my call is timely," Nando said. "I have completed a background check on Pavlin. She came from the city of Savinja in Slovenia, where her father was a wine merchant. She has been in Los Angeles for eighteen years and has a green card, although I could not verify the card's legitimacy. She worked as a nursing supervisor and is now retired. She pays her taxes and has no arrest record."

"Net worth?" I asked when he paused.

"I could obtain no banking records, but she drives a Tesla like me and owns a home in Beverly Hills worth at least two and a half million and another smaller place in Malibu with a nice view of the Pacific Ocean."

"Huh. Squeaky clean, but she owned and ran a notorious escort business," I said. "That takes skill and some pretty steely nerves."

"Indeed," Nando agreed. "The Queen has led two lives very successfully."

"Anything else?"

"Yes, there is one more thing," he said, his voice suddenly registering a conspiratorial tone. "You asked me to find out the name of the employer of Ferris Spielman when he was arrested for stealing drugs, but the charges were dropped."

"Oh, right. I'd almost forgotten about that."

"Well, I just learned this morning that he worked for the Arlington Wellness Center in Beverly Hills."

"What? You're kidding. He worked at the same place as Pavlin? You're certain?"

"Yes, I am certain, Calvin. I have numerous records to back this up. This man, Spielman, got around, sharing prison time with Tucker Bivens and work time with Natalia Pavlin. Of course, his overlap with Bivens was eight years before Krasnova's murder. But he was arrested, then released for drug theft at Arlington, just six months prior to Krasnova's murder."

"Why was he released?" I asked.

"I was unable to determine that."

"Send me every scrap of information you have on this. Great work, Nando."

After Nando and I disconnected, I immediately called Margie Bingham, my assistant who kept me organized and punctual for ten years back when I was a prosecutor. She still worked in City Hall, which was only eight blocks away, and she agreed to meet me there in twenty minutes.

As I pulled out into traffic, the sun broke through the haze, and the cars and trucks in front of me seemed to part like I was behind the wheel of a patrol car flashing red lights and blaring siren. "Maybe I'll get back to Oregon sooner than I thought," I said out loud to no one.

CHAPTER THIRTY-FOUR

"I HEARD YOU WERE IN TOWN, CAL, AND I'M HURT IT took this long for you to call me," Margie Bingham teased after we greeted each other in the City Hall Rotunda. She had the same quick, bright smile that activated a set of dimples, and except for a few gray strands woven into her short, auburn hair, she looked the same.

"I know, Margie, guilty as charged, but I've been slammed since I've been here, trust me. You look great. How have you been?"

She brought me up to date, a tale of how much can change in a mere thirteen years—the arrival of twins, a broken marriage, a recent engagement. Finally, I said, "I need your help," and went on to explain I was looking for any information she had on Ferris Spielman, a lifer at Corcoran who was now deceased. "I'm going over to see Todd Whipple for a half hour or so. Would that give you enough time?"

She flashed the teasing look again. "Haven't changed a bit, I see. Need everything ASAP. I'll see what I can do."

It took me about five minutes to hoof it over to LAPD Headquarters. Whipple was on the phone but waved me in when I arrived at his open office door. "I know, goddamn it," he was saying, "but you tell the FBI to take a flying fuck. And tell them who said it." With that he disconnected, turned to me, and rolled his eyes.

"Nothing ever changes, does it?"

"Nope. Same old shit from the feds," he said, motioning me to sit down. "What can I do for you, buddy?"

"I was just at the morgue at LA General. Don't know whether you heard, but one of the shooters who took out Tucker Bivens was found with a bullet in his head. I just identified him as one of the thugs who jumped me in Skid Row a few days ago." I waited, curious to see Whipple's reaction. Was the LAPD really as compartmentalized as I feared?

"Yeah, I heard the news from Banks," he answered, his lips curling into a cold, cop smile. "Another scumbag bites the dust. Banks still likes Imhoff for the Bivens' hit, by the way. And he still thinks those two were gunning for you. What's your read now?"

"I'm flattered that someone would actually pay to have me killed, but I still think Bivens was the target." I met his eyes and smiled. "Of course, I'm sure you know a hell of a lot more than I do about this. I mean, it's raining fentanyl in this town, right?"

Whipple nodded and avoided my gaze. "Believe me, I'm feeling the pressure from City Hall."

I smiled. "I feel your pain, but my focus is on who had Irena Krasnova killed. Along those lines, Mimi Ryerson recalls there was considerable tension between Jimmie and Moretti during the Krasnova investigation. Do you remember anything about—"

"Tension? Are you kidding me?" Whipple shot back. "What murder investigation doesn't create tension between investigating officers? Give me a break, Cal."

I half-raised my hands in retreat. "Okay, this came from Mimi not me. It was just an impression she had." I hesitated to ask the next question but decided to plunge ahead. "Is Moretti still in town?"

Whipple eyed me carefully. "Far as I know, why?"

Ignoring the question, I said, "When you two left the other night, did he mention seeing anything in my apartment, like a handwritten journal in the kitchen?"

"No." Whipple bunched his brows. "Where are you going with this?"

I told him about the journal and the break-ins at my place and Mimi Ryerson's. He pressed me for details about what I'd learned from the journals so far, but I kept it vague. For example, I didn't mention that, according to Ryerson's notes, Moretti seemed to be slow-walking the Krasnova investigation.

Finally, Whipple said, "This is really out there, Cal. You actually think Moretti could've had something to do with the Krasnova murder? Aldo? Really?"

"No. I'm not saying that. All I'm saying is that he's not happy with my investigation, and I don't necessarily buy that it's all about protecting LAPD's honor."

"Come on, Cal, you know Aldo bleeds blue, and besides, no one in the force is happy with your goddamn investigation."

We left it there, and I slunk out of Todd Whipple's office feeling like I'd overplayed my hand. I called Margie as I headed back to City Hall, and she was waiting for me in the lobby when I arrived.

"Why don't you come up?" she said. "A lot of the old gang's still around, you know."

I glanced at my watch. "I'd love to, but I need to get

back to Santa Monica within the hour." It was true that I didn't want to leave Archie unattended for any longer than I had to, but the real reason I demurred was that I knew there would be too many ghosts up there on the top floor, too many reminders of how I'd left the job I loved. Better to leave that chapter in the past.

We reminisced for a few minutes before she opened a small notebook. "I took some notes," she said. "The file was practically empty. First of all, Ferris Spielman was arrested for stealing prescription pain medications from the Arlington Wellness Center. However, the charges were dropped when a witness recanted their statement. The drugs were later recovered, having been quote-unquote 'misplaced.' Spielman threatened to sue the department, but nothing came of it."

"Who was the witness?"

"The name wasn't in the file."

"How about the arresting officer?"

She looked down at her notes. "Aldo, Aldo Moretti. He was in Narcotics then. He's retired now. I can get his address if you need it."

"No, I know where he lives, Margie." I stood up, thanked her, and hugged her goodbye, hoping she didn't notice that my heart was thumping at twice its normal rate.

CHAPTER THIRTY-FIVE

"OKAY, SO MAYBE THIS DETECTIVE'S GETTING LAID BY one of the Bitch Queen's girls. Maybe he's taking a little cash on the side to keep quiet, too," Dante said after I described what I'd just learned. He was waiting with Archie on my apartment patio when I got back from LAPD Headquarters. "Along comes Irena threatening to blow the whole thing up," he continued, "so the dude and the Queen hire Spielman to kill her and blame it on me. Is that what you're thinking?"

"Something like that," I said. "You were there. What do you think?"

He stroked his beard and focused on something at the far end of the patio. "I used to wonder how Good Company was able to operate without getting busted, you know? Somebody had to be protecting all those celebrities and millionaires. Those fuckers don't take risks." He nodded and looked at me. "Yeah, it could've gone down like that. Imhoff was probably in on it, too."

I raised my eyebrows at the last comment.

"He wouldn't have bought the operation without the protection, right? The guy's an asshole, but he's no dummy."

"Could be," I said. "You'd make a good detective, Dante."

He averted his eyes in modesty. "'Chess is the art of analysis,' you know. That's a quote from Mikhail Botvinnik, my favorite grandmaster. I'm all about analysis, man, but I believe in taking action, too. Maybe Imhoff could use a little persuasion, you know what I'm sayin'? A taste of his own medicine."

My heart froze for an instant. "No, Dante, don't even say that."

He gave me a gotcha smile. "I'm pullin' your leg, Cal. No way I'm giving anybody an excuse to put me back inside. I don't even jaywalk these days." He held the impish grin for a few beats. "Tell you what—neither one of us has been to the Impromptu since we got here, right? Let's go tonight and check out the vibe, show Imhoff we're not intimidated."

"Why not?" I replied.

—/ /—

Dante called Sherri Haller—the waitress I interviewed when I first arrived in LA—and she was able to snag us a table for an eight thirty arrival at the Impromptu. "No way I want Harry to know we've had any contact, so act surprised to see me," she told Dante. We took the 10 to the 405 and exited at West Pico Boulevard. The traffic was moderate, and we arrived at the restaurant right on time.

"Jesus, is that you, Ricardo?" Dante called out to the parking lot attendant, a tall, elegant looking man wearing a white shirt and a black bow tie. "You still parking cars here?"

Ricardo bent down and squinted into the driver's side window. "Dante! I heard they let your moldy ass out." Dante jumped out of the car, and the two bumped fists while I found a parking space.

A low, single-story structure with a flat roof, the

Impromptu wasn't impressive from the outside, but the interior was a different story. The lighting was subdued, but the ornate coffered ceiling, black and white checkerboard tile flooring, and marble pillars had visual impact, albeit a tad pretentious for my taste. We were shown to a corner table adjacent to stairs leading up to the bar area, which was set off with wrought iron railings that echoed the intricate ceiling patterns.

As instructed, Dante feigned surprise when Sherri Haller sauntered up to our table, oversized menus in hand. After we ordered—prime rib for Dante and wild-caught salmon for me—he went up to the bar area to check out the scene. Meanwhile, I sipped a Williams Selyem Pinot Noir, a fine California wine, to be sure, but lacking the complexity of the best Oregon pinots.

As I sat there, my mind turned to what made the opulence surrounding me possible. If sex workers were independent contractors, I'd feel better about the profession, I mused. But sadly, they hardly ever are. The thought of Harry Imhoff using fentanyl to enslave his sex workers was nauseating. And Imhoff's clientele—did they ever consider the human toll of their actions? My stomach tightened. Maybe Alec Macleod was right—maybe our species is lower on the evolutionary ladder than we'd like to admit.

I snapped out of my musings when Dante came back to the table. "One of my old buddies is tending bar tonight," he said as he sat down. "He told me Good Company's laying low, only taking known customers with good track records these days. No new johns or corporate accounts."

"Did he say why?"

"Orders from Imhoff. He's feeling the Claxton-Ellis heat, I guess."

I couldn't help but smile. "Have our names come up?"

Dante returned the smile. "Oh yeah, yours more than mine. You're the bumbling fool from Oregon who might fuck up the whole Good Company operation, you'll be happy to know."

I laughed despite myself. "Did you ask him about Bivens' death?"

"Yeah. He hadn't heard about it, and most of the staff here now weren't around when Tucker was customer *numero uno*. He said Imhoff walks around looking like he's gonna pop a blood vessel most of the time. The restaurant has always been a loss leader, so with the escort business throttled down, he's feeling the financial pinch."

"Is he here tonight?"

Dante nodded. "He's got an office in the back of the building, down from the men's room."

Sherri served our dinners, and as we ate, we watched the comings and goings in the restaurant. The clientele was mainly male, older, and not particularly well dressed. Some customers came in and went directly up to the bar and then exited with a companion in tow. This was a class operation, after all—no sex on the premises. Occasionally, escorts came down the stairs to join a customer or group of customers at one of the tables. The dining room action was all very pseudo-sophisticated with forced conviviality, like a Playboy Club back in the day. The bar action, I surmised, was probably more transactional.

When we finished our dinners—average fare, at best—I got up and said, "I'm going to say hello to Harry. I've got a question for him, and I want to see how he answers it."

Dante's eyes grew large. "You sure that's cool?"

"No worries. Like you said, Imhoff's not stupid."

"Oh, man, I'd love to be a fly on the wall."

I started up the staircase. The lighting in the bar area had a purplish tinge and was dimmer than in the dining room. It wasn't crowded—it was early, after all. Two women wearing low-cut cocktail dresses, black net stockings, and bored expressions sat next to each other at a small table. They both turned and eyed me appraisingly as I traversed the thickly carpeted space. I smiled back out of a sense of courtesy. A small sign above a double doorway to the left of the bar directed me to the gents. The hallway was better lit, and another sign a few doors down read Private Office. I knocked sharply, and a high-pitched voice I recognized invited me in.

Sitting behind a mahogany desk, Imhoff looked up from the tiny, snow-white dog perched in front of him—a fuzz ball with skinny legs, maybe a Bichon. His eyes widened, and his neck took on some color. He laid a grooming brush aside, put the dog into a crate beside his desk, and stood up. The bulk of the man seemed to fill half the room.

"I heard you were sniffing around here tonight, Claxton. What the fuck do you want?"

"Good to see you, too, Harry," I said over the yapping of the dog. "Got a minute?"

"Hush, Chloe," he said in a gentle tone, and the dog complied. Imhoff's hair looked grayer than I remembered, but even in the harsh light his full lips and smooth, chubby cheeks were a rosy pink. "I've got nothing to say to you, asshole. Make sure you pay your bill on the way out."

I stepped further into the office and closed the door behind me. "I visited the city morgue today. They have a body there with a hole in its head. Name's Eddie Conway. I recognized him as one of the men who assaulted me in

Skid Row." I fixed my eyes on him. "Know anything about that, Harry?"

He broke eye contact, and his jaw clenched . "I don't know what you're talking about, but I figure that if you got beat up you probably had it coming."

I smiled, keeping my eyes on him. "Well, that could be. The police tell me they're closing in on his idiot partner, the husky guy. They think Conway and his buddy killed Tucker Bivens. I'm sure they've discussed that with you."

His neck took on more color, and beads of sweat that had formed on his smooth upper lip caught the light. He pointed a thick, pinkish finger at me. "You need to get out of my restaurant now or I'll have you thrown out."

I raised my hands in mock surrender. "Okay. Okay. Just trying to keep you updated." I put my hand on the door-knob, then turned back to pose the one question I'd really come to ask. "Oh, one thing before I go, Harry," I said, my eyes locked back on his. "Do you remember an LAPD detective by the name of Aldo Moretti? Might've been a regular at your fine establishment. He was involved in the original Krasnova investigation."

Imhoff met my gaze and said without hesitation, "Moretti? Never heard of him. I don't do business with cops." He curled a lip in disgust. "Now get out of here."

I threaded my way back through the bar. The two women who'd eyed me coming in had been joined by two older men wearing suits and ties. Like all good salespeople, the escorts ignored me and put all their focus on the paying customers.

At the table, Dante said, "That was quick. How'd it go?"

"Interesting," I said, "but we've been asked to leave."

Dante got up, glanced at his watch, and said with a

deadpan expression, "Think we've been in here long enough for someone to plant a bomb in your car?"

I smiled. "We're about to find out."

The car started without exploding, and as we pulled out onto West Pico, I said, "Imhoff must be a lousy poker player. When I brought up the Bivens' hit, he lit up like a Christmas tree." I described the exchange, and his obvious tells.

"You'd do well in San Quentin, Cal," Dante said. "It's useful to be able to read people when you're inside, especially the ones who are about to go off on you."

"Next I asked him if he knew Moretti, and I got a pretty clear read—he'd never heard the name before, I'd be willing to bet."

"No shit?" Dante said. "Can we take that to the bank?"

"Not yet. We need solid proof, but my gut says that if Moretti and the Queen were behind the murder, it's unlikely that they would've involved Imhoff."

"Two's company, three's a crowd?" Dante asked.

"Exactly."

Dante leaned back in his seat. "So, it's the Queen and the dirty cop who put me away?"

"It's beginning to look that way," I answered.

CHAPTER THIRTY-SIX

"YOU'RE A WANTED MAN, BOSS," MY PART-TIME LAW clerk, Timoteo Fuentes, said with a chuckle when I called him the next morning. "I couldn't put off some of our clients anymore, so I've lined up a series of Zoom calls for the early afternoon between, say, one and four. If you're okay with that, I'll pull the trigger." I agreed, and he continued, "How are things going? Are you still on schedule to wrap it up down there?"

"We've caught a couple of breaks," I said. "I'm cautiously optimistic I can stick to my original timing."

"That's good news," Timoteo said. "We're having a great spring here in the Red Hills. The vineyards are in full bloom, and the tourists are starting to pour in."

I thanked him and signed off as I pictured the view of the vineyards from my Aerie—a profusion of white blossoms dusting the rolling hills. I felt a sharp pang of homesickness. Clearly, it wasn't just Zoe that I missed.

I fed Archie, went for a jog on the beach, and spent the rest of the morning preparing for my Zoom appointments. I slogged through the four calls that afternoon, and after making some notes and sending follow-up emails, opened another of the bottles I'd brought from Oregon—a six-year-old Lange Pinot Noir Reserve. It was a pricey bottle, but I figured I'd earned it. The wine didn't disappoint.

After the second glass, I called Mimi Ryerson. We chatted for a while before I brought up the real reason for my call. "Do you happen to have Aldo Moretti's cell phone number?"

"Yeah, I think I can find it. Why do you ask?"

"I think he's still in town. Why don't you call and invite him over."

She paused before saying, "And...?"

"You'll invite me over, too. You know, just for old times' sake. Although he discouraged you from cooperating with my investigation, you're not aware of the tension that's developed between him and me. So, it's all very innocent."

"Oh," she said, "I like the way you think. You're going to ask him some hard questions and see how he reacts, aren't you?"

"Exactly. I can't interrogate him, and I have no legal basis to depose him, so this is the next best thing. Hard to say where it might go, so just be open about the burglary and follow my lead. Be the good cop to my bad..."

"I can do that."

"This could be the man who attacked you, Mimi. Are you sure you're okay with this?"

"I'm a cop's wife," she reminded me.

—/ /—

I arrived at Mimi's place a little past eight that evening. The sun had slipped behind the mountains, leaving a vermillion sky and signaling the cicadas to commence churring.

Moretti had accepted her invitation for after-dinner drinks and dessert, and when informed I was also invited, he reacted with apparent enthusiasm. "Sounds great," he told her. "Drinks at Mimi's with some of the old gang."

I assumed the BMW i4 parked in front belonged to Moretti. *The cannabis business can't be all that bad,* I remember thinking. Mimi met me at the door wearing turquoise earrings, a cotton dress with an embroidered floral design, and sequined flat sandals. The pale violet halfmoon below her left eye was barely noticeable, and her demeaner was calm, belying the fact that she'd just been alone with the man who might've attacked her.

I followed her through the house and out to a lighted, covered patio. Her backyard was fenced, and I could smell the scent of spring flowers arrayed in a profusion of well-tended beds. Wearing boat shoes, khakis and a rumpled Hawaiian shirt, Aldo Moretti got up when he saw me. "Cal, good to see you again," he said, offering his hand. "Does this bring back good memories or what?"

"It certainly does," I said.

As we shook hands, I caught a whiff of alcohol on his breath, reminding me that he'd been drinking the last time we met. He looked at me without making eye contact and cleared his throat. "I'd like to apologize for the way I behaved over at your place the other night. I was out of line."

Out of the corner of my eye I saw Mimi stop pouring a glass of wine. I said, "Hey, no worries about that. I understand where you're coming from, Aldo. You have a lot of well-placed pride in the force."

Moretti nodded and Mimi finished filling his glass. "I'm serving a Riesling tonight, because I think it will work with the peach tart I made."

"Yum," Moretti said. "Your barbeque soirees in Huntington Park were always first class, Mimi. Jimmy tried to take credit for the cooking, but we all knew you were the brains behind the operation." The comment elicited a slightly strained smile from Mimi, and when she handed him his wine, he seemed to notice the bruise beneath her eye for the first time. "How'd you get the shiner?"

She hesitated for a moment, allowing me to cut in. "She was attacked by a burglar right here in the house a few nights ago."

Moretti set his glass down as a shocked look spread across his face. "You're kidding! That's terrible." He eyed Mimi. "Did you get a look at the bastard?"

She shook her head and touched the spot above her ear. "No. I saw nothing but stars, unfortunately."

He looked at me. "Any leads?"

"No, not yet. I think the break-in here is related to my investigation into who had Irena Krasnova murdered."

Moretti downed half the contents of his wine glass before asking, "How so?"

"Jimmy kept journals on some of the investigations he was involved in, including the Krasnova murder—"

"Oh, I remember that," Moretti said, showing another broad smile. "He was going to write the great American novel someday, right?" He turned to Mimi, "I think he would have, too. The man was brilliant."

She gave him an appreciative smile.

"Anyway," I continued, "Mimi gave me Jimmy's journal on the case, but someone broke into my apartment in Santa Monica last Saturday and stole it before I had a chance to review all the contents."

"That's shit for luck," Moretti said as he swung his gaze from Mimi to me. "Who knew you had it?"

"Just Mimi, as far as we know. It's probable the find at my place was fortuitous for the perp, who must have put two and two together that there were more journals here in Topanga Canyon."

"Were there more journals?" Moretti said before draining his wine glass.

"Yes," Mimi said. "The burglar found the rest, but none of them were related to the Krasnova murder."

"Damn," Moretti said, shifting his gaze back to Mimi, "Sounds dicey. I'm glad you're okay, kiddo." To me, he added with just a hint of sharpness, "Your investigation's having impact, Cal, but not all of it's good. Maybe you bit off more than you can chew."

I laughed good-naturedly. "The thought occurred to me."

Mimi crossed her arms and lifted her chin. "I'm all in on this, Aldo. What Cal's doing is righteous."

At that point, she excused herself, went into the house, and returned with a warm, golden-crusted peach tart nestled in a porcelain pie dish. While she cut us each a generous portion, I refilled our wine glasses. The night air filled with the aroma of warm peaches and cinnamon, the mood softened, and we began to reminisce.

"I remember that house-warming party you and Jimmy threw when you first moved to Huntington Park," Moretti said between bites of tart. "We all got wasted, and Todd dropped an entire pitcher of margaritas on your deck. Kaboom!"

Choking back laughter, Mimi said, "Yeah, and everyone was upset, not because of the mess but because of the wasted margaritas." More laughter.

"I was a newbie," Moretti went on, "and a little drunk. I made the mistake of yelling, 'The Whip strikes again' or something to that effect."

"Which wasn't appreciated by your new boss, remember?" Mimi added.

"Oh, yeah," Moretti said with a boozy grin. "I was worried about my job for a while."

When the stories finally subsided, I took a tack that chilled the mood: "Something I've been meaning to ask you, Aldo—does the name Ferris Spielman ring any bells?"

The grin melted on Moretti's face. "Should it?"

"He was the hitman who took out Irena Krasnova," I said as I sensed Mimi's gaze focusing on him as well.

"Oh, the guy who copped to the hit and then cashed in," Moretti responded, his speech faintly slurred. "Todd mentioned it, but the name didn't really stick."

"That's odd," I said, keeping the tone light but my eyes fixed on him. "Back when you were in Narcotics, you arrested him for stealing drugs from a medical facility in Beverly Hills where he worked—the Arlington. That was six months before the Krasnova murder. Does that ring a bell?"

He opened a hand. "Hey, I arrested a lot of bad guys in my day, and my ability to remember names is zero-shit. But I arrested the guy who capped Krasnova? *Really?*" He studied me for a few moments before adding, "So, what's your point?"

"Just trying to connect a few dots," I said.

His eyes went flat as he drew his lips into a straight line. "Oh, I see. And I thought this was a social event—"

"It is," Mimi cut in as she topped up Moretti's wine glass. "You know Cal—he doesn't know work from pleasure. Never did."

I turned to Mimi and showed my palm as if to silence her. "Give me a break here," I said, bleeding a bit of annoyance into my tone. Then I turned back to Moretti, whose eyes were slightly glassy. "I've got another question for you. The Bitch Queen. Can you tell me anything more about her?"

His hands opened, and he furrowed his brow. "No more than the last time you asked me."

I waited, hoping he might have more to say.

He cocked his head for a moment. "I don't think we ever identified who she was. I mean we zeroed in on Dante Ellis in a hurry. Didn't really need her to make the case."

"Her name's Natalia Pavlin," I said. "Spielman worked for her. You didn't make the connection? Another oddity, wouldn't you say?"

He set his wine glass down carefully on the tray table next to him and glared at me. "What the hell is this, Cal, some kind of shakedown?" He looked at Mimi. "Are you the good cop?"

Mimi forced a smile. "Oh, come on, Aldo, we were just hoping you could—"

Moretti sprang to his feet, knocking his chair and tray table over. His wine glass shattered on the stone patio. "Thanks for the dessert, Mimi. I'm out of here. You can both go fuck yourselves."

We sat there in stunned silence while he let himself out. As the low whine of his electric vehicle receded into the distance, Mimi looked at me with a wry expression. "That certainly went well. I feel kind of guilty for ambushing him."

"Don't," I said. "He could've cheerfully cooperated with us, but instead he couldn't get out of here fast enough when the questions started coming."

She absently stroked the side of her head where she'd

been struck and sighed. "I know I said I didn't trust him, but after seeing him here, it was the same old Aldo, you know? It's hard for me to imagine him attacking me."

I met her eyes. "We don't know if he attacked you, Mimi, but he's hiding something for sure."

"But what?"

"That's what I need to find out."

As we cleaned up the broken glass, we discussed the case but failed to turn up any new insights. I did manage to bum another piece of her tart before I headed back to Santa Monica. It was even better than the first serving. At the door, she said, "I meant what I said, you know. What you're doing is righteous, Cal. Jimmy would've approved. And you know what? Zoe is a lucky woman."

"I'm the lucky one, Mimi."

CHAPTER THIRTY-SEVEN

ARCHIE AND I WERE DOWN ON THE BEACH EARLY THE
next morning. A stiff, onshore breeze had flattened the surf
and was beginning to kick up whitecaps that flashed in the
slanting sunlight like tiny explosions. My dog, who'd spent
the better part of the day before inside the apartment, was
an animal possessed, racing up and down the wet sand,
barking and chasing receding waves into the water further than I'd ever seen him venture before. I felt good that
morning, and even better when my cell phone rang and I
saw Claire was on the line.

"Hi, Dad," she began in a bright voice. "Are you still in LA?"

"Yeah, but I'm starting to wrap things up," I said,
knowing full well I wasn't anywhere close to doing that.
"What's new with you?" I added quickly, hoping to divert
the conversation away from me and the sticky situation I
found myself in.

She brought me up to date before saying excitedly, "I'm
going on a backpacking trip in the Sierras with some of my
friends. We're going to tackle the High Sierra Trail, which
is seventy-two miles of gorgeous country. I'll be out of cell
phone range for probably ten days."

I knew the trail, which was known to be challenging

terrain, and my parental instincts kicked in. I said, "Claire, are you sure—"

She cut me off. "Dad, don't worry. I'll be fine. Gotta run, now. I'll call you when I get back."

After we disconnected, I looked at Archie. "Why did I think she'd ever listen to me anyway?"

We were back at the apartment when Zoe called. "Hi, Cal," she began, her voice all business. "I've got some information on Gabriela Belmonte."

"Great," I said. Hearing from Claire and now Zoe made my morning. Getting information on the case was a bonus.

"Well, it's not so great, it turns out. I finally caught up with someone who used to work at DeBarge Model Management who was willing to talk to me. She told me Gabriela's maiden name is Morales. According to the internet there are 347 women with the name Gabriela Morales in California, most of them in the LA area."

"Ouch," I said.

"Yeah, it's daunting. But the contact gave me the name of another DeBarge employee who knew Gabriela better. I've located him, and I'm waiting for a call back."

"Excellent," I said, and when she didn't respond, I added, "Are you okay?"

She sighed deeply. "Not really, but it's my fault, Cal. You've been completely open with me about the risks involved in what you do. And I told you I accepted the risks. To be honest, I didn't think anything could be more threatening than your last investigation, but here we are." She blew her breath out. "This is what it must be like to be married to a cop."

"Look, Zoe, I—"

"Hey, you've got enough on your plate. I'll work through

this. Just keep yourself and Archie safe and sound as you wrap this thing up. That's all I ask, Cal. I love you."

"I love you, too."

—//—

I was back at the apartment catching up on my email when Todd Whipple called. "Hey, buddy," he began, "what are you up to?"

"High level detection, why?"

"Yeah, right. Your friend, Harry Imhoff, is going down this morning for the murder of Tucker Bivens. Thought you might want to witness the arrest, you know, maybe blow him a kiss."

My hand went to my neck, and I absently stroked the abraded skin where a bullet had grazed me during the drive-by shooting. "Wouldn't miss it. So nice of you to include me."

"Hey, you're family. I'll swing by and pick you up at 11:30 sharp. We'll watch the perp-walk together from a distance. This is Charlie Banks' show, and a nice feather in his and LAPD's cap."

On the way to the Impromptu, Whipple briefed me on the situation. "The fingerprint found in the stolen car used in the shooting was traced to a guy named Altman, Sonny Altman. He's got a long rap sheet including assault and attempted rape. When he was brought in, he cracked like an egg—claimed Eddie Conway did the shooting, that he only drove the car."

"Did he say who the target was?"

"It was Bivens, according to Altman. You were, in fact,

in the wrong place at the wrong time. Anyway, he immediately fingered Imhoff as the person who hired him and Conway. Claims he was paid twenty thousand for the job."

"He'll be allowed to plea down if he swears to that in court?"

Whipple nodded. "Yep. It's a done deal."

"What about Conway's murder?"

"He claims he was in Vegas, and Banks is in the process of checking that out."

We arrived at the Impromptu at 11:50 and scored a parking space two blocks down from the restaurant. Whipple switched off the ignition and said, "The arrest is going down at twelve." He gave a head nod to two unmarked police cars on the other side of West Pico Boulevard, which was teeming with fast moving traffic. "Banks' team is already in place."

"Was it Banks' idea to invite me?" I asked.

"Yeah. You're his other star witness. He thinks you've earned a front row seat. I had to agree."

The team—Banks and another detective along with two uniformed officers—had planned to simply enter the restaurant and arrest Harry Imhoff, but the suspect flipped the script when he emerged from the restaurant before they had gotten out of their vehicles. Imhoff wore dark glasses, a pink golf shirt, and a pair of white linen slacks that matched the color of his dog, Chloe, who pranced on a leash in front of him like a circus pony.

The detectives and uniformed officers got out of their cars and approached him. Whipple and I managed to cross the busy street and approach the scene in time to hear Detective Banks make the arrest and inform the suspect of his Miranda rights.

When Imhoff saw me, I smiled cheerfully and waved. He glared back, his face contorted in rage, and uttered something—choice words, no doubt—that got lost in the traffic noise. As he was being handcuffed, Chloe's leash was dropped, and the dog, perhaps sensing a threat, dashed into the street in a complete panic.

"Chloe!" Imhoff screamed as he wrenched free of Banks' grasp and ran into the street to rescue his dog. Somehow Chloe made it across, but Imhoff didn't. The vehicle that hit him—an Amazon delivery truck—launched his three-hundred-pound body into the air and flung it more than forty feet. The sound of steel impacting flesh and bone was as loud as it was sickening, and it was followed by a cacophony of screeching brakes, shrieking horns, and crunching metal.

"Oh no!" Banks screamed out as he clutched his head with both hands. He pointed at the two uniformed cops. "Stop the traffic." To the other detective he barked, "Catch the damn dog, at least." Then he threaded his way through the stopped cars as he called in the accident. By the time he got to Imhoff, Chloe had already found her owner and was standing next to his crumpled body, guarding it with teeth bared.

Whipple and I stood stunned for a few moments. I felt what—a pang of sympathy? I despised the man and everything he stood for, but his selfless concern for his dog moved me. And the dog, at least, had survived. Whipple said, "There's no way we can help Banks at this point, and there are plenty of witnesses. Let's get the hell out of here."

I understood his motivation, but it didn't sit well with me. The accident promised to be a messy situation he wanted no part of, and it was complicated by my presence. Bringing a civilian like me to witness an arrest wasn't exactly LAPD protocol, even for a Captain. Fortunately, we were parked far enough downstream of the accident that we were able to leave the scene.

As we pulled back onto Pico, Whipple smacked the steering wheel with the heel of his hand. "This is fucked up on so many levels—a good cop like Banks will take the hit for bungling a straight-forward arrest, LAPD loses the arrest *and* a slam dunk conviction in a highly publicized murder. And mark my words, one of Imhoff's relatives will figure out a way to sue the department for millions."

And like Bivens, another one of my suspects is no longer prosecutable, I thought. Aloud, I said, "What about the drug angle on this, Todd? I mean it's clear now that Imhoff had Bivens hit over what must have been a drug squabble. Does his death impact any of your investigations?"

Whipple shook the question off. "Nah, not really. I've got bigger fish to fry." He paused for a moment, making it clear that was all he was going to say on the subject. "What about you? Does this wrap things up? I mean, Imhoff was a man who used contract killing to solve his problems. It's no stretch to imagine he hired Krasnova's killer, right? Maybe you're done here."

"Nah, not really," I said in a slightly mocking tone but with a smile. "Krasnova threatened to mess up Imhoff's purchase of the escort business, but I don't think he had her killed. Sure, he had his goons rough me up, but that was because he was worried my investigation would shed light on his operation. And he targeted Bivens in the drive-by, not me, right?"

Whipple smiled back. "High level detection? Sounds circumstantial to me. And there's obviously a lot you're not telling me. You could've been next on Imhoff's hit list, you know."

"Maybe," I said before changing the subject. "Did you know that when Aldo was in Narcotics, he arrested Krasnova's killer, Ferris Spielman?"

"You're kidding. When?"

"Six months before he came over to Robbery-Homicide."

"Have you asked him about it?"

"I tried to, but he got defensive and stormed off again."

"Huh, I don't blame you for asking him, but, you know, he made a lot of arrests out there…"

"That's what he said."

Whipple glanced over at me before returning his eyes to the road. "There you go again. It's Aldo, for Christ's sake. No way he's involved in this thing. Give it a rest, Cal. The vineyards must be greening up in Oregon. You don't want to miss that, do you?"

"I think you know me better than that, Todd. I'm not leaving LA until I figure out who had a beautiful young woman murdered and blamed it on an innocent man. I'm not there yet."

Whipple looked straight ahead with both hands on the wheel. "Goddamn zealot," he mumbled under his breath. Even though the comment was meant half in jest, it pissed me off. The rest of the drive back to my apartment proceeded in silence.

I called Dante to tell him what just happened, got his voicemail, and left a message for him to call me. After a dinner of leftovers, I sat out on the patio reviewing the day's events. The boulevard was quiet, and a light breeze off the ocean carried a faint scent of beached kelp and iodine, even a mile inland.

Archie lay dozing at my feet as my thoughts turned to Whipple's snarky comment on the trip back to Santa Monica. I'd never thought of myself as some kind of fanatic when it came to seeking justice, but I had to admit my friend had a point. I *was* a bit of a zealot. And that was probably the way Zoe was beginning to see me. Was the view worth the climb? I wondered. Could I really pull this off without jeopardizing our relationship? I wasn't so sure.

I rubbed Archie's back with a bare foot, and he turned his head and looked up at me. "Well, Big Boy," I said, "No pressure, but we better wrap this thing up fast."

CHAPTER THIRTY-EIGHT

I WAS ABOUT READY TO TURN IN THAT NIGHT WHEN Dante finally called back. "Got your message. You still up?" he asked.

"Barely. Glad you called, I've got something to tell—"

"I'm with Lara. We need to talk to you, too. Can we stop by?"

"Of course. What's—"

"We'll explain when we get there. You need to hear this."

A marine layer had moved in, chilling the night air and masking an almost full moon. I put on a windbreaker and waited on the patio with Archie. My client and his newly acquired girlfriend arrived fifteen minutes later. They were holding hands when they came through the gate. Archie, always the lady's man, immediately took to Lara Novak, and judging by her response the feeling was mutual. Her dark hair was pulled back, which served to accentuate her big liquid eyes and prominent cheekbones. She looked nervous.

Dante wore a sweatshirt with a UCLA logo on it. "Lara gave me this," he explained with a hint of pride showing through. "She thinks you're right, Cal. I should try to get into UCLA, study math."

"After you go to community college to pick up your

prep courses," Lara added, while gazing at him with unmistakable fondness.

"Yeah, that feels right, that feels like what I should do," Dante said, "but we didn't come here to discuss my future." He turned to Lara and waited.

"Please, sit," I said, gesturing toward the chairs.

Dante pulled out a chair for Lara. After she sat, she looked at me and swallowed. "I, uh, I have a confession. I was approached by Natalia to get close to Dante. She offered to pay me in exchange for any information I could give her about the progress of your investigation." She turned to Dante and then brought her glaze back to me, her chin quivering slightly. "She wanted me to spy on you both, and I agreed to do it."

I nodded. "Did she say why she wanted you to do this?"

"Yeah, she said she was worried about her immigration status, that you might find out she's undocumented and tip off ICE."

"She wasn't worried my investigation would reveal who had Irena killed?"

"She, uh, asked a lot of questions about how things were going, who you were zeroing in on, that sort of thing. So, yeah, she did seem interested in that."

"Did you tell her much?" I asked next, figuring Dante might've revealed even more than he admitted to me.

She again looked at Dante before answering. "Well, I didn't know very much. I told her you were suspecting Tucker Bivens before he got killed. I told her about the journal that the detective had written, the one you had here in your apartment." Her eyes welled up and a single tear slid into the hollow of her right cheek. "I'm so sorry it got stolen and that your friend's house was broken into."

"It's okay," I said. "Do you think Natalia was behind the break-ins?"

She opened both hands, palms up. "I don't know. Natalia's hard to read, you know? She was certainly interested when I told her." Lara took a tissue from her purse and dabbed her eyes. In a show of emotional support, Archie got up from his spot in the corner, walked over to her chair, and lay down next to her feet. She reached down and patted his head.

I said, "Why are you telling us this now, Lara?"

She looked at Dante before turning back to me, her damp eyes gleaming in the porch light. "I came to realize what a good man Dante is, and what I was doing started to feel like betrayal." She smiled and reached out for his hand. "Then I, uh, fell in love with him."

Dante reached over and squeezed her hand. "I love you, too."

Lara dropped her eyes and studied the table. "I'm ashamed I ever agreed to do something like that. At the beginning I honestly believed I was helping Natalia. I mean, I didn't want her to get deported or anything. But the more I got to know Dante, the more it bothered me. And the more I thought about it, the less it seemed about Natalia's immigration status."

"Have you said anything to Natalia about your change of heart?"

Her dark, tapering eyes got large, and she pursed her lips. "Oh, God no. I haven't said a word about this to her."

"Are you afraid of her?"

"Natalia is a powerful woman and vindictive." She swallowed and tried to smile. "I, uh, I feel like I'm caught in the middle."

"We'll protect you, Lara," Dante said.

I nodded to affirm Dante's pledge, and because I believed Lara was being truthful, went on to say, "We have reason to believe Natalia Pavlin was involved in Irena's murder. The confessed murderer—a man named Ferris Spielman—worked for her at Arlington Wellness Center, and she had a compelling financial motive to have Irena silenced. This was before your time at the center, but did Natalia ever mention the name Spielman?"

Lara shook her head. "No, I never heard the name." Her hand drifted to her face, which had lost some color. "So Natalia was the one who hired this man to kill Irena and blame it on Dante?"

"At the moment, it's a theory. We need more evidence, Lara." I paused for a moment and met her eyes. They were steady and unblinking. "Will you help us?"

She drew her lips into a thin, straight line and set her jaw. "I'll do whatever it takes." Then she smiled and raised an eyebrow. "Does this make me a double agent?"

That broke the tension, and the three of us shared a laugh.

"I have something else to tell you," I said and went on to describe the accident that had taken Harry Imhoff's life. When I finished, Lara smiled bitterly and said, simply, "I'm glad they found his dog."

Dante clinched his jaw, adding, "Couldn't have happened to a nicer guy."

Lara took his hand and sighed deeply. "Good Company was into prostitution, but when I was there it was done safely and with class and respect for the escorts. It was more about companionship then. Sex was optional." She lifted her chin up. "And I'm not ashamed to say I was part of that."

Dante shifted in his seat, and we both waited, knowing she had more to say.

"But Harry Imhoff took the business in a sick direction, mixing it with drugs and low life clients whose only interest was sex. He used drugs to keep his escorts in line, and he ruined the lives of many young women. It was disgusting, inhuman." The bitter smile returned. "He won't be missed."

The conversation turned to what disinformation to feed Natalia Pavlin going forward. I stressed the importance of conveying that our prime suspect was still Harry Imhoff, and how upset we were about his untimely death. Also, that we eliminated Tucker Bivens as a suspect and had no clue who stole Jimmie Ryerson's journal or how anyone could've known about it.

"I understand," Lara said, "I'll make her feel comfortable that she's not a suspect, that Imhoff's death has brought your investigation to a standstill."

"That'll work for openers," I said, and then turned to the last subject on my mind. I'd crossed the Rubicon on trusting Lara, but I still felt hesitant to reveal what I suspected about my former colleague. Was it simply the shame of having to admit that an old friend, an LAPD cop, could've been involved in such a heinous crime? I wasn't sure, but I barged ahead. "While you were at Good Company, did you ever hear anyone, Pavlin or one of the escorts, mention a man named Aldo Moretti?"

Lara paused, wrinkled her brow, and then shook her head. "No. I don't recall ever hearing that name, but that's not unusual. We only knew the names of a few of our regulars— you know, like Tucker Bivens—but we were forbidden to use a client's name. We gave some of them nicknames. How—"

"What was Bivens' nickname?" Dante asked, interrupting Lara to my annoyance.

She giggled and blushed slightly. "Irena called him Minute Man. He was, you know, quick to the finish line. Irena was good with the nicknames."

Dante laughed, and I couldn't help but join him.

"How does this guy, Moretti, fit in?" Lara asked.

"We're not sure, but he's a suspect." I decided to leave out the fact that he had been a cop. "If Natalia mentions the name, let us know. And if she does, whatever you do, don't react to it."

After they left, I went into the apartment and poured myself a nightcap. The evening had taken a surprising and promising turn, I mused. Having Lara Novak in place as a trusted ally of Natalia Pavlin offered a real opportunity to blow the case open. But how to exploit this turn of events? That was a complex question, and I was too tired to grapple with it.

Once in bed, my final thoughts turned to Dante Ellis. He had fallen in love, and Lara Novak seemed sincere and right for him, even encouraging him to go back to school. That was great progress for a man trying to rebuild his life after a traumatic prison stint, and it filled me with hope.

But I also knew that he was terribly vulnerable. My last thought before falling asleep that night was, *Don't hurt him, Lara. Don't hurt this man.*

CHAPTER THIRTY-NINE

I WAS ON THE BEACH THE NEXT MORNING WITH ARCHIE when a call came in. "Mr. Claxton?" a male voice asked, "My name is Jamare Gilpin. I understand you represent a man named Dante Ellis, who was recently released after spending thirteen years in prison for a murder he didn't commit."

The voice was firm and direct, and I felt a tremor of excitement. "Yes, Jamare, I'm working with your father to determine who framed him and for what reason."

A moment of silence and then, "So, you know who I am. How did you do that?"

"I work with a very good private investigator. It wasn't difficult. How did you find me?"

"Let me start at the beginning. A friend who's a big Innocence Project supporter happened to mention the exoneration to me. She had no idea the man was my father. She didn't even know he was in prison. Anyway, I was shocked when I read about it. So I called the Innocence Project. They wouldn't share my dad's contact information, but they mentioned you, so I called your office and talked your assistant into giving me your cell phone number." He paused before adding, "Any way we could meet, um, just you and me?"

—*/*—

I met Jamare Gilpin that afternoon at a little coffee shop just off the 405 in Torrance, about halfway between Santa Monica and Costa Mesa, where he lived. He was taller and broader than his dad but had the same chiseled physique and a face that brought his father to mind, although it was hard to say why. It was his eyes, I decided, as I drew nearer. Like Dante's, they were wide-spaced, honey-colored, and alert, the kind of eyes you knew wouldn't miss much.

He shook my outstretched hand. "I appreciate you coming all the way over here. Thanks." He nodded towards the counter. Get a coffee and join me."

I ordered a skinny, double cappuccino and sat at his table a few minutes later. "How can I help you, Jamare?"

"Thirteen years in San Quentin," he began. "That's gotta be rough. How is he?"

"Incarceration has traumatized him, but he's on a strong recovery path. He speaks of you often."

Jamare glared at me. "What brought that on? He washed his hands of me and Mom when he went to prison. Didn't want anything to do with us. I cried every night for a year at least, begged Mom to take me to see him. She said he never wanted to see us, that we were no longer a family. She—"

"I don't think that's accurate," I cut in. "Your dad told me he wrote to you all the time, that it was your mother who cut things off and never allowed you to visit. My guess is she probably destroyed his letters."

Jamare puffed a breath and shook his head. "You blame her? He was screwing around with some prostitute, the one who got murdered, right?"

"Wrong. He was friends with Irena Krasnova, but he wasn't having an affair with her. Your mother bought the case the prosecution brought against him. It was bullshit, designed to give your father a motive to kill Krasnova."

He leaned back in his chair and crossed his arms. "Oh, yeah? How the hell could you know that?"

This was *not* the way I wanted this part of the story to break, but there it was. "I was your dad's prosecutor for the Krasnova murder. I was the one who developed the case against him and sold it to his jury."

Jamare's coffee cup halted halfway to his mouth, sloshing its contents over the rim. "What? You were his prosecutor? I googled you. You're an attorney up in Oregon, a one-man law practice in some little village…"

I nodded. "I took an early retirement from the city not long after your dad's trial. Moved to Oregon."

He raised his eyebrows in bewilderment. "How did you reconnect? How is that possible?"

I had to smile. "Your dad found me, and it wasn't to reminisce about old times."

"He must've been furious. You wrecked his life. Come to think of it, you damn near wrecked mine."

I nodded. "You could say that, although I would argue I was following the evidence amassed against him. But I was the one who sold the affair to the jury. I don't deny that." I waved a hand. "In any case, your dad and I decided a more constructive way forward was to find out who set him up rather than blow my head off. I'm doing this pro bono, by the way."

We sat there awhile without speaking. An ambulance went by out on the boulevard, its siren shattering the silence. Finally, Jamare's eyes welled up. "I've been angry at him for so long, I'm not sure I know how to turn it off.

I mean, you tell me he wrote letters. I never saw one, *ever*. How do you explain that?"

"Your mother was determined to sever your relationship with your dad, so she withheld the letters he wrote to you. He told me that after you went into foster care, his letters started coming back to him. I think he still has those."

Jamare sighed deeply. "Does he really talk about me?"

"Yes, he does, and when I showed him your picture on LinkedIn, he nearly popped the buttons on his shirt."

Jamare smiled, and a tear made its way down his left cheek. "So why didn't you contact me?"

"Your dad gave me strict orders not to. He figures you have a good life now, and he doesn't want to intrude. Even though he was exonerated, he still feels the stigma of having done prison time."

Jamare studied the tabletop for a few moments. "Yeah, it's complicated. The Gilpins are family to me. They took me in after I ran away from my first foster parents. I don't want them to feel like I have divided loyalties. Then there's my wife and in-laws." He shook his head and grimaced. "I, uh, I haven't been totally honest with them about my background." He looked up at me with a sheepish smile. "I told them I was estranged from my dad, and then he was killed in a car wreck."

I winced. "Complicated, indeed. Why don't we do this—I'll talk to your dad about a possible reunion. Since you contacted me, I'm ethically free to do that. I think he'll come around. And you give some thought to how you want to handle your foster parents and in-laws. We can review the bidding in a week or so. How does that sound?"

"Like a plan," Jamare said. "I definitely have some

sorting out to do. By the way, if you're doing this pro bono, what's in it for you?"

"Nothing I do could ever make up for the time your dad spent in prison. But at least I can attempt to catch the person who set this whole thing in motion, the person who paid to have Irena Krasnova murdered. It seems the only course of action that assuages the guilt I feel. And I hope it'll bring some closure to your dad and to you."

"Closure? I've never understood what that means. The deed is done, the time is lost, and it'll never be recovered. I'm okay with what you're doing, but don't expect me to thank you. This was a massive injustice." With that, Jamare Gilpin got up and walked out of the coffee shop.

I sat there for a while feeling like I'd just been slapped hard across the face. *Closure?* I said to myself in disgust. *Why in hell did I use that term, anyway? Jamare's right. The damage is done, and there's nothing I can do about that.* I felt my resolve begin to waver, but then the stubborn side of my nature kicked in. *No, goddam it. Stick to the plan. Finding Krasnova's killer is the one positive thing you can do.*

CHAPTER FORTY

"ARE YOU ON YOUR FIRST OR SECOND CAPPUCCINO?" ZOE said in a teasing tone at eight sharp the next morning.

"Second," I said, chuckling. "Archie's fed and we're heading down to see if the ocean's still there."

"Tough duty," she said. "Wish I could get in on that. I've got a blank page staring back at me, chapter fourteen, and I don't have a clue how to start it."

"Write a really strong first sentence and you'll be off to the races," I suggested.

"Easy for you to say, but not bad writing advice for a lawyer."

"Says the Ph.D. psychologist," I countered, and that made us both laugh.

"I've got a strong lead on Gabriela Belmonte who now goes by Gabriela Morales," she went on, her tone ringing with seriousness. "The colleague I mentioned finally called me back. He told me she quit the modeling agency business and went to work for a cousin somewhere on the southern California coast. An art gallery of some kind."

"Crap," I said, "there must be a zillion galleries on the coast. What's your plan?"

"I started in San Diego, and I'm working my way north,

call by call. I've talked to twenty-six galleries so far with no luck."

"Sounds like a lot of work. What do you say when you call?"

"I just ask for her, like I expect her to be there. I don't give a name. So far, all I've gotten is 'I'm sorry, there's no one here by that name.'"

"What if she answers?"

"I'll confirm she was a friend of Irena Krasnova's and convince her to talk to you."

"And who could resist you, Zoe? That sounds like a great plan."

"I'm calling Laguna Beach galleries later today. I'm going to find her for you, Cal."

"I have no doubt of that," I said. "Laguna's got to be the epicenter of art galleries in SoCal."

"For sure. I've got more than two dozen on my list. Cross your fingers."

I brought her up to date on the meeting with Dante and Lara Novak, the demise of Harry Imhoff, and the surprise contact with Jamare Gilpin. When I finished describing the latter, Zoe said, "This is tricky territory, given what the mother chose to do. Father and son are essentially strangers despite their shared genes. These kinds of reunions don't always play out the way they do in the movies."

"I was planning on telling Dante about the contact today. Any thoughts?"

"The sooner the better, but I would ask Dante for the letters, so that Jamare can read them before they meet. That might help bridge the gap. Keep your expectations low, too."

"Got it. What if Dante balks? He seemed adamant about not disturbing his son's life."

"Don't push it, of course, but I think he'll come around since his son reached out first. It's pretty clear Dante loves the kid. If his son has any fond memories of him, it just might work."

Our conversation eventually turned to what was happening in the wine country. It was the start of Oregon Wine Month, and Dundee was now chockablock with tourists. Gertrude Johnson was worried about my lack of billable hours for the month, and my law clerk, Timoteo Fuentes, was planning to paint the interior of my office and wanted to talk to me about colors.

"I love you, Zoe, and I miss you like crazy," I told her as we were signing off.

She made a soft sound in her throat. "Come back to me in one piece, Cal, and bring that dog of yours, too. I love the pair of you."

—/⊢—

I was on the phone with an Oregon client an hour later when I heard the low throb of a motorcycle. Archie whined at the door, and by the time I ended the conversation he yelped with excitement as the patio gate rattled open. He knew who had come calling.

"I get a Friday off every now and then," Alec Macleod said as my dog and I joined him outside. "I was out running errands and wound up in your neighborhood. Thought maybe I could bum a cup of coffee, say hi to my favorite dog, and get caught up on the case. I read about Harry Imhoff getting whacked. Man, that was a shocker. Who said only the good die young?"

"Unfortunately, I witnessed it," I said and went on to describe the incident. "The man loved his dog, I'll say that. What's the word on the street?"

"There's no surprise out there that Imhoff was behind the Tucker Bivens shooting. Now a chunk of the fentanyl trade is up for grabs in LA. It's going to be a free-for-all, like flies on shit." He eyed me before continuing. "Is he still a suspect?"

I shook my head. "Unsavory, for sure, and he did have a financial motive to silence Krasnova, but he's way down my list." I paused for a moment. "Think back on your chauffeuring days at the Impromptu. Ever hear of a guy named Aldo Moretti? He was a cop, and he was on the team that investigated Krasnova's murder."

Macleod scratched Archie behind the ears while he considered my question. "No, that doesn't ring a bell, but names weren't bandied about much, of course. How does a cop fit in?"

I explained the situation, adding, "Do me a favor—go back to your contacts at the Impromptu and see if anyone's heard of him around the time of Krasnova's murder."

"Wouldn't people remember the name because of the investigation?"

"I don't think so. His partner, a detective named Jimmie Ryerson, probably did all the interviewing at the restaurant."

"Oh, I see. Sure, I'll ask around." After I returned with two coffees, he said, "Any luck finding Gabriela?"

I looked at my friend and smiled. "I thought that ship had sailed."

He shot me an annoyed look. "Just curious. I know how anxious you are to find her."

"We think she might be working at an art gallery somewhere on the coast, at least she could've been thirteen years ago. Zoe's on it, making cold calls and hoping someone who knows her will cooperate."

Macleod looked pensive and stroked his chin. "I remember something about a cousin in Dana Point. Don't know if he had a gallery or not, but Zoe might want to look there." He gave a shrug of resignation and brought his eyes back to mine. "You know, I was thinking about buying Gabriela a ring and proposing...but before I could scrape up enough money she vanished." He snapped his fingers. "Just like that."

"I think we're going to find her, Alec. When we do, maybe you could talk to her, at the very least find out what happened."

He swallowed and said, "Aw, that'd be a waste of time. She probably doesn't even remember me by now. She left for a reason, never bothered to contact me." He blinked rapidly. "What's to say now?"

"Who knows? Situations change."

His turn to smile. "How are you and Zoe getting on?"

"Oh, you know, she's been a big help, really going the extra mile to find Gabriela. It's been great..."

He eyed me. "And...?"

I surveyed the yard outside the patio for a few moments. "Nothing she's said, but I'm worried she might get tired of worrying about me..."

He nodded. "I wouldn't blame her much. I mean people seem to be dropping like flies around you."

"Come on. Imhoff's death was an accident," I said and immediately kicked myself for sounding defensive.

He smiled and pointed at me. "Maybe so, but I can still see the mark on your neck that a bullet meant for Tucker Bivens left. Did you tell Zoe about that near miss?"

I smiled sheepishly. "Well, no, not yet—"

"There you go," he said. "She has every right to be worried, and she probably senses you've been holding back on her." He looked at me, his eyes full of sadness. "You could lose her over this, you know."

His words felt like an ice pick to the heart. "Yeah, I know."

CHAPTER FORTY-ONE

AFTER MACLEOD ROARED OFF ON HIS HARLEY, I IMMEDI-ately called Zoe back. She didn't pick up, so I left a voicemail relaying my friend's tip that Gabriela Belmonte could have a cousin in Dana Point. "You might want to focus your next round of calls there," I suggested.

It must have been drop-by Friday, because a short time later Dante arrived with Lara Novak. I was glad to see Dante. I needed to tell him about his son, Jamare, but was concerned about Lara being there when I did so. The issue I was about to discuss with him was highly personal, after all. However, when I saw how the two of them basked in the glow of their newfound love, I decided there wasn't a problem.

Dante's beard was neatly trimmed, and his eyes were clear and eager. "All is not lost on the chess front," he announced with a broad smile.

"How so?"

"I have a rematch with the woman I insulted at the Venice Beach Knights chess club. A ranked opponent, you will recall." There was a spring in Dante's step, and his voice had a youthful energy I hadn't heard before.

"How did you pull that off?"

He beamed a smile. "Lara goaded me into apologizing to her for my behavior."

Lara shot me a mischievous look and squeezed Dante's hand. "It wasn't easy talking him into it, but I had a feeling it might work. If nothing else, I figured she'd relish a chance to crush him after what he did."

Dante smiled and shook his head. "Anyway, I called the club and apologized to them first. That went okay, but they refused to give me her cell phone number, so I left mine and asked them to have her call me—"

"And she did!" Lara said, her dark eyes crinkling at the corners in delight.

"Yep," Dante added, "and I poured my heart out to her." He paused for a moment, and when he spoke again his voice thickened. "Told her everything. I, uh, I couldn't believe how kind she was to me. The rematch is set for a week from this Saturday."

"And he's going to whip her, too," Lara said.

Dante smiled. "Oh, yeah. No mercy."

"I've got news, too," I said when the laughter died down. By this time, we were sitting at the patio table. Archie had positioned himself between my two guests, figuring—as he always did—that they had come to see him. "Your son, Jamare, called me yesterday. I met him and we talked. He wants to meet with you."

Lara sucked a sharp breath and then, except for the drone of traffic out on Colorado, the patio got quiet. Finally, Dante cleared his throat. "He called you, right?"

"That's right. Out of the blue. He got my name through the Innocence Project people and somehow came up with my cell phone number. He's a fine young man, very personable."

Dante leaned forward and placed his hands flat on the table, his face suddenly taut. "What did he say, exactly?"

"Bottom line, he wants to meet you, but he needs some time to prepare his wife, foster parents, and in-laws. That's understandable."

Dante swallowed and licked his lips. "Do they know about me?"

"The foster parents certainly do. I'm not sure about his wife and her family," I answered, deciding to let Jamare explain why he'd lied to them. "There's one complication," I went on. "He's pretty angry at you. He believed the story about the affair with Irena, and apparently your ex-wife never showed him any of your letters from prison and never let on that you wrote to him frequently."

Dante's face grew taut. "Of course, he bought the story about the affair, thanks to you, and it's no surprise that Shanice kept my letters from him."

Ignoring the sharp-edged barb, I said, "You still have the letters that were returned to you, right?"

He nodded. "They're packed in a suitcase in my motel room."

"Good. I'd like to give them to Jamare to read before you meet. You okay with that?"

"I'll give you the letters, but I never said I'd meet with him. The last thing he needs is—"

"No, Dante," Lara said as she stood up and faced him, her eyes flashing anger, her face filling with color. "Meet with your son. Let him see what an amazing man you are. You've never hurt anyone in your life, and you never should've been in prison. You're not an ex-con, you were exonerated."

Dante squeezed his eyes shut and ran both hands through his hair. He got to his feet and looked at me, his eyes suddenly shiny with a film of moisture. "I'll bring the letters over tomorrow." He turned to Lara. "Let's go. I need some time to think."

At the gate, Lara turned back to me as Dante made his way to the car. Her jaw was set, her mouth drawn into a firm line. "He'll come around. He's a man who needs to process things." She paused for a moment. "There's something else we came to tell you. Natalia's been in touch."

I snapped to attention. "Tell me about it."

"Well, she called and said she wanted to talk. I met her at a little bar in Beverly Hills. She must've been there most of the afternoon, because by the time I arrived she was pretty drunk."

"Margaritas, right?"

Lara frowned. "Her favorite drink. So, she proceeds to pump me about you and Dante, wants to know if you're going back to Oregon now that Imhoff's dead. Even though she was blitzed, she seemed anxious and nervous about something, you know?"

I nodded. "Do you have any idea what?"

"Your investigation, I guess, but I didn't get anything specific from her."

"What did you tell her about the investigation?"

"Like we agreed, I said you are upset about Imhoff but that Dante hasn't told me what your plans are yet. I gave her the impression you are deciding next steps."

"Good."

"She seemed to mull that over, and then she surprised me—she said she wants to meet with you."

"Did she say why?"

Lara shook her head. "She wouldn't say. Have you heard from her? It's been a couple of days."

"No, I haven't."

She smiled knowingly. "Keep your cell phone handy. I know this woman. She's got something important on her mind."

—/ /—

By the time Archie and I finally made it down to the beach, the surf was blown out and most of the surfers had called it a day. As we walked north, a nice wind at our backs caught and accelerated the frisbees I was tossing him. My dog made some leaping catches that would've made Willie Mays envious. When his tongue was finally hanging out, I stopped and called Nando.

"Calvin," he greeted me, "I was beginning to think you've been kidnapped by some crazy sun-worshipers down there. What is happening, my friend?"

I filled him in on the death of Harry Imhoff, the fact that I now had a mole in Natalia Pavlin's camp in the person of Lara Novak, and the sudden appearance of Dante's son, Jamare.

When I finished, he said, "My, a busy few days. You do not sound too broken up about Imhoff's death. Am I missing something?"

I thought about my encounter with Imhoff in his office at the restaurant, where he showed no reaction when I sprung the name Aldo Moretti on him. "I doubt there was any connection between him and Moretti, but it's just a gut feeling. He's off the board, in any case."

"So, it's down to the Queen and your former colleague at LAPD."

"It looks that way, and that's why I called. Your report on Natalia Pavlin mentioned she has a home in Beverly

Hills and another on the beach in Malibu. Can you send me the addresses?" I described what Lara had just told me about her meeting with Pavlin. "I'm going to pay the Queen a surprise visit."

Nando laughed, a deep baritone rumble. "Ah, the patented Cal Claxton surprise party. You are very sneaky, my friend."

"Also, I'm curious about Aldo Moretti's move to Oregon. He has quite a spread just outside Jacksonville, and he's got a lot of marijuana under cultivation there, too. I'm wondering how much he has invested and how he was able to swing that on an LAPD pension. See if you can shed any light on that."

I ended the conversation before Nando had a chance to ask me about Zoe or tell me about the beauty of the cherry blossoms along the Willamette River in Portland. The sooner you crack this case, the sooner you can go home, I reminded myself. And for the first time since arriving in LA, and despite a lack of tangible evidence, I felt I might be close to a breakthrough.

CHAPTER FORTY-TWO

THAT EVENING, I LEFT A DISAPPOINTED ARCHIE BEHIND with the admonition to 'guard the castle' and inched my way along Santa Monica Boulevard toward Beverly Hills. I realized the chances of catching Natalia Pavlin at home on a Friday night weren't that great, but calling her first was out, since I wanted to catch her unrehearsed.

The sun had just ducked behind a line of towering palms when I arrived at her place, a two-story white stucco and red-tile roof affair behind an elegant, if decidedly unwelcoming, wrought iron fence. The culmination of the American dream.

When I rang the bell, the only greeting I got came in the form of deep-throated barking and snarling from what must have been a very large dog. I retreated to my car, backtracked to the coast, and took Highway 1 north. The sun had set by the time I reached Malibu, and the cloud-speckled sky above the horizon was a palette-knife study in lavender and pinks that would've done Monet proud. Pavlin's second home was on Malibu Colony Road among a stretch of much older beach houses, all facing west and built on stilts. Her place was a flat-roof structure that conjured up Frank Lloyd Wright and afforded a spectacular view. A red model S Tesla sat in a carport out front, and there were a couple of lights on in the house.

I rang the rear bell and listened as it reverberated through the house. No one answered. I heard faint music—soft jazz—coming from the rear of the property. I took a catwalk that led around the south side of the structure to a large covered deck cantilevered over the sandy beach. The surf line wasn't that far from the deck pylons due to the rising sea levels along the coast. I wondered if the house would survive another decade. Probably not.

The dying sunset provided the only light, but I glimpsed a few wisps of condensation from a hot tub built into the center of the deck. The beat of the soft jazz seemed to match the rhythm of the waves breaking below me, and I found myself feeling an intense pang of envy. I wouldn't have traded this place for my Aerie in the Red Hills, mind you, but still...

"Hello?" I called out as I approached, thinking Pavlin could be sitting in a shadowy corner. But all I heard back was the slapping of the waves. A low bench next to the hot tub apparently served as a bar, because I could just make out some liquor bottles, an ice bucket, and a single glass. I walked past the whirring, unlit tub to the end of the deck to see if Pavlin might be taking a stroll down on the narrow ribbon of sand below the line of houses.

She wasn't. *Missed her,* I thought and turned around to leave. As I passed the hot tub, it occurred to me to see if the glass still had ice in it. As I bent to look closer, something in the tub caught my eye, so I flipped on the interior light.

Seaweed? I thought as a mass of dark, tangled filaments swirled into view. I looked more closely and saw the faint outline of a body beneath what I quickly realized must be human hair.

I grasped a handful of the hair and gently pulled. The body came up, and a face broke the surface of the warm water. The face was the color of plaster with open, lifeless eyes and bloodless lips that had somehow set into a faint but chilling smile.

Natalia Pavlin, no question. Her bloated body and the murkiness of the water suggested she'd been there a while, at least a day. The thought made me nauseous, and I nearly emptied my stomach on the deck.

I released my grip on her hair and backed away from what could possibly be a crime scene. I took a more careful look around. Nothing on the deck seemed disturbed or out of place. The single glass sat between an empty quart of Patron Silver tequila and a half empty fifth of De Kuyper triple sec. A bottle of lime juice, a small bowl of what looked like sea salt, and an ice bucket completed the margarita-making equipment.

I followed the catwalk back to the front of the house and called 911. A cruiser from the Malibu/Lost Hills Sheriff Station arrived eight minutes later, followed by an ambulance. I was told to wait by my car while the deputies and the ambulance team hurried around to the deck. Fifteen minutes later a deputy coroner arrived and joined the party. She would decide when and how to remove Pavlin's body from the hot tub.

Forty minutes later the covered body was carried out on a stretcher and loaded into the ambulance. A small crowd had gathered by that time and witnessed the event in silence. A young male deputy with a dark tan invited me to sit in his cruiser while he took my statement. "What do you think happened?" I asked after he took my name and contact information.

"Can't say at this point, but when people drink excessively, they can become overheated in a hot tub. Vessels dilate, blood pressure drops, and boom—they pass out and drown. It's happened before here in Malibu. There's a lot of drinking in this town and a hell of a lot of hot tubs."

"That may be," I said, "and I can attest to the victim's weakness for margaritas, but I urge you to treat this as a potential crime scene. I didn't touch anything except the light switch on the control panel. I hope you'll check thoroughly for fingerprints and DNA."

The deputy raised an eyebrow and eyed me more closely. "Of course. What brought you to Ms. Pavlin's home this evening?"

I told him about my law enforcement background and that I was investigating a murder that occurred thirteen years earlier. Natalia Pavlin was a person of interest, I explained, and I was there to interview her. "I got the impression she had important information to divulge," I said. "Now she's dead. That seems way too coincidental to me."

The deputy shrugged. "People have a habit of dying at the most inopportune times."

The interview lasted another twenty-five minutes, during which I gave the deputy a bare bones outline of my activities since arriving in LA. I didn't mention my suspicions about Aldo Moretti, since I had no hard evidence and felt he and the LAPD deserved the benefit of the doubt. The last thing I told him was that a dog at Pavlin's residence in Beverly Hills would probably need some attention.

I came away with little confidence that the LA Sheriff's Department was going to give this apparent accidental death a hard look. But why would they? I mean, my story, as I thought back on it, sounded weak and circumstantial, almost conspiratorial.

As I headed back to Santa Monica, the implications of Pavlin's death began to weigh on me. There was no question in my mind she was involved in Krasnova's murder, and now she was dead before I could talk to her. *I was so close,* I said to myself as a wave of frustration washed me clean of all the optimism I felt just hours earlier. Had she drunk herself into a stupor? Or had someone helped her, someone who feared what she might tell me and knew her weakness for tequila and lime juice? I didn't know yet, but it was clear I needed answers.

And it was also clear that it was going to be up to me to find those answers.

CHAPTER FORTY-THREE

"I DON'T KNOW WHERE THE HELL MORETTI IS," TODD Whipple said over the phone as I sped down Highway 1 toward Santa Monica. "I'm just a friend, not his nursemaid. Why are you asking this time?"

"Someone's dead who shouldn't be," I said. "Her name's Natalia Pavlin. She was the Madam at the Impromptu back then and a prime suspect of mine." I went on to describe the grisly scene at Pavlin's house in Malibu.

"Jesus, another body, Claxton? This is really getting old. But you know, just like Imhoff this one could've been an accident, too."

"Yeah, but the coincidences are mounting up. Ferris Spielman, the man who killed Irena Krasnova, used to work for Pavlin. And like I told you the other day, Moretti arrested Spielman back when he was working Narcotics, then he winds up on the Krasnova investigation and does his level best to throw sand in the gears."

"What, you think Pavlin and Moretti were *accomplices?*" Whipple said.

"Maybe. Moretti might've been sampling the wares at the Impromptu, and Pavlin wanted to sell the business. They both had something to gain in silencing Krasnova, who was threatening to blow the whistle on the operation."

"Did you tell the sheriff investigators in Malibu about your suspicions about Moretti?"

"No, I didn't feel like I had enough evidence to do that."

"Good. You owe that to Aldo. Why don't you just call him, a casual how's it going? He's probably got a solid alibi, you know, busy up in Oregon growing weed."

"I don't want to chance tipping him off any further than I already have. Maybe you could do that, Todd."

"Come on, Cal," he countered. "You know the old bromide about there being no coincidences is bullshit, right? Coincidences happen all the time."

I exhaled a breath in frustration. "Moretti shows up in LA, and a vital piece of evidence is stolen from my apartment. Then I find out that he had arrested the hitman, Spielman, over a drug theft case involving him and Pavlin, the madam of the escort service working out of the Impromptu. The charges on Spielman are suddenly dropped, and then he kills Krasnova. Following that, the escort service is sold by Pavlin for a large sum of money. That's a lot of coincidences, Todd."

"Okay, I hear you. I'll call and try to find out where he's been," Whipple said in a tone of resignation. "What's the time frame?"

"Pavlin probably died within the last two days. Try to ascertain if he has an alibi for that period."

"Got it. Anything else you want to squeeze out of me?"

"Since you asked, you could swing your LAPD weight around a little bit by calling the captain at the Malibu/Lost Hills Sheriff Station and asking her to take a careful look at Pavlin's death. You could say you got an anonymous tip that foul play was involved. Her name's Helen Thompson, I looked it up."

"I know Helen," Whipple said. "I guess I could do that. But the thought of it makes my skin crawl. It's Aldo, you know?"

"I know. Look, Todd, I don't want it to be Moretti any more than you do. I want to eliminate him as a suspect, that's all. Maybe it was just Pavlin who hired Spielman, and maybe she drank one too many margaritas. If that's the case, I'm done here. Believe me, LA's nice and all, but I'm missing Oregon."

He laughed, but it had a bitter tinge. "Come on, Claxton, you've got a hard-on for Moretti and you know it." With that, he disconnected.

Despite having just found a dead body in a bubbling cauldron, I was ravenous by the time I pulled up to my apartment. After feeding Archie and firing up the grill, I headed to Trader Joes and bought the fixings for a good meal. Forty-five minutes later I plated an ahi tuna steak seasoned with soy sauce and honey, steaming jasmine rice, and oven roasted asparagus. I paired the meal with a Brick House pinot and dug in.

I felt more resolve and less disappointment after the meal. Good food usually had that effect on me. After all, I told myself, if Pavlin was murdered—and I believed she was—then it was an act of desperation. And desperate people usually make mistakes. At the same time, I felt an annoying sense of helplessness. The probe into Pavlin's death would proceed without my direct involvement. Would Todd Whipple follow up with the Sheriff at Malibu? I hoped so, but I also knew my friend's blood ran almost as blue as Moretti's.

I called Nando Mendoza next, and when he didn't pick up, left this message—"I need another favor, old friend.

Would it be possible for you to use your considerable sleuthing skills to determine if Aldo Moretti has been at his home in Jacksonville for, say, the last three days? Or if not, try to find out where he's been? I have no suggestions on how to do this, but I'm sure you'll come up with something. You always do."

I could just see my friend rolling his eyes at my obvious flattery. The request was basically what I'd asked Todd Whipple to do. A little redundancy never hurts.

—⊣⊢—

Later that night, I was as restless as a caged lion, so I poured myself a Remy Martin and took it out on the patio. There wasn't a breath of wind, and the moon hung just above the rooflines like a tarnished, discarded coin. As I sipped my cognac, I imagined what that same moon would've looked like from the deck of my Aerie in the Red Hills. That moon shone bright and clear and beckoned to me—*leave all this nonsense and come back to Oregon*, it seemed to say...

But the reverie was cut short when Dante returned my earlier call. I broke the news about Natalia Pavlin, and I heard a gasp from Lara, who must have been listening in on speaker.

"Oh, my God," she said, "Natalia drowned? In her hot tub? How could that be? She loved that thing, had it built right into the middle of her deck at ridiculous expense. What happened?"

I described the bar adjacent to the hot tub with the single glass and margarita fixings and explained what the deputy told me about what can happen to people who drink and soak in hot water.

"That's hard to believe," Lara responded. "Natalia drank and used her hot tub all the time. And her ability to drink margaritas was legendary. She was...," Lara's voice faltered. "She was fun to be around, and she helped me get a life, too—"

"And she probably had your best friend killed," Dante said. "Is your cop buddy still in LA?" he added, directing his question to me. "Sounds like he got worried Pavlin might talk." His voice had the defeatist ring of someone who was used to bitter disappointments.

"I'm working on that," I said and described what I'd asked Todd Whipple and Nando Mendoza to do. "My gut says we're going to find out that Moretti's still in the area. I'm in your camp, Lara. I don't think this was an accident."

"Suppose the fucker's still around. Then what?" Dante said.

Leave it to Dante to ask the tough question. "I haven't worked that out yet," I said, trying not to sound defensive and worrying again that he might be contemplating violence.

"Thought so," was all he said in return.

CHAPTER FORTY-FOUR

I SLEPT FITFULLY THAT NIGHT, MY DREAMS SUFFUSED with images of bloated bodies rising out of deep, roiling pools like zombies. To top it off, I felt hungover, although I didn't think I drank all that much the night before. When I swung out of bed and put my feet on the floor, Archie came over from his spot in the corner, put his front paws in my lap, and stretched languorously. I stroked his broad back, and he looked up at me, his big coppery eyes earnest and full of concern.

"Yeah, Big Boy, I said, "I know you want to go home. I know you miss your five acres at the Aerie, and I know you miss Zoe, too. So do I."

The grogginess didn't abate, so after a double cappuccino, I took my dog down on the beach for a hard jog in the hopes of sweating out the last vestiges of my encounter with Natalia Pavlin's corpse. The tide was out, so Arch and I had a nice stretch to run on, and a brisk westerly breeze cooled what would have otherwise been a warm morning. We were nearly to Will Rogers State Park, about three miles out, when Zoe called.

"You sound winded," she said when I answered. "You're jogging on the beach, aren't you?" she added with a tease in her voice. It was good to hear a little levity from her.

"You caught me again," I said, chuckling. "What's up?"

"I think I just found Gabriela! Your friend in Skid Row was right—she works at a gallery in Dana Point called Capo Surf Art. It was the first gallery I called this morning."

"Did you talk to her?"

"No. A man answered the phone, and when I asked for her, he said she wouldn't be in until the afternoon. I told him I'd call back and didn't leave a name or number. It *has* to be her, Cal. I mean, what are the chances? Do you want me to call her back, or maybe you should?"

I considered her question for a few moments. "I agree with you. It's got to be her. I'll take a drive down there this afternoon to confirm it. This is good news, Zoe. You're a jewel."

When Archie and I got back to the apartment, a battered suitcase sat on the patio table with a note taped to it:

> Cal, here are the letters I wrote to my son. Most of them are unopened because I couldn't bear re-reading them when they came back to me. I hope Jamare reads at least some of them. If he still wants to meet me, then go ahead and set something up.
>
> Dante.

After scanning the note, I shouted "YES." A startled Archie sprang to his feet and barked a couple of sharp notes with his butt wagging. He knew by my tone it was some kind of good news.

It turned out Costa Mesa, where Jamare lived, was on the way to Dana Point, so I texted and asked for his home address. Next, I ate a hearty breakfast and loaded the suitcase and my dog into the car and headed south on the 405. Halfway to Costa Mesa a text pinged back giving his address and stating that he'd be there when we arrived.

"You weren't kidding about a lot of letters," Jamare said when I lifted the suitcase out of the backseat and motioned for Archie to hop out. "An Aussie," he added as he bent down and offered his hand for Archie to sniff. "Love this breed. What a handsome dog."

"Not too loud, it'll go to his head," I said as I set the suitcase down. "Your dad wanted you to have all of them." I smiled. "But he said you don't have to read them all."

"But I will," Jamare said, casting his eyes down. "My foster parents are cool, but I, uh, I still haven't told my wife or my in-laws that I have a living father who spent a decade in San Quentin. Joyce is going to hate that I lied to her, and my in-laws are socially connected up the wazoo around here. This will be a bitter pill for them to swallow, regardless of whether my dad's guilty or innocent."

"What are you going to do then?"

"I'm going to put this suitcase in my workshop in the garage and read every letter in private and then decide how to proceed."

I said, "I understand your dilemma, Jamare, but rightly or wrongly, your mother turned you against your father. It's understandable that you would want to distance yourself from the monster you were told he was. Tell them the truth. I think they'll understand."

Jamare's eyes filled, but he blinked back the tears. "I wish I could believe that. I'm caught in my own damn lies."

"Then end it," I said. "Don't underestimate the people who love you." Having offered more advice than I should have, I started for the car, then turned back to him. "Your dad also said that after you read the letters, he wants to meet with you. That is if you want to, of course."

Jamare nodded and wiped one eye with the heel of his hand. "I'll let you know."

I left Jamare feeling the full weight of the miscarriage of justice I'd orchestrated. The prosecution of Dante Ellis hadn't just impacted Dante, I was reminded. It had rippled out to affect a lot of other people, all innocent bystanders. I didn't need a reminder of how badly I'd mucked things up, but I got one anyway.

Forty minutes later, Archie and I were in Dana Point, a city on the south coast named after an American writer, if memory served. Tucked in next to a surfboard shop, Capo Surf Art sat just across the highway from Doheny State Park. Seemingly every genre from photographs to abstract paint-ings—all depicting the sport of surfing—were on display in a bay window that ran half the length of the building.

Taking a chance that it was a dog-friendly business, I leashed up Archie and brought him with me, since there wasn't a shady parking spot on the street. A bell attached to the front door announced our entry. The front of the shop was empty, so I browsed the artwork, noting that it may have been 'surf art,' but some of the pieces were com-manding eye-popping prices. I was standing in front of an oil painting of a young surfer slicing across a wave at sunset when someone approached.

"That's one of my favorite pieces," a voice said from behind me. Archie and I both turned to the speaker, a woman in her early forties with a confident stride and an engaging smile. Long, chestnut brown hair framed a perfectly oval face, and her radiant eyes were the color of caramel.

I extended my hand, feeling in my gut it was Gabriela

Morales. "I'm Cal Claxton. This is Archie. I hope it's okay for him to be in here."

She shook my hand, probably wondering why a customer would introduce himself let alone bring a dog to an art gallery. "Gabby, Gabby Morales," she said, then added with an impish grin, "Sure, we like dogs here, but if he pees on anything, you've bought it."

I laughed, then cleared my throat and met her eyes. "I'm an attorney representing Dante Ellis." I handed her a card. "Dante was recently fully exonerated and released from prison for the murder of Irena Krasnova. I'd like to talk to you about Irena. It's vitally important."

She took a step back as her eyes got huge and a hand drifted up to her face. "Oh, dear Jesus," she said, "I had no idea. That's, that's shocking and…wonderful. Is Dante all right?"

"He's fine and sends his regards."

She put her hand on her breast and exhaled. "Excuse me a moment," she said and then went to the front door of the shop, locked it, and flipped the Open sign to Closed. "We can talk in my office."

Archie fell in behind her as she led us down a back hallway with long, purposeful strides. As I followed, I noticed my pulse rate had ticked up a few notches. *It's her,* I said to myself, *and it looks like she's willing to talk. That's two for two.*

CHAPTER FORTY-FIVE

GABRIELA MORALES' OFFICE WAS A STUDY IN GOOD taste—leather and wood furnishings, interesting art on the walls, and an array of plants strategically placed around the room. A large, framed picture of a young girl on a swing sat on her desk. She looked to be about ten years old.

After I sat down with Archie settled next to me, Gabby said, "So, how did you find me?"

"It wasn't easy. I traced you to the DeBarge Model Agency, and a former co-worker had a vague memory of you moving to the coast and working in an art gallery. Dozens of phone calls later, here I am."

"So, what can I do for you, Mr. Claxton?"

"Call me Cal," I said, and began by describing the deathbed confession of Ferris Spielman and how Innocence Project was able to secure Dante's release after a lengthy court battle. When I finished, Gabby looked at the card I'd given her and said, "If Dante's fully exonerated, why does he need an attorney?"

"Good question. I'm conducting an investigation on his behalf to find who actually hired Spielman to kill Irena. That person is still at large."

Gabby made a face. "Creepy. Yeah, I was shocked when Dante was arrested. He and Irena were close, but like brother and sister, you know? I was devastated when they convicted him. At the time, everybody was saying the evidence against him was overwhelming."

"It was a clever frame-up, for sure, but that's no excuse for what happened in court." I shifted in my seat and looked directly at her. "I was the city prosecutor who secured Dante's conviction. I'm in private practice now and doing this investigation pro bono. It's one small way—the only one open to me—of making it up to him."

Gabby sat back in her chair and looked at me full on, her mouth agape. "You're serious, aren't you?" She cocked her head as if considering my statement. "Irena was a beautiful person, and the coward who paid that man to kill her should rot in jail before rotting in hell. I applaud your efforts, Cal." Then she gave me a wry smile. "How are you and Dante getting on? He was pretty fiery, as I recall."

"Actually," I said, showing a smile, "he came to Oregon to kill me, but I talked him out of it. I offered him this deal, instead. He tolerates me."

She laughed despite herself. "Oh, God, I'm glad he didn't kill you, for your sake and his."

To set the stage, I went on to tell her some of what I'd learned about Irena as related to me by Dante, Lara, and the waitress, Sheri Haller. When I finished, I said, "I understand you were helping Irena break into the modeling business. Can you tell me a little bit about that?"

"Sure. I met Irena at a Pilates class. I was a model talent scout at the time. Irena was one of the most beautiful women I'd ever seen, so I approached her about modeling, and then we became best friends. She wasn't just physically beautiful, she was beautiful on the inside, too. I started getting her some modeling gigs here and there. Some magazine photo shoots. She was very popular with portrait artists too, you know, at private studios, even some art classes at universities." She rolled her eyes. "Most of them wanted her to pose nude."

"I know she wanted to get out of the life," I said. "She told Lara Novak about some sort of scheme she was working on around the time of her murder. Do you know anything about that?"

Gabby wrinkled her brow and squinted for a few moments. "Actually, I do remember something…Irena told me one of her johns was a detective, pretty high up at LAPD. She was planning on, well, blackmailing the guy for a significant amount of money. It wasn't like Irena, and I told her it was a terrible idea, but she was fixated on it. The guy was a shit, too, obsessed with her." Gabby leaned forward and locked eyes with me. "She was just trying to better her situation, you know?"

I nodded as a cold chill slithered down my spine. "Did she mention the name of the john?"

Gabby squinted again. "Not that I can remember."

"Did she ever describe him?"

She shook her head. "No, I don't think so, but I know she knew his name. She told me she looked at his ID one night when he was asleep. She had a nickname for him, too. I don't remember that, either." She blew out a breath in disgust. "Jeez, I must be getting senile."

"No worries," I said. "Does the name Aldo or Moretti ring a bell? Or any play on those two names?"

She shook her head again. "Sorry. It's been too long. The truth is it wasn't a happy time for me. I must've blanked out a lot of memories." Then she smiled and raised a finger. "Oh, there was something else—one of her modeling gigs was sitting for a portrait artist who had a husband who was some big cheese in city government. Irena said she was going to drop his name with the john to let him know she meant business."

I said, "Why didn't you come forward with this at the time?"

She opened her hands. "It was an open and shut case, right? Besides, it didn't put Irena in the best light. And I wasn't anxious to get crosswise with some LAPD detective, either."

I nodded. "So you left LA to come down here shortly after that?"

"Yeah," she said, nodding toward the picture on her desk. I figured Dana Point was a better place than LA to bring up my little girl."

"Makes sense," I said. "She's beautiful." Then I added something I really hadn't planned on saying. "I ran into an old friend of yours during the course of this investigation—Alec Macleod. He says hi."

Her face lit up at the sound of his name, but only until she was able to tamp down her emotions a moment later. "How is he?"

"He's fine. He's a counselor at the Rock of Hope Mission in Skid Row. Works the streets. Folks there call him The Rev. He's doing a lot of good down there. He, uh, told me to tell you he hopes you found what you were looking for."

Her chin quivered slightly, but she managed to smile after nearly tearing up. "That's wonderful. When I knew Alec he had a dreadful job working for a despicable man. I'm glad he's found something else, something more meaningful." She paused for a moment, as if considering what to do next. Then she opened a desk drawer, took out a card, and handed it to me. "Give him this if you see him again. It has my cell phone number on it."

I told her to call the number on my card if she thought of anything else. As we were saying our goodbyes at the front door, I lingered for a moment, because a loose end was rattling around in my head. The thought finally crystallized. I said, "You mentioned that Irena was a model for a portrait artist whose husband worked for the city. Do you remember the name of the artist by any chance?"

Gabby squinted again for a few moments. "No, sorry. I had a lot of clients then. I do remember that she was at Occidental College. Maybe she taught art there."

I'm not sure if Gabby noticed when my face turned white. I know it did, because I could feel the blood drain from my head. My wife, Nancy, taught art at Occidental back then and was a prolific portrait artist. In fact, she was the only professor in the art department who specialized in portraiture. I was a Chief Prosecutor for the city of Los Angeles, which would qualify me as a 'big cheese,' I supposed.

My head was spinning. *Had Irena Krasnova been an artist's model for my wife, Nancy? How in the hell could that be? And if it was true, what did it mean?*

CHAPTER FORTY-SIX

WHEN ARCHIE AND I GOT TO THE CAR, I SAT FOR A WHILE trying to think my way through what I'd just learned from Gabriela Morales. First, I now had strong evidence that an LAPD cop was involved with Irena when she was killed. That finding bolstered my theory that Aldo Moretti had—with the probable complicity of Natalia Pavlin—hired Ferris Spielman to kill Irena. I knew how discreetly the escort service operated, but was it possible that someone involved, someone I hadn't interviewed yet, would be able to identify him? Not likely, I decided. After all, it was over a decade ago and memories fade as Gabby had just so amply demonstrated.

The second thing I learned was that Irena Krasnova might've been posing for my wife in the time period leading up to her murder. That was such a mind-blowing thought that I couldn't wrap my head around it. But I did think of a way I might be able to determine whether it was true or not.

I called Timoteo and luckily caught him at home on a Saturday. "I need something right away," I said. "Go to the internet and find the best photos you can of Irena Krasnova, head shots, full body, whatever you can find."

"She's the woman whose murder you're investigating, right?"

"Yes. Your best bet is probably the LA Times and the

LA Daily News around the time of the murder or when the court case began. You have the records there. Maybe cable news covered it, too. I need you to email the pictures to Zoe as fast as you possibly can. I'll make sure she's standing by."

"Got it," he said.

Next, I called Zoe. "I just left a meeting with Gabriela Morales, thanks to you. She was more than willing to talk, too."

"Oh, I'm so glad that turned out to be her. And I'm so glad I don't have to make any more damn phone calls. You owe me big time, Cal Claxton. How did it go?"

"I'll fill you in later," I said. "Right now, I need another huge favor. I need you to go to the Aerie and look at some of my wife's artwork. You know where the key is. The paintings are in the attic."

"Sure. How do I get up there?"

"There's a trap door in the master closet ceiling. You'll need a stepladder. There's one in the pantry. Timoteo will be emailing you some pictures of Irena Krasnova, the woman Dante was accused of murdering. I want you to see if any of the portraits up there could possibly be of Krasnova. The paintings are wrapped up, so take a pair of scissors with you."

A long pause ensued. Finally, Zoe said in a voice edged with fear, "How could that be? What's going on, Cal?"

I sighed into the phone. "I'm not sure yet. I think—" Just then a call came in from Todd Whipple. "I gotta get off and take a call," I said. "I'll get back to you, Zoe. Good hunting in the attic."

Todd Whipple said, "Hey, Cal, I wanted to let you know I tried to chase down Aldo. He's not picking up, so I called his wife, and she told me he's still down here in LA trying to sell his most recent marijuana crop. So, just in case you're right about him, watch your back. I also talked to the Sheriff at Malibu/Lost Hills. She said a preliminary autopsy on Pavlin didn't find any evidence of foul play, but they're still investigating. What's new at your end?"

"I just met with Gabriela Morales, a good friend of Irena Krasnova. She told me an LAPD detective was definitely involved with Irena before her murder. And she was trying to squeeze him for money."

"Whoa. Did she have a name?"

"Nope. But I'm working on it. It wasn't that she ruled out Moretti. She just couldn't remember that name or any nickname that might fit. There's something else I'm trying to understand, something crazy," I went on. "Morales told me Irena was posing for a portrait artist at Occidental College around that time. The artist could've been Nancy. As bizarre as that sounds, it might be another way into this thing. Maybe Nancy said something to one of her coworkers at Oxy. I'm going to follow up on that."

"Do you remember her saying anything to *you* at that time?"

"No, but you know how she was. I'll bet Irena was baring her soul to her."

"Goddamn interesting, Cal. Keep me appraised. I'm over on Catalina Island with the wife right now, but let me think a bit about how to proceed with Aldo. I'm sick about this and furious at him. All his bravado about the integrity of the force. What total bullshit. This is going to be a mess if we're not careful."

I wondered what 'if we're not careful' meant but ended the conversation without asking. And I wasn't about to involve LAPD until I had all my ducks in a row.

The traffic on the 405 was slow, and I was hungry, so

I turned off just outside of Long Beach and found a taco truck that served up some pretty decent carne asada tacos. I wolfed down three and then took Arch for a quick walk at a park across the street. We were back on the highway twenty minutes later.

The sun had just crossed the horizon when a call came in. "Cal? This is Gabby. I thought of something that might help. After you left, I was looking through some old pictures of Irena and me that I'd stashed away in a shoe box after her funeral. I couldn't stand to look at them at the time. Anyway, the nickname of that john she was planning to blackmail finally came back to me. She called him The Whip."

My heart stopped beating. "The Whip," I repeated slowly. "Irena called him The Whip. You're sure of that?"

"Yes. I'm positive. She had a nickname for all her regulars."

"Did you remember anything else about The Whip? Even the smallest detail can be important here."

"No, but if I do, I'll get back to you. I hope this helps you catch the bastard."

As we disconnected, a horn from a semi blared at me, because I had drifted across the white line. I jerked my car back into my lane and continued. My brain felt numb, leveled, like a grenade had gone off in it.

I was still reeling from Gabby's phone call when Zoe rang back. "I'm up in your attic, Cal. I received the photos from Timoteo, which included one really good headshot. I've found two paintings up here that match Irena almost perfectly. One is finished, and the other has her features drawn in with pencil. The resemblance to the photo is striking but in an artistic way."

"You're sure, Zoe?"

"Yes. She was a beautiful woman, and your wife brought her to life on the canvas, especially her gorgeous eyes and Mona Lisa smile. No doubt in my mind." She paused for a moment. "What does this mean, Cal? I'm frightened for you."

"Don't be," I said. "It may mean nothing, or it may mean everything. I've got to think it through. I'm on the road now. I'll call you back when I get to Santa Monica."

I was a menace on the highway, so I pulled off the 405 at the next exit and parked on the outer edges of a Costco parking lot. The night was cool, and the moon hung like a big grapefruit on the western horizon. I took myself back to that traumatic time. Nancy's suicide was totally unexpected. Even though she had bouts of depression and was on medication, I never dreamed she'd take her own life.

My daughter Claire and I somehow got through the funeral and did our best to prop each other up in our shared grief. I was told to take extensive time off, but two weeks later I was back at work. I felt like it was the only way to keep my sanity. And the case of the city of Los Angeles versus Dante Ellis was on my docket.

Was it possible that the deaths of Irena Krasnova and my wife were somehow related? I thought about the gift Nancy had—an aura of trustworthiness that drew people to her. How many times had she come home saying she'd just made a new best friend and then proceeded to tell me the intimate details they had shared? I smiled at the memories.

It was no stretch then to assume Irena would feel comfortable enough with Nancy to share her 'scheme' of shaking down Todd Whipple, known by the nickname, The Whip. And Nancy would've known immediately who The Whip was.

Then it hit me. It was Whipple who offered to get the

coroner to skip Nancy's autopsy. I remembered him saying, "You don't want them sawing and slicing on her, Cal, trust me." I was in shock. I readily took him up on his offer.

A wave of nausea drenched me. Did my trusted friend kill my wife? I didn't know how, but I was almost certain that he had. The knowledge of that fact, as it seeped into my consciousness, was like something straight out of a nightmare. And I felt a growing sense of anxiety bordering on panic. Although Whipple didn't know I just learned he was the killer, I was sure he considered me an existential threat, given what I'd just divulged to him.

It was only a matter of time before he came for me.

I knew this needed to be handled delicately, so I called the best contact I had at LAPD—Detective Banks. He didn't pick up, so I left a voicemail requesting him to get back to me as soon as possible. After disconnecting, I wondered how the call would've gone. After all, from an evidentiary standpoint, the case I had against Whipple was circumstantial, at best. And to accuse an LAPD cop of multiple murders I needed something rock solid, and I needed it fast.

I calmed down enough to drive and pulled up to the apartment forty minutes later. Instead of parking, I drove around the block once as a precaution, since I had no way of knowing if Whipple lied about being on Catalina Island. I didn't see anything suspicious, like an unmarked patrol car, and reminded myself that he didn't know what Gabby just told me. I let myself through the gate into the darkened patio. As soon as Archie growled a warning, I knew I'd made a terrible mistake.

"I told you to watch your back, buddy," a familiar voice said. "You never listen, do you."

CHAPTER FORTY-SEVEN

ARCHIE GROWLED AGAIN AND BARED HIS TEETH AS TODD Whipple came out of the shadows holding a gun. "Keep your hands where I can see them and cool your dog, Cal, or I'll put a bullet in his head. Your neighbors won't hear a thing." He nodded towards the silencer fitted on the barrel of his Glock. "This is a Banish 45 suppressor, best in the business. A shot from this baby is softer than a baby's fart."

My throat went dry, but I managed to say, "It's okay, Archie. Calm down." My dog sat down next to me but kept his eyes locked on Whipple. I shook my head slowly and said, "What the hell, Todd?"

He averted his eyes. "It's a long story. We can chat on the way over to Mimi's. I called her and said we would drop by, you know, just like old times out on her back deck. But first put your dog in the apartment. He'll be just fine."

I opened the door and told Archie to go in. He obeyed but stopped just past the threshold and turned to me, his big eyes troubled. He knew instinctively something was wrong and didn't want to leave my side. "It's okay, Big Boy," I told him. "I'll be back soon." I shut the door and turned to Whipple. "Leave Mimi out of this, Todd. This is between you and me."

He shook his head, feigning disappointment. "Oh, come

on, you two have been as thick as thieves. Just like you, it's not in my nature to leave any loose ends." He waved the gun barrel in the direction of the street. "Now, come on. We don't want to keep Mimi waiting. You're driving, and don't try any heroics along the way. I can always go back and shoot your dog, and I know where your girlfriend, Zoe, lives, too."

I flinched inwardly at his words but didn't react. I wasn't about to give him the satisfaction. We got underway, with Whipple resting the suppressor against my rib cage as I drove. Once we were out on the road, I said, "You killed Nancy, didn't you?"

He sighed heavily. "Jesus, I didn't have a choice. I mean, to your wife's credit she came to me first, instead of spilling the beans to you about my relationship with Irena. I told her I regretted the whole thing and asked her to let me be the one to explain the situation to you. She agreed, of course. It was thoughtful, empathetic Nancy, after all. Meanwhile, Irena had already demanded big money from me, and I had lined up Spielman to kill her." Whipple sighed deeply. "I'm sorry, buddy, but your wife was a loose end, and I had to act fast. You know what they say—timing is everything."

"How did you kill her?" I said, feeling like I'd slipped into some parallel universe where up was down, black was white, and a good friend, a respected police captain, was a cold-blooded murderer.

Whipple sighed again. "When I stopped by to see Nancy the next day, she was in her bathrobe, depressed. Overcoming her was easy, and I gave her an ether compound to put her under. Six breaths and she was out. Then I injected her with a lethal dose of Xanax between her toes, staging it to look like suicide. She didn't feel a thing, Cal."

I felt an enveloping sense of rage as tears blurred my

eyes, but my instincts told me to keep him talking. "And then like a nice guy you arranged for the autopsy to be skipped," I said. "No sawing or slicing, right?"

"Yeah. Autopsies are horrible. The Chief Coroner owed me one. No big deal. I mean, Nancy had a history of depression, and this looked like a garden variety suicide."

"Pavlin gave you the drugs, right?"

"Very good, Cal. Yes, the woman had amazing medical knowledge, including what ether to use and how to make Xanax injectable. And she introduced me to Ferris Spielman when it became apparent that Irena was going to blow my cover and threaten the sale of the business."

"What about Moretti?"

"Ah, the useful idiot. I put him on the case with Ryerson and told him to steer the investigation away from Impromptu's clientele, that I knew of some important people who had used the service and didn't want their names to come up. Of course, he never dreamed I was behind the killing. That couldn't happen in his universe. And I knew he would keep me well informed and slow things down with his lazy-ass detective work."

"So, Moretti's prior arrest of Spielman was a coincidence?" I asked reflexively.

Whipple nodded. "Yep. I told you they happen all the time, didn't I?"

"Did you kill Pavlin, too?"

He waved a dismissive hand. "I can hardly take credit for that. I just got her drunk on margaritas and then gently held her head down. Blub, blub, blub, it was all over in a few minutes, and I didn't leave a mark on her. Should've done that a long time ago. She knew way too much, and then you came along and started asking questions."

I flinched when he poked me in the ribs with the gun barrel for emphasis.

"I told you to let it be, but you had to keep digging. I should've known you were the same old Cal, like a dog with a bone." He huffed out a breath. "I never planned all this mayhem, believe me. It all started with Irena. I couldn't get her out of my head. Then the dominoes just started to fall, you know?"

I drove on without answering, forcing down my rage so I could at least think straight. I needed a hail-Mary strategy, or Mimi and I were going to die. This murderous sociopath actually enjoyed talking about his exploits. And I knew he would have more to say when we reached Mimi's. *He'll have to watch both of us*, I told myself. *Keep him chatting and look for an opening.*

It wasn't much of a hail-Mary strategy, but it was all I had.

—/—

Mimi's isolated house in Topanga Canyon was well-lit and cheery when we arrived. The moon had set, the stars were brilliant against a pitch-black sky, and the cicadas were out in force. The front door was halfway open, and music wafted in from the back of the house. Whipple was behind me, and when he prodded me with the gun barrel, I reluctantly pushed the door open and stepped in.

"Mimi," he called out in a disgustingly friendly tone. "We're here."

"I'm in the kitchen," she called back, matching the tone. "Come on in and join me."

Whipple stayed behind me as we entered the kitchen. Mimi turned around to greet us with a broad smile. She stood next to the stove, wearing an apron and holding a wooden spoon.

The smile melted when she saw the look on my face. "What's wrong?" she said, her eyes large and questioning.

Whipple shoved me into the room and then pointed the Glock at her. Mimi gasped, and the spoon hit the floor with a clatter.

"Get over there," he commanded. I stumbled forward, caught my balance, and turned around to face him. I looked at Mimi and said, "It was him, not Moretti. He was hung up on Irena and had her killed when she tried to blackmail him."

Mimi's face lost all its color. She started to speak, but Whipple glared at me and cut her off. "Hung up? I wasn't hung up, I was addicted. Being with Irena was like mainlining heroin. I tried but I couldn't stay away from her. Stupid, stupid me. I thought there was something between us, something special." His voice grew thick with emotion. "I was even thinking about chucking everything in and taking her away somewhere."

"Oh, my God, Todd," Mimi said. "How could you?"

He kept the Glock leveled on the space between us and continued in a whining tone. "She turned on me. All she wanted was my money. Anyway, it was easy framing Dante Ellis, but that asshole, Spielman, had to get all gooey on his deathbed and admit to killing her." His look turned incredulous. "Pavlin and I paid him twenty thousand bucks for that hit."

While Whipple spoke, Mimi had been inching to her right along the kitchen counter toward a vertical row of drawers. At one point, she met my eyes, and I gave her a barely perceptible nod of encouragement. *Yes,* I tried to say with my eyes, *go for it.*

She looked at Whipple, and her face hardened like a piece of granite. "You killed Jimmy, didn't you?"

Whipple sighed and shook his head. "Oh, God, don't remind me. Jimmy, the man with a sixth sense. He was about to screw everything up." The incredulous look again. "He came to me after the conviction, said he had new evidence, that we'd convicted the wrong guy, that Dante Ellis had been set up by someone." He gestured toward Mimi with his free hand. "That's why I had to get those damn journals back. God knows what he had on me. I burned the whole lot without even reading them."

Mimi uttered something between a groan and a sigh, and then when Whipple's eyes swung to me, she inched to her right a fraction more.

"I tried to talk him down, but he was adamant," Whipple went on. "You know what he was like, Cal. Anyway, he threatened to go over my head. What was I supposed to do with that?"

"So, you shot him in cold blood," Mimi said, her jaw set, her eyes slits. "You're a sniveling coward, Todd."

"Okay, enough about me," Whipple said with sarcasm. "Let's get on with it. I know this lacks originality, but it's going to have to be another burglary gone bad." He looked at me and shook his head. "I didn't want it to come to this, but you give me no choice, Cal." To Mimi, he added, "Sorry, dear. You're collateral damage."

By this time, Mimi had managed to position herself next to the row of drawers without Whipple noticing. She met my eyes again and gave a slight nod. I wasn't completely sure we were on the same page, but I did the only thing open to me—I looked over Whipple's shoulder into the empty dining room, opened my eyes wide, and said, "Oh, thank God you've come..."

Whipple swiveled slightly in response to my ploy, taking his eyes off Mimi. In that instant, she opened the top drawer and extracted her Sig Sauer. Sensing the movement, Whipple swung back around but he was a beat too slow.

Mimi braced her extended right hand with her left and pulled the trigger three times in succession. BAM BAM BAM. The noise shattered the Topanga Canyon stillness.

Whipple grunted, lurched backward, and left a bloody smear as he slid down the wall. He was dead before he hit the floor.

Mimi set the gun on the counter and said through gritted teeth, "That's for Nancy and Jimmy."

CHAPTER FORTY-EIGHT

Two Weeks Later

I was on the patio wire-brushing the barbeque grate when the gate rattled. Archie perked up and ran over to greet Alec Macleod with enthusiastic butt wags. I was delighted to see that Alec wasn't alone. I put the brush down. "You're the first to arrive, Alec, and I see you brought a guest. Great to see you again, Gabby."

I was hosting a get-together following Dante's chess match with the ranked player from the Venice Beach chess club. Mimi Ryerson's place out in Topanga Canyon would have been a more scenic venue, of course, and she laughed when I suggested it, tongue in cheek. "The holes in the wall where they dug out the bullets still haven't been patched and painted," she explained. "That's not a good look."

I sat Alec and Gabby down, anxious to hear what had brought them together, a surprise to me. "Well," Alec began, "you gave me her card, so I screwed up my courage and called her." He looked at Gabby and smiled. "This is our first date. It's been a long time. We're taking it slow."

"Ya think?" Gabby said, her face glowing. "He's a man of the cloth working in Skid Row. I sell surf art and have a teenage daughter. And we live sixty miles apart." She laughed and took his hand. "We have some issues to work out."

"Why did you leave LA back then?" I asked, feeling Gabby's candor had given me permission to ask something personal.

She looked at Alec, then back at me. "I got pregnant with a man I didn't love, a stupid one-nighter, and was ashamed to face Alec. And my best friend, one of the few people besides him I could confide in, had just been brutally murdered. It was too much to deal with, and I couldn't handle it. I snuck off to Dana Point and got caught up in raising Daisy and learning about the art of the sale." She met my eyes. "Thanks to you, Cal, Alec and I have another shot."

"If it works out," I said, "I'm taking full credit. Nothing that a couple of stubborn, headstrong adults can't work out."

We shared a laugh, and then Gabby said, "What's the latest on Mimi Ryerson? The police took my statement last week. I was nervous, but I got through it."

"She's here, as a matter of fact," I said, "inside making potato salad. She was detained after the shooting—that's pro-forma for an incident like that—but the judge released her on her own recognizance at her preliminary hearing. which is a good sign. In addition to Mimi and you, the police have taken statements from me, Lara Novak, and Aldo Moretti, a retired LAPD detective who has bolstered our claim that Whipple was going to kill us both to hide three brutal crimes he committed thirteen years ago, plus one more recent one."

"I've been contacted for a statement, too," Alec said. "But I don't have much to add." He raised an eyebrow. "An LAPD cop crossed the blue line? That doesn't happen very often."

I nodded. "Aldo Moretti is a man who was proud to

serve and still has enormous affection for the force. He's been reluctant to cooperate, but when Mimi and I told him what happened the night Whipple kidnapped us, he didn't hesitate to come forward."

"Is all that going to be enough to get her off?" Alec said, his voice edged with concern.

"There's more," I said. "We have a video showing my abduction, including a clear view of the gun and silencer Whipple was brandishing that night, the same gun that was in his dead hand when the police arrived at Mimi's."

"Where did the video come from?" Alec said.

I pointed across the street. "My neighbor had just gotten around to putting batteries in his security camera last week, so I guess you could say the Fates intervened."

Gabby said, "An experienced cop forgets about those pesky security cams, huh?"

I chuckled. "Yeah, there's plenty of irony to go around. Maybe it was the fact that he rode a desk for twenty years. He was out of touch with field work."

"What are you hearing from your previous law enforcement associates about him?" Alec said.

"Nothing at the moment. They're all in shock, and they're keeping their heads down. But, you know, even a good barrel can have a bad apple."

"What drove him to such extremes?" Gabby said.

"I guess we'll never know. The only thing I can tell you is that it started with his obsession with Irena, and then when she turned on him, he snapped, I guess. He told me that after Irena's death, the rest of the killings were like dominoes falling."

"Has Mimi lawyered up?" Alec said.

"Yes," I answered, relieved my friend had steered the

conversation away from Nancy's death. "She's retained one of the best criminal defense lawyers in LA, an old foe of mine back in my prosecutorial days. Dante Ellis and I are going to cover her legal expenses, if in fact she needs defending."

"You mean she might not? What happens next?" Alec said.

"The police will file a report of their findings to the District Attorney any day now. It's the DA's call, then. My sources inside the justice department tell me he won't bring charges, that he'll make a finding of justifiable homicide."

"What about the death of Natalia Pavlin?" Alec asked next. "How will that be handled?"

"Todd Whipple confessed to Mimi and me that he killed Pavlin, but the preliminary autopsy report ruled her death an accident. The coroner has ordered a second, more thorough autopsy, but I'll be very surprised if it reveals anything incriminating. In any case, the two individuals behind the murder of Irena have both met their maker."

At that point, Zoe came out of the apartment. She'd flown down two days earlier, and we were planning to drive back to Oregon together with Archie the next day. Barefoot, in white shorts and a blue cotton blouse, her hair bounced carelessly on her shoulders. After introductions, she said to me, "Where do you want these, Chef?" referring to the two wooden planks dripping water she held in her hands.

"What are those?" Gabby said.

"Western red cedar planks I've been soaking," I said. "I'm going to cook some salmon filets on them, Oregon style."

"It's his specialty," Zoe said with a grin. "Wait till you taste it."

The gate rattled again, and in came Dante Ellis and

Lara Novak, followed by Jamare Gilpin and his wife, Stephanie. "Behold, the conquering hero," I said.

Dante smiled modestly, and a beaming Jamare pumped a fist. "Oh, man, did he smoke her or what? It was game over in fifty minutes. And she's got a chess rating number of 1950, which is damn high."

Dante's son had read his father's letters, and like Zoe thought, the letters had won him over. I wasn't present at their reunion, but I heard it was an emotional affair, and since that time the father and son were almost inseparable. Stephanie had readily forgiven Jamare for the lie he told about Dante, but her parents had yet to come around. Knowing Jamare as I now did, I figured they would. They were lucky to have him as a son-in-law.

Mimi Ryerson came out to join us next. Beverages were opened, and the chess match was replayed move by move. Finally, Dante got up and said, "I'm no good at this, but I want to propose a toast."

He looked at me. "Some of you probably wonder why I hang out with his dude. I mean, he caused me to spend thirteen years in San Quentin, which wasn't a lot of fun, believe me." A patter of nervous laughter ensued. "But I came to realize Cal was just doing his job, using the evidence the cops dug up. It wasn't his fault they got suckered." He swallowed and shook his head. "I'm not proud of this, but most of you know I went up to Oregon to kill him after I got out." The patio fell absolutely silent. He looked at me again with a thin smile. "He'll tell you he talked me out of it, but it was really Archie who saved his ass. Who could've orphaned a dog like that?"

We all laughed, relieving the tension.

"So, I'll tell you why I'm here and not dead or back in

prison," Dante went on. "It's because of this man. Sure, the Innocence Project people worked their asses off to get me out, and I love them for it. But I was totally lost when I was released, filled with nothing but hatred and self-loathing." He opened a hand in my direction. "Cal helped me to believe in myself again, and he showed me what can result from the most goddam stubborn determination I've ever seen."

That brought another round of laughter.

The truth is," Dante continued, "if I hadn't gone hunting for him in Oregon, I wouldn't be reunited with my son, in love with a beautiful woman, and satisfied that the people who caused all this grief got what was coming to them."

Dante raised his glass of iced tea. "To Cal. Thanks for the help and thanks for the friendship. I love you, man."

—⊣⊢—

Two days later, Zoe and I were sitting on the side deck at the Aerie sipping a particularly good Oregon pinot noir. Archie was curled up at Zoe's bare feet, sound asleep, as was his habit during our evening ritual. The sun was setting, and the sky above the horizon was a tapestry of swirling gold and vermilion. The vineyards falling away to the south were fully leafed and vibrantly green, even in the fading light.

Zoe took a sip of her wine and studied me over the rim of the glass. "You've been quiet since we've been back. Want to talk about it?"

I exhaled a deep sigh. "I'm still reeling. When I think

back on it now, why the hell did I buy in so readily? Nancy wouldn't have left us willingly. Okay, her depression was real, but still I..."

Zoe's eyes flashed at me. "Don't you dare blame yourself, Cal Claxton. You had absolutely no reason to believe your wife had been murdered by a good friend, a man you trusted. Give yourself a break."

I got up and stood with my hands on the deck railing, gazing out at the sunset. A brisk breeze blew in off the valley and gently swayed the Douglas firs on the east side of the property. "It wasn't just that I blamed myself," I went on. "I was angry at Nancy, too. How could she have done something so horrible to herself? Surely, she knew how this would devastate our daughter. How could she have done that to Claire?"

"Your anger has colored your memories of Nancy, but you can turn the page on that now."

Tears welled up, blurring my vision. "She didn't deserve that. It went unspoken, but a lot of our friends blamed her, too."

"You can't change the past, but you can let go of your guilt and anger now. Can you do that, Cal?"

I nodded. "Yeah, I'm getting there." I raised my arms and spread them as the wind ruffled my hair. "I feel like someone just took a thousand-pound weight off my shoulders. I feel so light this breeze could blow me off the deck."

Zoe got up, put her arms around my waist, and snuggled into my back. "No worries," she said. "I've got you now."

"Well, Dr. Bennett, what I think I need right now is a good therapist. Are you up for the job?"

She playfully kicked me in the foot. Then she took my hand. "Come on. I've got an idea. Let's go hang some of

Nancy's pictures. They're gorgeous. and they'll really perk up this dreary bachelor's pad of yours."

An hour later we had hung a half dozen of Nancy's paintings on the first floor and were now in my bedroom hanging a landscape I'd forgotten how much I loved. I'd just pounded a nail into the wall when a call came in.

"Hey, Dad," Claire said, "I'm home from my back-packing trip. Are you back in Oregon?"

"I am."

"Great. I'm missing you and Archie, so I thought I'd pop up to see you."

"That would be wonderful, sweetheart."

"How was LA?"

"Memorable. When you get here, I'll have a lot to tell you."

The End

ACKNOWLEDGEMENTS

A COLLECTIVE SIGH OF RELIEF WENT UP IN THE EASLEY household when I finished the first draft of this book. After twenty-eight years in the same place, we decided to move to another, smaller home in Oregon, which put me on a collision course with a self-imposed deadline of getting book 10 in the Claxton series out this year. But thanks to Marge Easley's support, unflagging encouragement, and unsurpassed editing skills, we made it.

As always, thanks to my incredible critique group, which has been going strong for what, fourteen years now? Lisa Alber, LeeAnn McLennan, Debby Dobbs, and Janice Maxson—you are extraordinary writers who provide encouragement, insight, and inspiration that *always* strengthens my work. Special thanks to the brilliant Karen Bassett for advising me on psychological issues, particularly on the nature of incarceration syndrome. I'm also indebted to first readers Barbara McReal, Pat Marshall, and Richard Marshall, who caught numerous errors and made sage suggestions that further strengthened the manuscript. A hearty thanks to Tom Smith, who advised me on some sticky legal plot points and, more importantly, has been a steadfast supporter of the series.

ABOUT THE AUTHOR

Formerly a research scientist and international business executive, Warren C. Easley lives in Oregon, where he writes fiction, hikes, skis, and fly fishes. As the author of the Cal Claxton Mysteries, he received a Kay Snow national award for fiction and was named the Northwest's Up and Coming Author by Willamette Writers. His fifth book in the series, *Blood for Wine*, was short-listed for the coveted Nero Wolfe Award and his eight book, *No Witness*, won the Spotted Owl Award for the best mystery written by an author living in the greater Northwest. For more information visit: warreneasley.com and facebook.com/WarrenCEasley.